CUST

Free Planet Book One

MIKE PHILBIN

ISBN: 1490448799
ISBN-13: 978-1490448794

ACKNOWLEDGEMENTS

And Did Those Feet in Ancient Time (1804)
by William Blake

Poem is also the lyrics of the anthem *Jerusalem* (1916)
Music composed by Sir Hubert Parry

We'll Meet Again (1939)
Composed by Ross Parker and Hugh Charles

Eton Boating Song (Circa 1863)
(inspiration for the *Oxford Boat Song* in this novel)

Words by William Johnson Cory

Music composed by
Captain Algernon Drummond and Evelyn Wodehouse

COVER CREDITS

Cover image and design by Mike Philbin

CUSTODIAN – FREE PLANET BOOK ONE
1
THE CUSTODIANS
NINETY BILLION SOULS

Local time: 2102 hours.

Miss Asalah Al Faghori is one of Oxford University's finest post-graduate researchers. This is the fourth year of her five-year D-Phil in Biochemistry, majoring in The Commercial Applications of RNA Research. A twenty-three year old from the London Borough of Tower Hamlets. Her stridently Christian parents, natives of the Egyptian town of Qena on the eastern shore of the River Nile, came to Britain in the 1980's following the assassination of President Anwar Sadat.

Can you imagine how driven, how focussed, how dedicated their 'little girl' must have been to have (within one immigrant generation) secured approval to study in the hallowed halls and libraries of Oxford University?

Neither her younger brother nor her elder sister had so embraced the English way; fitted in so cleverly. And it's the way she is with others that really sets her apart. It's like, even though she's no obvious leader, you'd go to war for her. In many ways she's the dark horse, quiet and considered, but gathered around her are a loyal network of avid researchers and close friends from all aspects of Oxford life, more than sterile colleagues or clock-watching associates.

There's a bond, a spiritual connection with a higher plain, that you see only after you've spent time in her presence.

Asalah Al Faghori has contributed to ESI or Eye Sys Industries in very-profitable ways during her four year tenure at Oxford University and has been well remunerated for her commercial exploitation in the form of a well-equipped lab and external access to all relevant files, a corporate expense account and regular appearances at trade conferences around the world in the field of biogenetic research. She has her mother's dark hair and her father's darker eyes. She's not a practising Christian herself, but that sort of structured up-bringing rubs off on one, shapes one's mind. She stands five-foot nothing in her stocking feet and has a bell-peeling laugh that could melt an iceberg with its sonority, its song. Though she has 'adult curves', there's not one ounce of excess fat on her.

Asalah Al Faghori will die tonight and we shall share the moment of her passing so that she can fulfil her promise of a brand-new future so far denied the inhabitants of this cruelly commercial world.

She will die so that you the people can understand Creativity.
She will die so that you the people can translate Passion.
She will die so that you the people can share Kinship.

She's not going to die strapped to a chair receiving four hundred stab wounds from some lunatic home invader like unlucky French biochemists.

She's not going to be discovered in some GCHQ safe house, zipped into a locked pink sports bag, decomposed well beyond the few days since her demise.

She's not going to be discovered with her wrists slit in the wrong way, undigested paracetamol in her gut and no blood near her corpse in the woods.

She's going to offer her life to the whole world, the scientific world, the political world, the living world. She's going to commit the ultimate sacrifice of her flesh so that there'll be no doubting her dedication, her resolve. She believes this to be the right thing to do. She believes that her sacrifice will be judged right and proper in the great accounting table of history's more significant events. God is on her side, or so she believes.

The walls of her bedsit are bare, painted limestone-white over embossed Edwardian wallpaper which you can still see during early morning hours. No student posters. No family portraits. No flat screen TV crucified on high. Along the far wall, sprawls a large foldaway cushion bed the Japanese call a *F'ton.*

Here's a list of the additional fixtures and fittings:

An ancient oak double-bookshelf groaning with biochemistry books fills the back wall.

A white porcelain sink, where a single toothbrush stands guard in a clear glass beaker.

CUSTODIAN – FREE PLANET BOOK ONE

A clock radio, red LED, black Casio model from the year dot.

A white tourist coffee mug from the Mena House Hotel in Cairo.

A top of the range Dell laptop, with four co-processors and an 18.4 inch screen, donated by ESI so that she can be logged in 24/7/365, for the good of The Corporation.

The beige carpet is too plush, too clean, compared with the age of the building. It was probably relaid before she took this room at the start of her tenure. No expense spared so that the golden egg-laying goose could roost.

Outside, below the open window of this Spartan bedsit, the Yellow Buses are transporting the last of the day's summer tourists down High Street and out through The Wall, heading east out of the town centre, obedient to the Law of Curfew. Asalah Al Faghori has cleared a big space in the middle of her bed-sitting room for tonight's rite.

"Ninety billion souls," she reminds herself as she prepares the backdrop her laptop camera will pickup, re-arranging some books, tidying a few nick-nacks. These will be the theatrical props, the elemental spectres, behind her head as she commits suicide online to one of those private forums where its become something of a grunge sport; an acquired taste for when there's nothing on the TV or you just wanna see how the nutter-half live, or die - or don't die, as is often the case.

She kneels down in front of her ESI laptop, on the floor. Sets the timer on her camera; ten minutes is all she'll need.

"Ninety billion souls..." she says this like it's the start of some personal performance she's been practising, rehearsing, troubled by, for quite some time. It's the start of something she wants to get right. It's the three most important words of an emotional outpouring that'll probably even bore the investigative psychologist who'll look upon this desperate *exeunt stage left* as just another sad condemnation of student life in Oxford and the utter lack of anything to take your mind off the educational grind.

It's not easy to kill yourself, right? You know what they say - *it's the people you leave behind who have to bear the pain.*

CUSTODIAN – FREE PLANET BOOK ONE

"Ninety billion souls," she starts again, trying another voice a half octave deeper, and clears her throat, "Ninety billion souls..." happy with the way the sound reverberates within the sterile space. In a neighbouring student room, someone's cooking a curry.

She had been dressed in jeans and t-shirt but now she is completely naked. There's a glass of distilled water beside her right knee. The camera on her enormous laptop won't pick up any of these details. She's not filming a porn death, only a talking-head shot death. She's filming her ideological death, and a state of undress (a return to primal purity) is essential.

To be exact she is ritualising the *death of all dogma*, that's how Miss Asalah Al Faghori would like this moment of transition to be remembered. That's her intention. But that's getting slightly ahead of ourselves. We're looking for too many extenuating circumstances behind the death of this spirited young female from an Arabic country that's just seen so much trauma and revolution, that's still pushing and bearing through the gut-busting contractions of *Democracy*.

Broadcasting to the world, eventually.

Unblinking eye, intentionally.

Red light recording, for posterity.

Having noted the time on her LED clock radio, she begins her prepared monologue to camera...

"I had a dream last night. It was a dream about our little house in the English countryside. A cottage with a thatched roof and heavy oak doors. Beams in the lounge, the kitchen and the bedrooms. Lead in the windows. It was snowing outside. All the foxes and deer brought their families to our house to avoid The Cull. You could hear the hunt dogs barking in the distance. Getting nearer. On the TV was the story about the foxes and deer arriving because we'd saved one or two of them every year.

"I don't have such a 'little house in the English countryside'. My family live in a council block of flats. I don't even have a TV. And these contradictions have helped me ... understand ... what the events of the next few minutes are going to cause. I realised this dream is about us. Our little group, our little *coalition of the willing* I've called The Custodians. You have no

4

idea who we are. Neither do our bosses, our superiors, our sponsors. Tonight, The Custodians are going to cut the heads of innovation free from their enslavement to the dollar, the yuan, the t-bill. The Custodians are no longer going to allow the yoke of corporate slavery to polish the necks of mankind. It is going to be a routing of Historical Proportions. Real Freedom for all is going to Sprout. And Flourish. And Thrive."

She pauses there, and places the transparent hundreds-and-thousands-filled capsule onto her tongue in a proscriptive fashion. She takes the glass of distilled water and sips from it. Swallows, with obvious effort. Looks about nostalgically and makes a frown. Then a smile appears on one side of her mouth. She drains the glass in big, loud gulps. Wipes her glistening mouth with the back of her hand. Takes a deep breath. Sets the glass down out of harm's reach.

Waits...

"Oh, ninety billion souls. I nearly forgot," she adjusts her position, seems rushed.

"I've done some calculations, as part of my 'thesis'," she snorts ironically, "Without getting too technical … the human brain contains approximately ninety billion or so neurones. And ninety billion or so is an estimate of the number of humans that have ever lived, throughout history. Ninety billion. Recently, the earth's human population passed seven billion and I wondered one day whether this planet could actually sustain ninety billion souls at the same time. What sacrifices would we all have to make for that to become a reality? What would the collateral damage figures be? … and I realised..."

She flinches. Just the once. Beads of sweat blossom on her forehead. A worried look skitters across her face. Her eyes dart about, then settle. She gulps. As she's about to continue, she creases over in a blaze of pain. Dropping out of the shot from her laptop camera. You can hear her muffled groans of agony. You cannot see the arch of her back, three or four vertebrae protruding.

"I realised..." a sweat-mottled forehead re-surfaces, comes back into shot, shoulders drawn up by her ears, the back of a fist across the opposite cheek like a boxer defending against a right cross, "I realised that..."

A lip-bitten scream erupts within her throat. She tries to keep it in. Her face goes bright red and tears pour down her face. She keeps screaming like this for nearly a minute. Literally sixty seconds of pure pain are carved across her face in tortured freeze-frame. She doesn't blink once, keeps looking right into the camera as the crescendo of pain rises and rises then cascades away draining the horror from the crevices in her face in tumbling blocks of marbled relief.

Sweat pours down her forehead from inside her hairline. She performs a series of deep, heavy gasps and pants before continuing, "...this planet has a limited resource.

"I'm not talking about gold or diamonds or rare earth elements or carbon, air, water. I'm talking about souls. Yes, souls. There's something about the way the Earth is wired such that only ninety billion souls are allowed to exist. Ever. Like there's some sort of dislocate between time and souls. Eternity is written into the human equation and we ignore this at our peril. And by souls I mean neurones, the ability to process, to share information.

"That is fundamentally what a soul is, a converter from star light to intention. The physical...." she doubles over again like she's been gut-punched by Stanley Kubrick's Gunnery Sgt. Hartman.

Asalah has fallen off the shot entirely while the sounds of vomiting can be heard. Asalah is on her side, naked on the carpet of her room, in front of her devoted laptop. Her knees are drawn in. Her forearms wrapped around her shins. Her fingers balled into fists. Her toes curled in like claws. There is a watery puddle of puke in front of her, dangerously close to the laptop.

Back on camera now, we can see how the sweat is pouring off our young heroine. Shivers sword-swipe through her body in chaotic choreography. The facial skin actually seems to twitch jaggedly; one wonders if it won't tear or rip into sinister lesions. Remember those images from childhood where someone in a science lab touches the electrostatic generator and their hair billows out?

"The physical world.

"A mathematical expression.

"Of man's intent," she gasps, rapidly gulping horror.

"But it is. Not just this. There are animals. Birds, insects. Computers. With 'neurones'. That process. Energy converters...!!!" that last word raised into a shrill shriek.

"It is a… rapidly soul-stripped Earth. And. There's no stopping. The onslaught. The nightmare. The Earth may already. Always be. Full of souls!" she part-shouts, part-sobs, blurting out the last word like it was the most important thing she'd ever do in her life.

"I can't..." blood issues from her lips in a pink spray where she's tried to bite off the scream, imprison the pain, retain the agony, her gum-line reddened; vampyric. A tooth comes loose.

Without warning, while you're looking right at her, she soft-explodes with a barely-audible thud and what remains is like a festering apple caught in the last frame of a time-lapse-movie documenting its rapid rot.

Poof, in the blink of an eye, Asalah Al Faghori is nothing more than a multi-coloured fur ball on the too clean carpet of her bed sitting room. A vaguely human silhouette and palette, no sharp definition. No movement. No final exaltation or disclaimer. Just this pile of drying fibres, like wind-blown grass, settling, finally relaxing, released from its gusty turmoil.

* * *

Twenty-four hours later, to the second, the mound has filled out. Ballooned to a satin sheen. Splayed into the room. This off-colour assortment of thread and lattice now occupies most of the area of the floor. The laptop is nowhere to be seen. Subsumed maybe, integrated into the mesh.

Exploratory fronds have taken an interest in the bookshelf like the shivering hand of a drowning person reaching out to the river's edge, looking for a way out, leafing through pages, fibre by fibre. Monochrome filaments skitter about on the walls like writhing spider webs looking for flies to catch. The mound inhales.

Just once.

And you're not even sure you saw it. There was no jet-engine turbo-prop accompaniment, no guttural rasping sound. Just this single movement in the mound. Not even a breath, not a full one, anyway. It just seemed to adjust, like a human face stifling a yawn in polite company. You'd have missed it if you weren't as vigilant as you've been. Sitting here. Watching. Waiting for something truly revelatory to happen.

But that's it.

Maybe it was a trick of the eye. A photonic sleight of hand, shadow play. A dalliance of time/space, weary at the attention, trying to offset the interest. Here, have a ripple, an adjustment, a butterfly effect.

A living vector slices lazily through one side of the thing on the floor while you try to escape the quicksand of contravention. A metallic rainbow soars up obliquely out of the felt-covered mound, reminding one of the Egyptian *khopesh* or Canaanite *sickle-sword*. This lethal sculpture counts a beat then splits, along its outer edge, in a shower of shrapnel causing a single musical phrase to hang in the air like mint-scented mist.

Organic detail crinkles through the uniformity of the softened wing-edge and fractal complexity starts to obligate itself out across the rainbow, trespassing upon the cubic geometry of the room.

2
YOU THE PEOPLE
EARTHQUAKES IN EAST OXFORD

Localised seismic tremors worry the London Road housing estate, on the eastern outskirts of the City of Oxford; a deep, thrumming sound that gets louder and louder over the course of Thursday afternoon. Soon, antique crockery will have fallen from display cabinets, Edwardian and Victorian money pits will have settled unevenly onto their fungus-rotted foundations, street after terraced street will have been flattened in one long path of collateral damage.

Soon, pregnant women, wailing babies, shrieking children, brothers and sisters, old grandmothers, toothless grandfathers, wage slave fathers and working mothers will have succumbed to a pitiless machine that crushes hopes and dreams to so much biscuit base in an American cheesecake.

This earthquake maker is the property of **R³** - Relocation, Relocation, Relocation, or *the Largest Corporate Removal Service catering to the global relocation market.*

The technology that powers the R³ is licensed through ESI or Eye Sys Industries, an offshoot of the Global Money Making Scam that regularly schedules *flights* from one Gulag territory to the next for purposes of corporate consolidation and bottomline easing. Remember, what's happening on Earth is not like Communism, this is Free Market Capitalism (that's Sanctions plus Taxes) in its most beautiful form, its most perfect expression. The algorhythms work, this time, and the administration ain't gonna lose sleep over a few 'worthless eaters' who got in the way of a bit of profit.

This enormous corporate conveyance apparatus (the R³) had set out on its journey from the heart of Europe just eight hours ago, leaving former office location, Dusseldorf, at a top speed of fifty miles per hour on the successive-bailouts-funded superhighways of the Greater European Union like a massive rolling bowling ball. This ball, this R³, this matt-black sheep-poop shat from the conglomerate sphincter, is so enormous that it's really hard to get a grasp of its size. On the horizon, it's just another sphere in a long line of spheres bumping and jostling their way down private highways the way stacked phone calls push themselves down fibre-optic cable. Think of something the size of the dome of St Paul's Cathedral in the City of London. Imagine two domes of that size placed together so that they form a sphere. Imagine a sphere of that diameter rolling away from East London one day, taking with it all the indentured employees of The City.

In fact every method of corporational to-and-fro is taken care of by R^3. *"Across the globe, in the blink of an eye,"* is their cunning slogan. The Company Name R^3 is so ingenious, it even describes the mode of relocation, the R^3 itself. The cubed sphere. The triple-axis Pi-R-Cubed of whole-company removal; lock, stock and barrel. What the name doesn't tell you is how the personnel get into position within the relocation device. What the name doesn't tell you is even within this relocation agreement is the clause concerning collateral damage, and not just of crushed locals.

Dead Peasant Insurance policies orchestrated by BIR or the *Bank of International Resettlement* will have taken care of their obligation to the Citizens of a Nation 'rendered creditless' during the arrival of another arm of Unified Europe to new shores. It will also have taken care of any losses or 'settling' during transit of one conglomerate unit from point A to point B.

One simple digital pay-off to numbered government accounts will ensure that no legal action will be taken against PERSON or persons responsible for the deaths of 2985 people on this occasion crushed under the bloated scrotum of Industry – or rather The Industry.

That's the name given to most of what happens (commercially) across Europe in the name of rampant Consumerism. The Industry is a Mega Corporation, a multinational 'country' with its own pin-striped kings and queens, its own population of skilled tech-whores, its own population of scurrilous middle-management pimps dressed in 70s garb, its own Pepto-Bismol-pink-o tax rules and office regs, its serfs and slaves all tied up behind iron-clad NDAs or *Non Disclosure Agreements* enforced by scurrilous legal representatives.

Remember when Corporations achieved Legal Person status?

That's why *You* (The People) live like this, obsessively under the kosh; because you fucking love it. At least you deserve it, you grumbling, do nothing slackers.

There's nothing sicklier and more grotesque than a Captivated Workforce, it's like Stockholm Syndrome on a global scale. Sympathy (TM) is directed towards Team Pizza and Incestuous Work Practises; the unpaid overtime, the active ostracisation of the Unwilling to Comply like a new religion, a new model army. 'Oorah!' being the clarion cry among the work-soldiers who've united, fists raised in unison, those cliqued-up morons who belligerently serve their dark master ensconced in his Plexiglass shell in the far corner of every corporate dug-out.

You're not getting this, are you?

There are too many words, aren't there? Too many complex realities and elaborate military escarpments to rappel? Too many ethical sacrifices being advertised on your part? Like how can a company just heartlessly detach itself from a locality and make its way to greener tax pastures? What of the families split up or left behind? What of the communities shattered by the loss of such a corporate partner, the slaughtering of peripheral earner industries who supply and supplicate those marauders, those pirates?

Well, it's evident that you haven't been listening much to the rumble of the death ball in your general direction, have you?

The Industry legally detached a branch of its German office and conveyed it west to take advantage of government grants and legal tax incentives offered in the name of the Old East India Company that effectively rules (and financially lures to its shore) the scumbag murder mechanisms that have brutally cudgelled planet Earth to this day.

Get over that.

Off-shore became such a dirty term in the 1980's and the moniker *Satellites* was formally adopted to appease the PR crowd. Corporate Parents (spawners of these legal persons) protect their own offspring, their patent chattel – and that's it. Everyone and everything else is potentially a virus to be wiped away by the disinfecting cloth of Consumerist Manipulation.

You are expendable, blithe resident of this planet. You are nothing more than an irritating grain-of-sand in the Eye of Sauron to these literal psychopaths.

So, on to today's grammar lesson.

The *Kevlar Kubitz* (another ESI-derived innovation) has become the universal unit of occupancy in today's business world; the yardstick measure of corporate personnel who are the real power of any corporation. Technically speaking, a Kevlar Kubitz expresses the number of private insurance candidates the policy holder can safely transport from sealed premises A to sealed premises B as befits the the CCC or *Corporate Courier Covenant* agreed across the European Union.

Every corporate serf signs a rigid NDA (Non Disclosure Agreement) that states they are, believe this - *the property of their co-sponsor*.

No more than eight of these owned employees can be crammed into every living Kevlar Kubitz for secure removal to and from the work place, into and out of pre-arranged work hours (refer to contract for exemptions).

They're not really made of the trademarked para-aramid synthetic fibre *Kevlar*, these hunter-seeker units, but the first prototypes had a unique *filo pastry*-like method of electro-chemical propulsion and the name stuck through successive technical revisions.

Your modern day Kevlar Kubitz is a top-secret organism with some very special armaments and modes of self-preservation, multiple tactical-scenario search and chauffeur capabilities; the ultimate caring shepherd.

One of the really sexy things about the Kevlar Kubitz is the way a spherical volume of them (not exceeding 300,000) can swarm-transport an entire Satellite office from one location on the global game board to any other location on the global game board at a moment's notice due to its ProM.I.S. driver software that sings songs to a space-based network of quantum relay stations.

While the Kevlar Kubitz has been proven to be a secure method of personnel transportation, a certain percentage of transportees suffer brain damage during the geo-psychological trauma of Corporate Relocation.

Other side-effects known to manifest are irrational reality formation as a cushioning effect and chronic diahorrea. There's a patent to cover all these symptoms: it's called IED or

Intermittent Evertainment Dislocation. Has its own sexy corporate ident and everything.

And this is what you are witnessing right now - *you*, the people of Oxford. You are witnessing, and some of you are dying from, the crushing tonnage of the R³ ball-buster settling within your eastern outskirts. And you know why, don't you? You understand the price you're being asked to pay whenever a foreign company resettles onto cheap British soil?

The European Union.

Britain is, and always will be, a non-participant in Unified Europe. Britain has its own proud heritage of corporate espionage firms, its own shrivelled currency and its own legal system while all across Europe one voice rings loud from Brussels, telling all what to do and how to do it.

Or that's what Europe has been told to think.

In truth Europe hasn't existed for over two thousand years.

The old Roman Empire has been imprinted upon the legislative system of 'europe' for the last twenty centuries.

* * *

A siren sounds across east Oxford scattering the crows that had gathered on and around the enormous black sphere of R³'s relocation relocation relocation machine.

A second rumbling earthquake commences as a single orange spot appears on the surface R³, pointing directly west toward Oxford Wall.

In a gloriously concentric wave, like a sperm impregnating an egg or an enormous Eye of Sauron peeling open, the Kevlar Kubitz that make up the R³ begin to softly alter their colour. A glowing iris opening opening opening, the entire R³ rippling from matt black to burnished bronze maturing as a prominent tangcrine hue.

When all the outer-surface Kevlar Kubitz have taken part in this transformation, a bolt of lightning shoots out from the core of the R³ device, and a clap of thunder finishes off the gay drama.

All around, the critically damaged buildings ruined by the R³'s arrival finally succumb to the demand of gravity, crushing yet more hapless victims and ruining yet more families.

Then silence.

Suddenly, the bright orange surface of the R^3 shatters and singular Kevlar Kubitz spill down from their positions within the sphere exhibiting laminar flow properties. The fallen Kubitz settle and start to dig themselves in.

Burrowing into the ground, taking their corporate charge, their building foundations and their employees deep underground where seeding technology unpacks from the core of the R^3.

A new foundation buries itself in the debris of eastern Oxford, pouring its fungal tendrils miles into the earth to the north, the south, the east, and the west, and down, ever deeper into the Earth's crust, securing itself, latching onto the rock of the city, buried deep under clay.

Further to the west, concrete residential blocks rise from the earth, auto-architecturing themselves based on a corporate ground plan seeded moments earlier by the R&D department, the glowing core of the parked R^3. This is where *You* will live for the remainder of your corporate tenure. This is where the Kevlar Kubitz will come capture you on a daily basis while you remain a serf to The Industry.

If you survived the journey sane.

If your productive mind is intact.

If.

3
THE CUSTODIANS
AS MOTHER NATURE INTENDED

Local time: 2132 hours.

Forty two years old mature Engineering Degree student Rotimi Ogunjobi, from Lagos in Nigeria, is another of ESI's *would-be-traitors*.

He lives on the third floor of a set of flashy student apartments on St Giles, in central Oxford. His rooms are directly opposite the Martyr's Memorial dedicated to bishops Cranmer, Ridley and Lattimer who were burnt at the stake in nearby Broad Street in the year 1555 under the orders of Queen Mary.

While it is technically correct to say Rotimi *lives on the third floor,* we're back in lurid-paradox territory where terminology and appearance might be vastly at odds until forensic examination of the scene has been undertaken. For now, let's have a little chuckle to ourselves and say yes, Timi, as his friends call him, is alive in his apartment.

Like his bright-spark Uni friend across town, Asalah Al Faghori, he'd also remembered to leave a window open. The vertical hinge allows easy access to his apartment to man or beast able to scale the eastern face of this residence hall.

A muted swooshing sound, a scrabble of claws and a ruffling of feathered wings as some bird lands on the window ledge of Timi's apartment. A gleeful wheezing sound, like a keenly-aspiring turbo-charger, reverberates from the bird's asthmatic chest. Its clawed feet attain purchase on the fibrous wood of the window ledge and it cautiously pokes its feathery head in to see what's cooking.

Timi's room is a mess, as usual. All kinds of second-hand-shop trinkets in brass and glass and painted papier mache litter every surface. Framed iconic pictures from a bye-gone era crowd the wall space. Not necessarily antique, just rubbish, old furniture clutters the place; there seems to be a little table for every medium-sized knick-knack. There's even an African bead curtain separating off the kitchenette area. A bead curtain, in this decade. *Really.* A bamboo wind chime is softly percussing to itself.

In the middle of the room, on the carpetless floor, is another familiar multi-threaded fur ball. Familiar to the bird, that is. Bird, how would you define that? Chest, beak, feathers, feet, wings? There can't be many people out there who've seen a bird like this. She stands just under three foot tall, with an extended wingspan of about nine foot across. Her feathers are so fresh they're still moulting a soft white powder every time she moves. There's a vaguely owl-like appearance to the bird, but look again, and other genetic stuff refract through the viewfinder and it all feels wrong. Too many unrecognisable branches of the ancient tree of life poking out of the same long-forgotten forest.

The bird knows exactly what this mound means. Look into her eyes. Doesn't she have the dark eyes of Asalah Al Faghori; the cunning, the curled up lashes? Have you ever seen eyes so human on a bird? Is it so hard to imagine that this is what erupted from Asalah's mound over on the High Street just half an hour ago?

Asalah Al Faghori, knows exactly what's going on inside Rotimi's mound. It was she, after all who'd schooled The Custodians Group (LLP), this *coalition of the willing*, one member from each of Oxford's 38 private universities, how to use free-form visualisation to navigate the geneline once her clandestine chemistry spell was under way, once their old self was primed for replacement by AGP or *Archaic Genetic Preference*.

Asalah trained her pupating genomers to do this. There was no vulgar splicing involved in what she'd *code-cocted*. It was all there, within the heredity of each person in the team, no need for surrogates, simulations or mimicry. All's you had to do was dream in four dimensions. And as new-age-hippy as that sounds, that's exactly what you had to do. Dream down the iterative timeline. You controlled the depth of your submersion in the double helix's hereditary maze, to stretch back all the way to pre-historic times if you're self-knowledge could remain that intact, or you could take the coward's option and remain an ape-like retard. It was up to you.

Asalah scrambles down from the window ledge, avoiding the assault course of ornaments on the window ledge, and hops around inside the room, allowing her head to swivel all the way round to take in all the crap with her newly-honed eyesight.

Nothing much has changed. Man-made stuff looks just the same as it always had. You have to go outside, into nature, to see a truly revelatory rendition of what we've all taken for granted for so long. Just allow the wavelength of light to stretch a little and the whole natural world takes on this psychedelic shimmer, this visual fattening. Rainbow patterns of plummeting infra-red or soaring ultra-violet reveal themselves like snakes in grass. Hidden perplexity inveigled.

Asalah's enhanced attention now turns to the mound, within which a beast is dreaming. She blinks with those hauntingly human eyes, as she hops around it. Pecks at the outer surface of the mound with her beak. It isn't as soft as she'd expected, harder than her own had been; the woven mass of fibres has a texture not unlike dried chamois leather. She wonders how whatever-it-is Timi's creative magic is conjuring up will be equipped to break free from that prison. She resolves to help him a little, pull a few strands free.

A razor-clawed hand reaches out of the mound like a bolt of lightning and fixes around her scrawny neck.

Asalah flaps her nine-foot wingspan in utter horror, struggling with all her might to back away into the upper corner of the room. Kicking up a huge dust cloud, back illuminated by the last of the mid-summer sunlight streaming through the window.

Her wing beats are so strong that all the ephemera of Timi's life are blasted across the room with each explosive down stroke. Her clawed feet scrabble for purchase on the bare wooden floor. The grip tightens around her throat.

She beats furiously with her wings, pulling back from the mound, a scaled arm extrudes out of the mound with each frantic beat of her enormous wings. A carnivorous stink erupts from the mound as the shoulder and then the full torso slithers free, all glistening and muscular.

It's all arms and head, this newborn. Not much below but a carapaced ribcage and a spine. But what a head. It has the appearance of Sobek, one of those ancient Egyptian river gods. But there's a curvature to the snout makes you think of a T-Rex. But that's just insane. Unbelievable.

The nostrils twitch. The lips pull back revealing curved flint for teeth. Then the rest of it scuttles free. And what an athlete, that's the only way to describe Timi. A super-charged testosterone-rippling athlete.

His lips (though pared back to their basic function) still have that Timi-ness to them, still have the same smile-snear that seems to constitute his entire emotional repertoire.

Another razor-clawed hand reaches out for Asalah and only by the grace of god does she finally escape the clutches of this thing, this abomination of imagination, Timi has become.

Timi lashes out at her again and saliva sprays out of his growling throat.

"Shut up, you fucking idiot!" she reprimands him with a voice that sounds more like the lip-disabled efforts of a trainee ventriloquist, "Shut up!"

This stripping away of her former female layer takes her by surprise. Actually makes her more angry than fearful. She lands on the floor in a defiant pose, hissing like a cobra. Folding her wings up; first the left, then the right. Determined she will not be dominated by this... mongrel.

Mexican stand off, hybrid versus hybrid. Timi snarls and digs his clawed hands into the faux-Persian rug his mound half-covers, the architectural weave crumples under his grip.

"Come on, Timi, you morOn," there's a mechanical Icelandic-like trilling tone to the back end of every plosive, to the core of the word *moron.*

"Enough of this primEval posing. Its only fucking mE. Your mate Asi, you knOw?" she gasps and pants metallically

"I know, sis..." Timi quivers in his ready-to-slaughter four-pawed stance, shaking off the birthing pangs, "I was just enjoying the blood surge. The blood surge, Asi," that smile-snear staggers across his face like a drunken dance.

"I feel *more* than alive," he murmurs.

"Your arms are bigger than your legs," Asalah bows her head.

"What's wrong with you, have you looked in the mirror, sis?" he adjusts his pose, ready to pounce. Licking his chops. Totally prepared to murder, slaughter, annihilate anything that opposes it, friend or foe.

"Don't do that."

"What?"

"Don't call me *sis* like that. Feels, I dunno, *incestuous,*" she says, swoops in suddenly and beaks him under the sculptural jawline.

He exposes his jugular on that side. She sniffs at it. Can see the pulse of blood surging up it with every claxon heart beat. A vibrant hunger buzzes through her like an ice-cream chill in the sinuses.

"Eat it," she whispers, "What's left of the birthing process. It's not delicious considering where it comes from, but.."

"You are such a mumsy," Timi pulls back his head so he can see her, examine her owl-like closeness, look at what she has become, "You are a bit of a page-3 stunner, Asi." chuckles Timi, so that the protective plates of his outer surface seemed to jiggle loosely.

Asalah suspects that Timi is mustering whatever charm he can from his new body chemistry to ensnare the role of leader for himself; momentarily forgetting who Asalah Al Faghori is, and how she'll never rescind her role as the self-appointed head of operations, the Egyptian Queen (so to speak) of The Custodian Liberation.

"How then may the cat kiss the canary?" mischief returns to Timi's eyes.

"You have a tongue, still?"

Timi shows it her, all the length of it.

"Oh, my," Asalah gawps at the forked specimen, "What is a girl supposed to say?"

"Now who's being a carnivorous bore?"

Timi faces off against her before turning to his meal, tucks in with sloppy glee, devouring his velvet-encrusted placenta, "You can have some if you want," he slobbers, tearing off a strip and offering it to her. She hops in, side on, and takes the offering with her beak. Transferring it to her right foot to secure it, while her beak shreds it.

"It is share and share alike, *Chez Timi*." he tucks into another slice, ripping up a bit of faux-Persian rug with the morsel.

They both laugh at the ruin, the recycling of the old, for the new.

"Enough of this pratting about, Timi-boy," she swirls around, opens her wings and lifts, momentarily, into the air, "If all the team's on schedule. There'll be two more Custodians. Nearby. Just like us. About to hatch."

 * * *

While they're making their way down a deserted sunset-reddened Turl Street to their colleagues in crime, in this insane chemical chess game they've set in motion, Asalah and Rotimi come across their first live meal.

Timi, having scaled up the face of his apartment building, is leaping from roof to roof within the Gothic skyline of Oxford's dreaming spires.

Asalah is gliding overhead, keeping an eye on their destination, which she can already see from her hovering altitude; an ochre light in another rooming house.

They spot some kid. Some street urchin in a dark hoodie. Smoking Spanish cigarettes as he moves from shadow to shadow. He doesn't seem attached to a Corporation, there are no Ownership logos on his clothing, which is odd. Everybody has an owner, everyone has a corporate uniform. He doesn't seem old enough to be a student. But here he is, within Oxford's wall after curfew; freelancing? This was either some professor's kid out when he shouldn't be or there was a serious security breach, somewhere. It's always nice to know that security breaches exist, gives the boffins something to scratch their heads about, something to put in an invoice for.

Asalah catches a whiff of him and something primal goes off in here like a small bomb in the brain, a burning suffusing down to the grumbling pit of her stomach. She is about to swoop down to let Rotimi know that there's a Live Meal down below when she notices he's also spotted the youth. The chase is suddenly on.

The kid's a canny young thing and he knows he's being preyed upon. He takes to his heels and dashes down Market Street, crossing the road to then dash left down what's left of Cornmarket, and right again down Queen Street. He seems to know where he's going. Like he has an escape plan. Maybe he's heading back to the *crack in the wall* where he first got in.

Asalah swoops down silently and pulls the lad to the ground, dragging him through the dust. She hangs onto his shoulders with both feet as he kicks and screams, flailing around as arterial blood spurts over both of them. One of her taloned feet comes loose, the kid gets to his knees, purest anger in his eyes. He swings at her and nearly dislodges her remaining foot. He's spins round in the dust and the dirt of late-nite Oxford, determined to struggle free. Suddenly, Rotimi pounces, clamps his T-Rex-like jaws either side of the lad's face. One quick twist of the head. The lad is dead. A bloodied ragdoll dangles from a panting pre-historic monster.

Asala rights herself before a very-defensive Timi-beast, his plates of protective keratin as tight as a clam. Patent-leather shiny. Asalah keeps her distance, as yet unsure of the loyalty of her old friend compared to his need to feed. Nature is a razor-edge of potential. She has lost first claim to this meal, but there'll be others.

Timi drops the meal and starts to tuck in, opening the soft belly first; slurping at the soup bowl. You know, if you're a Re-Wilded, human meat is as good as it gets. After your first taste of human flesh, animal meat is like eating dog turds, there's definitely something missing. It's human meat or nothing for the Re-Wilded, though nobody actually told them of this side-effect. Why should they? Ah, unless...

"Wayward children, ill-equipped ramblers, the aged, the infirm and the careless," Timi says, licking blood from his front claws while Asalah tucks into the remains of his kill. "Had once again become food for the preying elite. As Mother Nature intended."

And there would lie their undoing, just that one sentence. Concrete evidence that The Custodians would fail in their Mission Objective. It's literally unavoidable with the human race, give them enough rope and they'll always end up hanged.

For now, bellies were full, egos also.

Someone would pay.

MIKE PHILBIN

4
YOU THE PEOPLE
KEVLAR KUBITZ, A RECAP

If you've never seen them before, they're real freakish-looking, these Kevlar Kubitz. Crawling up the concrete towerblocks of a CDZ or *Corporate Dorm Zone* housing estate like reverse slinkies tipping flexibly end-over-end, sniffing out today's scheduled roster of attendees to the global whorehouse.

A Kevlar Kubitz's outer surface is covered in microscopic cilia so that they can either scale tall buildings in this bending-over-backward fashion, or travel along commercial superhighways like snails on slime.

A Kevlar Kubitz is the best commuter device ever invented, like a Truancy Officer of old with his sniffer dogs bred to track you down, keep you off the streets. When a Kevlar Kubitz arrives in your Corporate Dorm Zone it'll sniff you out, home in on you, chemically. It'll ferret you out of your stinking pit of Evertainment slumber where you're allowed to be who you really wanna be. This is the perfect tactic for a ruthless organism like The Industry who may need to apply *Leverage* later on in your career cycle. You know, when your role as an asset for the Corporation, your paid-for loyalty, is put under *ethical pressure.*

Of course corporate employees can't WFH or *Work From Home*, don't be naïve. That romantic pipe dream was never gonna take wing. Mankind was sold the technological lie of DSL or *Direct Secure Live,* aka *work when you want, live where you want*.

There will always be deadlines, there will always be security issues, there will always be Team Pizza crunch time and *Dunkin Donuts* crisis meetings. Wasn't that obvious to any of you? WFH was just another well-marketed counter strategy to cyberlink the whole world in the name of Global Enslavement.

Remember, any system, any massively-parallel neural-network can be hacked into. Everybody knows this. What everybody doesn't know is they're designed to be hacked into. It's the golden rule in the three-year-consumables market. Make systems undefendable. There's always Commerce in Maintenance. It's the insidiousness of it all that gets to you, if you study the mindset; the never-ending out-flow of cash from *You* to *Them*.

So, the Kevlar Kubitz steal you from your Evertainment Socket in the *worker housing* and abduct you as part of a conscription army to the corporate office where you work out your contractual hours. They're made of this material that seems to absorb the employee, suffocate them almost, but keep them alive just enough until they're at the office gates.

If necessary, the Kevlar Kubitz can pacify you with one of its taser-like feelers to ferry you back to its owner, your corporate employer i.e. The Industry, which is really a single entity smeared across the world like rancid butter.

The Industry's sub-corporations shiver under ridiculously up-tempo umbrella names like *Highpoint* or *Pinnacle* or *Echelon* to convince the working-slave-population that it's not all some cynical money-making scam at your expense, i.e. monopolism gone global. The really bad thing about Kevlar Kubitz is their CIS or placement-funded Corporate Infotainment System.

P.V.s or Psyche-Vertisements, another ESI *ready-to-wear*, will push any old marketing to the core of your brain during your daily commute: here's a classic.

January, 1932. Dusseldorf, Germany.
Everyone knows the story about Lord Adolfus Hitler, 'cos you can't unknow a psyche-vertisement until its contractual erosion time has expired'. Heil Hitler, so the story goes, had just given a rousing speech before the Industrial Club in Elberfelder Strasse, just round the corner from where you recently worked in Wupper Strasse in what's still known as Dusseldorf in what once was called Germany. Heil Hitler was leaving the meeting, his protective entourage surrounding him, and he just slipped on something in Elberfelder Strasse, right outside the steps of the Industrial Club.

Died on the spot.

Everybody knows this … it's part of your Industry Education.

It isn't the arbitrariness of this probing psyche-vertisement nor the manner of Heil Hitler's death that really bugs you. Something shiny underfoot, so reports have it, something like mercury? Mercury all over a German street fatally tripping the destined-to-be leader of Your Country? Assassinated by Living Metal? Assassinated by a killer hiding among the Periodic Table of Elements? Something of grave importance, something fundamental, had happened to your beautiful, unified world this morning. A crack had appeared in space and time. And a sinister hand had reached down to throttle you to death.

Is that infotainment to you?

Maybe you're just starting to dislike the paste-like gruel of prison planet disinformation that saturates the microwave frequencies of your day in the office. Damn those obtrusive Psyche-Vertisements, selling their sluttish rot to the captive corporate Persons, drilling the garish neon-lit message home like a lurid gang rape. Right to the very core of the cerebellum, down to the root of man's ego-drive.

As you hang there in the suffocating stasis of your Kevlar Kubitz, they play this corporate muzak into your soul and you never seem to forget it. Even during the day, a micro-vert can spark off another stanza of neuronic reinforcement and the newest jingle or the shiniest logo presentation from 'some off-shore tax haven' company, some *Satellite*, leaps into your mind as fresh as spring lilacs, as solid as a fist punching your front teeth.

There was a phrase used in Thatcher's Britain at the end of the twentieth century, "Get on your bike, and find a job;" that was back when there used to be something called *Nostalgia* and a guiding principle called *Family*. None of that exists anymore. At a moment's notice a Corporation can up sticks and cart all its employees off to *greener pastures* aka *minimised overhead*.

There's an Emergency Exit demo all new corporate employees are shown where the Kevlar Kubitz conglomerate on the shore or the border of some 'country', as they used to be called, into these absolutely enormous balls of interconnectedness. Kubit after Kubit wedges in together. A maximum of eight employees per Kubit crammed into these enormous rolling spheres... you see them sometimes, when Relocations are afoot, like glaciers flattening private housing along their Relocation Route.

They seem grotesquely cumbersome, so heavy that the lower Kubit might get crushed were they not programmed to be in constant motion, sliding like convection currents from the upper to the lower strata of the Relocation Sphere. The whole thing softly rolling as more Kevlar Kubitz insinuate themselves into Escape Configuration.

It's this sudden realisation, that The Industry can be relocated from Zone to Zone at a moment's notice (or at least by Overnight Courier) that makes you feel less secure in your working life than you did before you were finally offered this Dream Job. It's not the fact that you might lose your dream job. On Earth, everybody works. Let's rephrase that to be more legally relevant, "Everybody (who can) contributes their daily quota of hard labour to The Industry."

You're an integral part of the money game, your personal contribution to paying back the global debt to the *DIM* or *Derivative Instrument Makers*.

Think about that, it's worse than *Original Sin* the Catholics tormented their hapless flock with. This debt is your responsibility, fuckers; that's what you're reminded every time a Kevlar Kubitz comes to drag you off to the factory.

If, before you plug back into the work node and take the fascism of office doctrine in the amygdala, you wonder, *What if The Industry isn't where I should be?* then you're probably on the way to becoming a petty criminal. If you're the sort of person who's not 'contributing their daily quota of hard labour' like all the rest, you're probably already involved in some sort of illegal money-making scheme; you're a gambler, a thief, a gangster. We're talking here about activities of this nature at the summit or the base or all points in between of the *GCP* or *Great Control Pyramid*.

The Penal System already has an estimate of your incept date in its database. There'll be some algorithm. There are algorithms for everything these days. Remember, this won't be your first job in The Industry.

Oh, no.

You'll have worked hard to get where you are today. You'll have even gone to University, or spent time at Night School, and/or gone through all the online/hardcopy Psyche-tut' and Psyche-pup' documentation to get you past Psyche-eval' and onto Second-int' and into one of only a few of the exalted positions in this global entertainment hub that, despite its voracious appetite, is more like a small village within every newly incorporated country.

You'll have done some amount of paid or unpaid freelance work, building up your portfolio. You'll be a stubborn and honest hard worker. You'll pride yourself on your ability to adapt to change and be a dependable soldier in The Industry's flirtation with the Consumer as Enemy.

And don't kid yourself, it's a war you've gotten yourself involved in.

Somehow, when you first joined this Dusseldorf arm of The Industry, you spidey-sensed the precarious dog-eat-dog nature of The Permanent Contract. Such was the initial torrent of methodologies, working practises and non-disclosure-agreements to authorise for every gigabit of information you processed, those first three months in the office seemed to fly by. You got in nice and early. You kept your head down. You kept your Psyche-soc' locked and loaded. You worked diligently through your assigned list of assorted mediocre tasks and you left for home a few minutes after your contractual hours.

Always treading lightly, like something blood-smeared and musky stepping round a slumbering carnivore. Your aim was to not only show that you should be regarded as an indispensable member of Your Team but to secure your passage through the legal wilderness of those first three months, thus making it harder for management to fuck with you when they suddenly find you surplus to requirements at the end of your current project.

That's how you have to play this game. Embed yourself like a tick they just can't afford to get rid of. Become an integral part, an essential cog or gear or grease.

You're really a bit of an old hand at it, this survival lark. You'd have done your research while you grafted in lower-grade jobs over the years. A successful spider is the one who spends his time finding the right location to build the right sort of web for the pickings of the region. And what excellent pickings this company is offering. You know this one company is really worth the fight, the dishonour and the scandal. You're willing to put your heart and soul into every aspect of your tedious working life.

You are not a total moron for wanting to work here.

You are a total moron for not realising earlier in your employ that, sometimes, being a total moron is a lot better than the alternative.

5
THE CUSTODIANS
EVERYBODY HATES SPIDERS

Local time: 2240 hours.

Due to their impromptu meal of fresh warm *poached* meat, Asalah and Rotimi arrive later than they'd planned at their next destination, a studio apartment on Merton's cobbled street shared by Sarah and Adam Sitwell. An inseperable pair of twins who many at Oxford University's Real Tennis Club, circa 1798, where they were avid *nee* fanatical players, suspected 'something was not quite right with them'.

The apartment is empty when Asalah and Rotimi arrive, as before gaining entry through the open window. On the floor, only a stain remains from where the 'evolutionary experiment' had taken place.

"Could they have been found, do you think?" asks Asalah.

Rotimi sniffs the air with his pre-historic snout, "Bad smell, I don't like this."

"Yeah, my feathers are tingling, you know?"

"We have to get out of this place. I think we've been compromised." Rotimi says, starts to back away.

"We could have just walked into a trap?" Asalah asks.

"Worse..." Rotimi prepares to fight with whomever is still in this room.

A nose-itching fibre of silk floats across the scene like a ghostly gossamer in the wind. The pair of them freeze with dread, and terror. No one breathes. No one moves.

At the back of the building, a police car speeds down High Street, on its way to arrest 'some other criminals' this time. They are safe, Timi and Asi are both off the hook, this time.

"How do you do that?" Rotimi asks her, starting to relax.

"What?"

"Talk without lips."

"H-uk yoo!" she replies, her beak partially closed like a ventriloquist, her feathers fluff spasmodically "Gottle o' geer? Gottle o' geer," she jeers up close to the man-dog-thing. Rotimi shows his rows of flint teeth. But something's still not right. And they can both feel it. A static charge in the air. Something's still watching them. Eyes on their flesh like itching hairs...

"No seriously, it's bugging me. It doesn't make sense," Timi snuffles through his dinosaur-like snout, the enormous sheets of jaw muscle throb and pulse.

"And you've heard *how* many dog-alligators talking recently?" Asalah tries to lighten the tone.

"Touché." there's that Rotimi snear-smile, that break in the tension, "But where are the..."

"What?" Asalah looks around, her owl-head swivelling all the way round in a mad panic. She goes into attack mode, her throat constricts such that a short shriek erupts from somewhere deep inside her horrorbox.

She looks up. Into the corner of the room. Nearly fecal sacs. *Everybody* hates spiders. And that's exactly what sits up there in the corner of the birthing room, breathing like a sauna. A big fucking spider. Upside down, pressed into the upper corner of the room. Bigger than one person. Four human legs with feet. Four human arms with hands. Four human eyes. Two human mouths, two human tongues. Ready to pounce.

"Aaarrrgh!" Asalah screams as the 'spider' starts to move. It's just the inertialess nature of spider movement. It's too much to comprehend rationally. You just react and that's it. All other considerations go out of the window. Nature takes flight. And you go with it. You move. You keep a safe distance from it.

The spider's eight appendages are just too long. And how did they get that extra joint in the middle? An arm with two elbows is just *wrong*. Asalah is looking at it, a down-turned expression at the corners of her beak. Asalah doesn't even see the spider-thing leap down between herself and Rotimi until its happened. They both react instinctively. Both drop going into attack crouches, ready to kill.

Two central eyes larger than the two outer eyes, spider-thing quips to itself in one voice. "Look, sister, a dog and its pet pigeon."

Rotimi bares his three-inch-long teeth, tatters of flesh from his recent meal still littering his gumline. He settles into his low-slung attack crouch, murder-ready. A snarl shudders across his feral face.

"Guys, guys! Chill the fuck out!" a second voice issues from the spider-thing.

"I'm gonna ride you if you don't quit that trash," Asalah takes wing with a staggering down-sweep of her snow-blinding wingspan.

Back to the first voice, "Come on, little pigeon, leap upon us," spider-thing crabs to the left.

Asalah presses herself against the far wall, an acidic bubble rising in her throat. Her mind in flames of horror.

"Ride us like an eight legged pony," the compound-voice, mocking laughter erupts out of the rippling double mouth doesn't sound reminiscent of either Sarah or Adam.

"Yeah, ride you like a spider," Asalah effects bravado, "I'm shitting myself over here. I properly hate spiders. Properly hate them. What the hell?"

"They were screwing each other," Rotimi has the instinctive answer, "Weren't you?"

"Man, we were roasting each other. And I mean really fuckin'," Adam-Sarah bangs one of its eight fists onto the floor. Elsewhere among the twin life form, a cheek reddens. Can a spider blush?

"We were fuckin'"

"And we were buckin'"

"We were lickin'"

"And we were suckin'" they take it in turns to catalogue the grotesquery of their salacious union.

"It got so dirty, so really really really really insanely dirty. Then genius here," Sarah-Adam refers to itself like it's still two separate entities, 'goes, you wanna do it now?' so I says, 'We're already fuckin' doin' it lover,' as you do, and he thumbs his pill into my mouth, so deep and so fuckin' delicious you can only imagine how fuckin' turned on it got me. Spat in my fuckin' mouth to make the medicine go down."

"Got us both," Adam-Sarah has a slightly different timbre to its voice. Now, that's freakish, that shift of timbre from the same thing like a bi-polar shift, a schizophrenic rift.

"And you survived, intact? As one?" Asalah landed and skipped around to examine the spider-thing, it was spider-like, no doubt about it, but the skin under the moulting spider hairs was human enough; you could even make out the remnants of both the male and female anatomy. Only remnants mind. Nothing distinctive. Softened into its new dual-role.

"Please don't move. Just stay as still as you can. Cos if you move, I'll..." Asalah is inspecting a raised glove of skin on the back of the spider-thing when it screams. It races into the upper corner of the room again, leaving a choking shower of silk in its wake.

Asalah screams. She does this every time it moves. She really fucking hates spiders. Her heart pounds in her throat. Rotimi watches the farce like it's funny, and it sorta is.

"Don't touch our spinnerettes, that tickles us." Sarah-Adam giggles from on high, its whole body shuddering as its eight human hands and feet affix them into the high altitude of the mock Tudor dining room.

"Don't tickle their spinnerettes, sis'." parrots Rotimi, "That tickles them."

And suddenly, there's a massive rugby scrum in motion. Rotimi and Asalah launch their pincer move without further ado. It's a spinerette attack of enormous proportions. The dog and its pet pigeon dash around the ever-spinning hiccoughing spider-thing, tickling and playing with it. Putting their hands and wings over its eyes. Rotimi pulling one of the eight legs. Asalah underneath the damned thing, her tail feathers scattering loose hairs from the manly-womanly 12-packed underbelly of the pseudo-arachnid.

Spider thing spins onto its back, eight legs in the air. Giggling like an enormous ungainly teen. Asalah scrambles back and launches herself in the air. At the same time across the room, Rotimi bounces off the far corner and is on a counter-tickle-attack trajectory.

A knock at the door. Three sharp knuckle raps.

Everyone lands in total silence.

Spidey on its back, legs akimbo.

Rotimi hands on spidey-belly.

Asalah crouches with her wings spread wide apart, frozen in time. Like a sculpture.

Nobody breathes.

"Can you keep it down in there?" comes the muffled threat.

"It's the landlady..." Sarah-Adam whispers in total embarrassment. She scuttles back over onto all eight arms and legs. Goes to the door. One of her four hands on the door handle.

Asalah hisses, "What are you doing?"

"I'm just gonna... oh," Adam-Sarah is back in control. Clears his throat, "Sorry about that Mrs Greenaway, got family over. We're sorry. Get back in there and sit down..." he fakes a reprimand to imaginary nephews or nieces.

Silence from the other side of the door. Then slippered footseps shuffle off down the creaking wooden stairs.

The four of them, if you're counting human hosts, three if you're counting Re-Wilded creature units, look at each other, smiles and raised eyebrows, a soft chuckle ripples through the group. Asalah exhales; a soft trill escapes the back of her throat.

"Guys, you're looking real good," Timi prowls around the spider-thing, "Phew … you smell funny, of course," he jumps out of the way of a brief spinnerette dusting of silk, "I say 'smell funny' but you're not even hearing me, are you? What you got for sense? What's special about you?" he's like a puppy finding a toilet roll hanging down in front of his nose, a kitten finding a butterfly on the wing.

"What's special about us?" Sarah-Adam asks with her side of the face.

"Let me," Adam-Sarah takes over the baton, "We've been thinking about this. You see us. Come on, have a good look. What do you see?"

"Spider," Asalah flinches.

"Spider," Adam-Sarah parrots her, "Then you're not seeing it."

"What are we missing?" Timi asks.

"We've been wondering," Sarah-Adam jumps in, "We're a couple, and we love each other. But let's say we're eight, nine, ten people who love each other with as much sheer ferocity," the hairs on the back of this spider-thing ripple as if a fox had just raced through a corn-field.

"You say the sweetest thing, cutey," Adam-Sarah breathes.

"Please, I'm about to puke," Asalah mocks them.

"We were thinking Centipede," Adam-Sarah just puts it out there, like it's the most obvious conclusion you could possible have, "We are Centipede."

"That is sick, man." Timi is strangely impressed by the suggestion, "Centipede?"

Asalah shrugs her shoulders, doesn't get it.

MIKE PHILBIN

6
YOU THE PEOPLE
INTERMITTENT EVERTAINMENT DISLOCATION

There's a phrase, *FUCK EARTH,* that appears, inscribed in block capitals on the frowning forehead of someone who's sat in a pilot's chair, someone *sick of the plane he's piloting.* You've no idea what that inscription means. You've no understanding of why it has scored itself across a pilot's sweating forehead in vicious drops of acid-like blood, crenelating in the crevices and folds of skin as the power, the sense of power at least, courses through an angered man's veins.

To understand what's really going on, we're going to have to take you back.

Back to the first time this ever happened, back to the time you first thought that you could actually achieve something with your life, the first time you dared to dream that there was something more to this existence waiting inside you maybe, the way cancer waits, to realise that there was something coming, to realise that you, *You* were that answer to all your problems.

But imagine the burden.

You're just *You.* As we've already stated. How can *You* make the Earth turn on a different axis? Little lonely, emasculated and isolated you. The scale of the task is just too daunting, is just too immense. Where's your imagined fulcrum?

But relax, we're here to help you.

You out there, reading this right now, we're hear to help *You* get over the worry and the fear and the anxiety of such an enormous task. But most of all, we're here to help you get rid of your ambivalence to the horror of ECO or Everyday Covert Operations.

We're here to take you on a journey into True Awakening™. We're here to make sure you know why your entire world is falling apart and why Earth must be allowed to die. So that New Shoots™ can spring up, so that Humanity™ can be re-born, so that the Earth can re-plenish and re-vitalise, recover from its assault by You The People™, the indentured masses.

If you're ready, we'll begin.

Take a deep breath before reading any further. This is the most important step. Take a deep breath and don't think about action...yet. That's not the way this is going to work. You don't even know what thing to do to make this right, so relax. Think only of breathing deeply. Think only of the sound of your own voice inside your own head. That voice, there. You can hear it, can't you? Making sounds of these lines of text? That's the voice of your fear and your anger and your inability to DO anything worthwhile. That's the sound of your misery, your rejections, your losses.

Embrace that voice, like it was really yours... Are you still breathing? Never forget to breathe. That is the most important aspect of survival. Breathe deeply, dear reader, breathe deeply. And exhale. Feel all the tension holding this book releasing from your hands, your wrists, your arms, your shoulders, your neck and your forehead. Breathe in again as the tension flows away into the ether and you can feel that constant hiss-droning tone in the centre of your skull start to melt like chocolate ice cream left out on a summer's day. Relax and breathe and let the stress and strain of modern living just float away. It's not why we're here. It's not why you're reading this book. It's neither the beginning nor the end, it's just about *breathing*.

Breathe!

Don't even think about doing anything just yet, that comes later, much later. Now, we need to listen to that inner voice, the voice that you use when reading books and newspapers and the internet. It's not even *Your* voice. It's a voice someone else put there so they could control what you think, so that someone could temper your critical thinking process, so that you would jump when you are told and urinate on your own stomach on cue. You are not the person you thought you were. *You* are something else.

A toy?

A pawn?

A plaything?

Maybe not, and possibly all three at once. Fact is, that voice there...Breathe! Breathe deeply, dear reader, please don't forget to breathe. And exhale. You're feeling much better now. Much better about everything. That voice, that *incubated persona* who reads things for you, in your own head, it will change, the timbre will alter, the intonation will mutate, the insistence will crumble eventually, given enough time, with enough reason and rhyme, you will hear a new You, a clearer thinker, a more compassionate and natural tactician, coming to the fore.

You will hear the sound, like a soldier hears the shouted commands of his sergeant-major. That's how it'll sound at first, but then you will hear a new voice that allows You to command where you're going. You, as a race of over seven billion individuals. But first you must breathe, breathe deeply, dear reader and soon we will allow you to dream once again. We will teach you how to BE, and not just do.

First of all, Fuck Earth.

That's the shock over with. Fuck it. It ain't working. It's broken. Reject the lie. Turn your back on the propaganda. End your own confusion. You don't need it. Never have. It's a goner. You will survive, so fear not. You must remember that breathing is your only aim. Breathe deeply now. Forget the fear, concentrate on the voice in your head, taste its intent, but be suspicious, don't trust it, not yet. Not fully. This will be a long process of re-wiring and re-education, but it will be worth it. If you're brave enough. If you can stand the horror, the sheer horror of the indoctrination your whole life has been. If you have the courage of your own conviction. If you believe there's a better way.

"What?" you say, a better life than in The City™?

How could this be possible? For hundreds of years, you've realised that all your needs were supplied, all your dreams catered for, by *The City*. Be it the City of Oxford, the City of London, Vatican City or D.C....And this can mean whatever you want it to. This is, after all, Your Story.

But something's not right about The City today. You look around and it's not apparent. You recognise it for what it is. But it's like something is missing. Don't think too hard about it, just accept its limestone brick legacy, its dreaming spires legacy. Just enjoy The City for what it is, an historical reference to Empire.

Relax

Breathe deeply

Because this is still all just part of a fantasy. Breathe deeply. Breathe...a noise.

Yes, a noise, in The City.

Why should that strike you as odd?

Isn't The City normally fractured by the random hiss of stocks and shares, assets and commodities, being bought and sold? Maybe it's a Bank Holiday today. But it's normally never *this* quiet. Punctuation of such an obvious nature is absurd, and horrifying. To your right.

A blue thing in the sky. A plane landing. A passenger airline. Its engines at full roar. But there is no runway in The City. All runways are out of town. Where the poor people live. Nothing as filthy as a runway would be built in The City, so why is a plane trying to land?

No. It's a plane you've seen before in press releases and TV specials. They call this plane Air Force One, a Boeing 747/200B is the actual model, and it's trying to land in The City. It's so close, you can see the pilot's face, your face, in the tiny window as it banks to the right, aiming down High Street for a landing.

But there's a struggle. Air Force One doesn't want to land. In fact, Air Force One is fighting with all its metal might to keep its snub nose in the sky. Its jet engines are screaming bright red as burning kerosene sprays out the back. Trying to keep aloft, trying not to crash. You can see the ripple of super-heated air bombarding High Street's cobblestoned road.

Air Force One yaws drunkenly round a corner, wildly rolling from port to starboard.

You don't see the crash. You don't see the flash. You don't see the clean-up operation nor the casualties. That's not why you're here. You hear someone tell you it landed in that open sewer, smoking in the middle of the road. But you know that's a lie. There is no debris around the hole and that size of aperture would never garage a plane so large. The math doesn't work, just like on 9-11 at the Pentagon; the gold don't pan out.

What you've just witnessed is the near-death of Reality™, the near-death of Profit™, the near-death of Peace™. But that's okay because this is not your concern, just yet. Just, look away...for now. Don't think about the logic in what you think you see. Don't try to understand the sacrifice you've all been making, day in, day out for a tyrannical global agenda. All will be revealed, in time. For now you're having a SCS or Severe Culture Shock.

Keep breathing.

It's about time you were distracted by the tangerine dream served up by the Kevlar Kubitz. Hadn't you thought it odd that there were no pedestrians on the streets of The City, only Kevlar Kubitz? Watch them zoom by, cubicle-sized cubes of jelly sliding along the cobbled streets of The City, a manic orange blur. You can see the corporate lackeys trapped in their capture poses like mosquitoes caught in amber. Look how they move at speed, navigating with pin-point accuracy around The City aiming for corporate targets where they can offload their issue. Berth their cargo. Certify a slave for another day of meaningless toil.

These corporate transportation devices are normally set to 'stun' in case they come across a disoriented employee in their path. They stun as they surge around the person. Not killing them, just welcoming them into their luke-warm petro-chemical embrace. A warm place where they can recover, refreshed to continue the work of the day. There are always more Kevlar Kubitz to tidy up any glitch in the machine. That's their job. Look at how they climb the walls of The City, like a soft cube of corporate loveliness, rolling end over end as they ascend to their assigned floors, opening up square-sphinctered apertures in the face of these corporate work houses where they disgorge their comatose contents into their relevant working cubicles and go about their hunter-seeker transportation duties.

You've never been in one of these Kevlar Kubitz. And that's probably a good thing as they'd dissolve you. You are not on their list of clients, they don't have your 'chain'. You are a germ in their gauntlet, a nasty fungus that must be cleansed from the equipment. You are an abomination. A stain. A disease.

Plus, nobody likes a thinker.

As smoke continues to billow up from the open sewer, you wander round aimlessly in this strange dead place. Kevlar Kubitz ferrying employees to and from their dead-end slavery for the Corporate War Machine, clocking them on when they're disgorged, clocking them off when it's time to pick them up and ferry them back to the stinking, festering, spore-choked outer limits of Urban Sprawl.

You know you shouldn't be here, right?

You shouldn't be out in the open, like this. Seeing this machine in action like this. Loose. Aware. Unregulated. This hasn't happened for several years. There was a case of one person, like yourself, who wandered about at a loss for purpose and structure in their life. That person had a good life for seven weeks, then he started to Under.Stand.

That's when the machines came for him.

And they were not set to STUN.

You find a pile of money in a derelict red public phone box and start to stuff your pockets with it. It's heavy and you can't go anywhere with it. Can't put such a suspicious amount in a bank, can't pay with change, can't get on a plane as the weighing apparatus will pick up your 'excess baggage'.

Before putting the last coin in your pocket you see something shimmer, it's not a high specularity error. It's something in the embossed surface of the coin. A tick tock ticking twitch in the living metal, heads becomes tails becomes nuclear weapons becomes a soaring dove, its wings spread apart. You put the coin in your pocket. Can you feel it still twitching, converting, warping from symbol to symbol?

In your pocket, the coin settles on two letters set in Times Roman, E.T.

7
THE CUSTODIANS
STEALTH MODE ENGAGED

Local time: 2303 hours.

"Look at it – it's big. But, it's a dud," Rotimi sniffs at the still intact but sadly deflated birthing mound. A sneer crawls across his face. He grabs a corner of the thing with a paw and pulls his head back fast as the stink hits him.

"Hungry as I am, Timi, I'm not eating that. It doesn't even smell right from here," Asalah shudders.

"This place does not smell right. You know what I mean, Asi?" Timi shows his flint-like rows of teeth, looking around the modern space as he tries to see if he's missing any clue, any detail as to why all this doesn't feel right.

"Does not smell right."

They are stood in the faux-marble floored dining area of the Private Residence of Robert Hennessy on Cambridge Terrace, just north of Speedwell Street, a purpose-built complex of one-bed and two-bed modern accommodation for the Bank of Mum & Dad student who just needs the sexiest modern apartment in Oxford to show off to their Bollinger-supping and Caviar-slurping Bullingdon/Piers Gaveston Clubbers.

Nineteen years old, Hennessey is as spoiled-a-rich-kid as they come; and clever, too. He is studying both a B.A. in English and a B.S. in Economics.

What they couldn't see was what had happened moments before their arrival...

Hennessey takes the pill.

Hennessey goes a funny colour.

Hennessey gulps and squirms like a fish on a hook.

Hennessey pukes up his part-digested evening meal of Edamame, Udon and Asahi beer.

Hennessey clutches at his throat like he's being strangled by some maniacal WCW wrestler.

Hennessey goes an undersea colour, coral blue, but with shimmers of edge through it. Edge is the sort of colour you get on those cars that've been painted with special refractive paint and the front of the car is a different colour from the back of it. And as the car passes you by the rainbow courses through its enamelled surface and you're like, "Wow, that's nutz!"

Hennessey shits himself and the brown-green stain spreads out underneath him. A sewer stink like nothing you've ever smelled pours out from under his foetal spasm on the faux-marbled floor. And this is where it gets mad and wrong and just so insane that your rational mind doesn't even comprehend what you're seeing.

Hennessey curses his Masters at the Uni.

Hennessey takes the Lord's name in vain.

Hennessey is having a really bad time of his transformation.

Hennessey is not a wimp. Don't take this as a shiftless-character assassination – this is not trolling or anything cheap-shot-ish. He's a man and he can take his punishment better than most – it's how he's been brought up.

From his earliest years, you can rely on Hennessy to just grin and bear any pain, any suffering. He just isn't taking it as well as those who've already made the journey into the festering bowels of their geneline, his parental quadrisplice stretching back through parallel branches of his family tree as far back as – that's not even physically anywhere in anyone's geneline, so where should such a kink in the matrix come from?

Admittedly, nobody's had an easy time of their transformation yet. It's a process that's fraught with horror and tortured by nerve-bursting surgery, heated knives at the molecular level. And, yeah, that hurts. And Hennessey's not some sort of wuss, he can take it. He's proven time and again he's got what it takes to 'move on to the next level' of existence. He's a liver, a healer, a deal-with-the-pain don't-show-it hero, ya dig?

But what Hennessey's become…well, it's not even physically possible. His abominable miracle is just a disgrace to Mother Nature. Its never existed before. And it's probably all his own fault. Hennessey is carrying an awful lot of psychological luggage around his everyday existence. Shit that stretches back through when he was a little kid in what remained of Kosovo after the Corporate War Game stomped through that once-beautiful country for benefits of a financial nature.

Yeah, "Hennessey" is an Escape Name, the cover identity of the remnants of a family torn to fucking bits by the ethnic cleansing of that Al Qaeda-murdered Eastern Bloc country. It's horrific the monsters that we all carry around with ourselves, but this?

We all have skin, some of us may have scales/feathers.

We all have bones, some of us may have our bones on the outside.

We all have blood rushing through our living systems, pushed around by our heart muscle – some of us may have many more than one heart.

But this…*this*, what is it? Plasma? No, it's not plasma. It's not like the separated parts of human blood. It can't even be considered human, not one single string of his original DNA remains. He's become this weird physics-slippery thing. A slug. No, more than that. A slug can't slip and slide through physical (supposedly solid) reality the way Hennessey can.

He's got form, delicious form – don't go thinking Hennessey's an amorphous blob or something, that'd at least give a reason for his insanely wrong abilities. No, the big insult is Hennessey has a perfect outer form that resembles something loved by young and old, male and female.

If you could see him outside of his 'natural element' you'd see that he looks a lot like a Bottle Nose Dolphin, but his face is adorned with mottled Peregrine Falcon markings. In fact, the mottling, the falcon-like softly-fluttering surface permeates the entire silhouette. But they're not feathers, they're like diamond edged flesh pockets that allow Hennessey to grip onto any medium at the molecular level; think of little hands gripping, swinging from rung to rung on some electrostatic monkey ladder in an adventure playground.

If you could see him, you'd notice the bulbous yolk sac depending from his navel like an undescended testicle – that thing has to sustain him for as long as he can prevent himself falling to the centre of the earth. You'd understand why his weird sucker-like mouth would inhibit his feeding on solids. You know, if you could actually see him; that is, separate him from his medium. But you can't – unless you trapped him inside a re-engineered electromagnetic MRI scanner. Hennesey, you must understand, epitomises 'dependent duality,' both part of his environment and aware of his own topology, all at once.

Sure, look at Rotimi. He's like from another era altogether, a prehistoric throwback to pre-dog, pre-cat, pre-quadruped. But this. This is a whole lot uglier. A whole lot more of an abortion of fate than the rest of the sad bunch called The Custodians. This freak couldn't even remain in its womb.

Even during a simple 24-hour gestation period, it was an immense mental effort for Robert Hennessey to actually stay within the confines of his amniotic fluid. But he did it. He completed his term. He could then 'relax' and have the easiest birth of all the Re-Wilded creatures.

"So where is our clever lad?" Timi sniffs the deflated mound again.

"This doesn't seem like him, right, this *failure*," Asi does this funny inflaty-thing with both cheeks of her feathery bird face, an odd whizzing sound escapes her birdy nostrils.

"You think Henny's still around? Watching us?" Timi asks.

"Not only is he still around, he's most definitely playing a game with us," Asalah said.

Both are wrong, Hennessey isn't watching them; he is nowhere in the vicinity.

Robert Hennessy had long since fallen down through the architectural maze of the building's concreted blueprint. Like some new complex sea, Henny (that was who he was known as among Oxford's elite) has discovered his own personal medium – a convoluted electromagnetic forcefield where no man had ever ventured.

And as the open ocean is a delight for any aquatic lifeform, so is the architectural ocean of concrete and steel and brick and rock and soil as exciting to Henny. You can be as near the surface or as deep in the trench as you wanna be. You can leap into the air and look at the sun shimmering off the surface of your beautiful abode. And it's the same for a creature like Hennessey, only with him it's a more lethal game. For Hennessey, the sun is flipped, the sun lives in the centre of the earth.

This is the beautiful place for a creature like Hennessey, skirting deeper than anyone has ever gone. Deeper than the deepest trenches in the ocean, skirting below the grumbling crust of the earth, virtually licking the super-heated magma below the tectonic rock.

Then totally going for it, plunging as close to the metallic core of the earth, withstanding the electronic pressure, withstanding the torrent of heat, resisting the urge to just allow his atoms to float apart into boiling soup bubbles, fritter away to hydrogen and helium and carbon and the other raw elements of existence.

Do you understand how delicious the centre of the earth tastes to the likes of Hennessey, this unique lifeform that has never existed on the Earth before? There's something that's almost too alluring about the centre of the earth, there's literally nothing like this that anyone's ever seen. You go *this* deep, you don't even want to breathe, ever again. You just wanna plunge, as deep as you can go. And suddenly, before you've even swum directly to the core of this delicate homeworld, this profit-ruined living surface, this oasis of life as we know it, you're on the other side.

You've surfaced in some other location, some other part of the planet.

You could do this all day, and why not? Well, obviously, feeling this free, this liberated, is a real bonus, but there's still a tightrope to walk, there's still a Free Planet to protect. And Hennessey's one of the protective Custodians who has pledged his life to ensure that a dream comes true.

"Where next?" Timi asks her. He doesn't even realise that Hennessey is back in the room, up in the far corner, giving off no scent; just a single eye sitting up there, like a sentinel.

"We all know what's coming next," Asalah announces. "The grand opening of this year's PGC or Piers Gaveston Club. The latest foray into booze, birds and debauchery."

"You got an invite to that?" Timi sneers.

"When did you become a comedian?" she asks.

"When I met you, my love," Timi's whole external surface shifts to a high-specularity mode that reminds Asalah of laughing metal.

Asalah knows all too well what this means, what a sly shift in Rotimi's skin means. She can already see the swelling of his genitals, the panting, pulsating proboscis depending wetly.

Timi is upon her in a second. It's infuriating, because he has such a low centre of gravity, you can't even anticipate that he'll be launching himself at you. He's just there, on you, before you can take evasive action.

And when Timi wants to be on top of you, that's it. You will be mounted. Shall we look away while Timi and Asi scrub their mutual itch to some sort of grotesque climax? Come on, let's leave the little love bird/love cat to their lickings and peckings and womb fuckery.

Even Hennessey backs away, folds back into the electromagnetic matrix. Flicks his powerful tail, dismally.

8
YOU THE PEOPLE
LAMBY IS YOUR ROCK

And that's what it is, this fiat money, this fake coinage, this excess baggage – it's how you're supposed to empathise with the Global War Game. You don't get it, but we'll continue on until you really see The Big Picture.

Remember, you're still in the same City where you piloted Air Force One into an opening no bigger than a manhole, where you witnessed The Crash, where you saw a glimpse of the future steaming from an opened sewer. There are still no 'humans' on the street apart from the briefest glimpse of a cocooned workslave deposited in a speeding Kevlar Kubitz like a mosquito caught in amber.

Focus on the pocket money you've just found. What a bonanza! Your pockets are so full of cash. Don't you feel like you've achieved something real, something tangibly positive in your life? You're going places. You've made it. You shall not go hungry if there's a jingling sound in your pocket.

Except you haven't made it.

You've been scammed.

Look around you again, what do you see?

The City is what you see, sure. But do you see the logos? The over-engineered symbolic faces off all the banks? Do you see any doors, any lobbies, any means of entrance to these banks?

Go up to any one of them. Choose where you might hope to deposit your heavy pockets of cash. Try to make a deposit into that public vault of corporate crime. You can hammer on the disturbingly translucent face of any building with the side of your fist until the meat turns to bruise and the bone turns to pulverised chalk, you'll not gain access.

It's not where you should be.

So, where are you at?

You have a pocket full of scrap metal with some 'symbolism' on it.

Keep hammering on the side of the public edifice of that WFI or Worshipful Financial Institute and you'll see what happens. You'll see what happens when the Kevlar Kubitz sniff your alien DNA. Nothing's gonna happen to you though, not you. There's something real special about your life mission. But you don't need to know what that is, not yet. You're special for a very insane reason, you're invisible to the Corporate War Machine. They can't target you. Not here, at this time. And nobody knows why.

But keep breathing.

Your breath is the only thing that's gotten you this far. So let's stop hammering on the wall of this bank. Let's calm down. You've picked up a dog turd. Empty your pockets of all that chump change. Let that shit spill out of your pockets onto the streets. You don't need it. Nobody ever has. You're alive, for now. Keep breathing, this is about to get exciting.

Ready?

Look again, look at The City.

What is it doing to you?

Have you not noticed that The City appears to be getting smaller and smaller? You've not noticed the encroachment? You can keep moving. It's not local to any part of this crooked place. It's all around you, you're the focal point of this gradual entombment.

Accept your fate, for now, you can fight later.

For now, accept that this world is crushing in around you.

You'll not die, that's a promise.

You'll only experience a brief sensation of bodily assault.

You'll survive the next bit but you'll be a different you than the one who was enclosed in this insane asylum's gasping cell. Watch the walls cubically move in around you. Even while you're running like a madman, tearing out your hair and slavering like a rabid animal. You're self-cornered. You're self-imprisoned. You're self-punished. But it's what you need. It's the solution that'll liberate you, in time. Once you've re-learned what it all means to be alive.

The City has moved all around you now and you can't escape. This will be your holding cell for the next few chapters. You hammer on the cubic forcefield and you feel like you're baking under the intense heat that pours in through the five outer faces of your imprisonment. You can scream. You can kick. You can bite your forearms until you reveal the bones. But you won't die. You won't be here forever. You won't die of anything that happens to you in this place. It will only be for your benefit.

Breathe!

At least there's grass on the floor.

You hadn't noticed that, had you? The grass, it sorta grew while you weren't watching. And, though the walls of your cell are barely translucent, you can still see The City outside. So, why is grass growing in your special zone within The City?

And what is that Lamb standing there for? Are you hungry yet?

Do you realise what you'll be asked to do in the name of your own survival? It'll be for your own good that you understand how the world works. How limited is your time within this cell. What, you haven't noticed? The air's thinning within this sealed cell. You're slowly drowning in your own exhalation. Your heart starts to thump like a big bass drum but you can't face it. You can't surge your system the way it'll need to be surged for you to do what you have to do.

The Hammer.

Pick it up from the newly-grown grass. Feel the weight of it in your hand. That lump could easily crush such a soft delicate lamb skull, right? Well, it's about time you did what you have to do to escape this cell before your air runs out. The lamb looks over at you, munching on the fresh green grass in its chops. You've never seen such a beautiful young animal close up. Look at its inquisitive eyes. Look at the softness of its fleece. Look at the way it wags its tail and leaps about in the butterflies and the daisies.

You can even hear the birds, twittering somewhere, off into the distance beyond The City.

And you have a hammer in your hand, and you're starting to sweat. Your stomach gurgles reflexively, and you feel a wave of disgusted nausea pour all over you like hot needles. You have a sense of self-loathing that you've never ever dreamt of before. You could never imagine hating anybody else as much as you hate yourself.

Gotta breathe! Gotta stop trembling. Gotta control the heartbeat. Gotta stay alive. Yes, stay alive – you'll have to. It's what you're here for, so how are you going to resolve it?

You throw the hammer at the cubic forcefield surrounding you. But you've already been told. You can't escape by hammering your way out. You only succeed in startling the lamb, who races into the farthest corner from where the hammer lands and bangs face-first into that corner. Bouncing back, comically stunned. Now would be your perfect moment to strike, deliver the *coup de grace*. While the lamb's short senses are addled by the collision. While the gorgeous dear thing wasn't gazing at you, teary-eyed, the way it will do later once you've drained it of milk and tried umpteen other ways not to dispatch its sorry little life.

You know what you have to do to survive.

But not now, now will be messy. Relax. We can wait for quite a while yet. No one's going anywhere. So, hang back. Faint if it helps to be dramatic. But don't worry about having to kill that delicate creature yet. Maybe you'll find another way to escape this cell. Maybe you're truly not like all the others who've been trapped in similar circumstance over the years, in this City that might be like any other City all over the world.

Countless days into your exhausting incarceration, You and Lamby, as you've decided to call her, have really shared the shit. You've cuddled together in the chill of the night in The City. You've experimented sexually in a hallucinatory day-dream of moral lassitude. You've sustained each other with piss and sweat and milk. You are a pair, united - dependent. And you still think life can go on, like this mini-paradise in a sealed box, for ever and ever, amen?

But now there are scowling faces at the glass. Human hands wiping clean patches in the wall of your cell. Human tongues licking windows onto your public humiliation. Human eyes staring in at you like you're some sort of living exhibit in the middle of the still-crumbling City. How many of them are out there, gawping in at your shame? Inviting more of their kind to come see the freak show. Do you recognise any of their questioning visages? Are these any of your friends, relatives, colleagues?

More and more of them turn up as the day's sun carves a migraine heat across the skin of your box, the prison cell of your mind. Yes, the mind. Didn't you know that all the worst prisons are prisons of the mind? Forget Alcatraz. Forget Guantanamo. Forget the Bangkok Hilton. The really scary places are wrapped inside your skull.

More and more hands squeak across the surface of your mind, smeared noses face-crushed in curious frowns and scowls. The light starts to fade as the living day draws to a close. As you and Lamby succumb to the enormous weight of your mission. There's a rumble of thunder from the sky, and a soft settling earthquake-type oscillation under your cube. The whole world starts to tip inwards, pulling you underground. Lamby cuddles up to you, its big round eyes flitting here and there, its tail between its hind legs.

More faces and fists appear at the glass, smearing together, melding into new faces, part faces. Fists hammer the glass, causing a pizo-electric reaction on impact.

Lamby is panic-stricken by the lights as (surely) the filthy glass cube is sinking.

You gasp a big breath, realising that you hadn't been breathing for god knows how long. Lamby bounces from your embrace and leaps around on the soft green grass, bleating and back-leg kicking, bucking like a fluffy white bronco.

Someone leaps on top of your cube, his bare feet giving off sparks. First one. And then the other. And another, and soon, all these naked pedestrians are jumping up and down on your cube, slamming, jamming and cramming you into the earth. Bright fireworks going off on the roof of your cube.

"Fuck Earth," you shout at them. "And fuck all of you, you fuckers!"

But still the crowd gathers like a wave bearing down from deep in the Paleolithic ocean! The insane weight of their combined hatred slamming, jamming and cramming you down down down into the soil. Their assault on the glass sparking and radiating a shower of slugs into the glowing letters that spell out E.T.

MIKE PHILBIN

9
THE CUSTODIANS
FIE, FOH, AND FUM

Local time: 2304 hours.

James Mellon Hall is a purpose-built residence for students of Oriel College. It's about a mile east of the city, just off St Clements. Residence of one Abigail Chopsticks.

This is where Hennessy is at this exact moment.

After all, it's his self-appointed role within the Custodian Liberation to make sure the agreed-upon plan is carried out to the fullest extent of the biogenetic brief. And that means every little feature. Leaving it in the hands of the enthusiastic amateurs of the group is surely just a Recipe For Disaster. Hennessey considers himself a true professional, in comparison; as exemplified by the subversive covert iconography of his own secret biogenetic recipe.

The Custodian *Coterie-thus-far-hatched* won't be making the journey to examine if this one's worked. This one's completely on its own. And that's probably the way it should be with her, for a while, you know, until she gets used to what she actually is.

Alone, yes alone, if and only if you can ignore the presence of Hennessey, the matter-swimming dolphin-peregrine hybrid. Hennessey's already shuffled up close under the eggshell that bore this weird sight, this vertical peanut-shaped amoeba.

Look at the cilia-covered surface of this thing, it remind you of anything?

It reminds you of the locomotive surface of a Kevlar Kubitz, doesn't it?

It should, as (technically) they're based on the same Patent, *Locomotion by Method of Inductive Cilia.* Hennessy is a clever lad and knows exactly what he's looking at, *If a sphere is Zero Order surface, we can equate the human object with a First Order surface or doughnut.* He did, after all, contribute significantly to the original ESI patent, named above. But whereas that 'organic extrusional topology' is designed to keep the Kevlar Kubitz crawling across any surface, this application has found adaptation as a flight surface.

This peanut-shaped entity is floating vertically, about one meter off the floor; an air sculpture. It's stationary in the air. No heat haze. No down draft. No discernible movement. The way a squid hangs in the water against the tide. All over it, the rainbow-flickering cilia seem to scurry around like a summer breeze in long grass. You can see the ripples of six-degree locomotion all over it as all the pitch, the yaw and the roll are demonstrated with expert proficiency. This thing was 'born to fly,' literally.

Hennessey bobs his dolphin-like, peregrine-falcon-decorated face out from the softly vibrating matter that makes up the electrodynamic substance of the floorboards, the carpet, the dustified years of student wear and tear, the soft matting of dead skin cells like tiny waves lapping against his blinking eyelids.

Abigail Chopsticks isn't her real name. Her first name *is* Abigail. And she did used to wear a pair of Japanese chopsticks in her hair, when it was gathered up into a bun. But that's the only connection. It's her chosen name, her Custodian Name. Maybe one day we'll all have these Custodian Names that speak more about our useful function to Free Planet rather than to the arbitrary naming fancies of our parents. Instead of being called Bob or Ted or Judy, we'll have names like Watches For Wolves or Finds New Species or Wise Pathfinder the way the Cherokee and Iroquois and the Apache used to name their children; later in life, once they'd earned the right.

Abigail, then, is the Christian name of the woman who took the pill that changed her existence into this strange peanut-like shape. Abi, as she asks to be called, swoops down instinctively toward the briefly surfaced Hennessey and a girlish musical giggle of inquisitive deceleration squeaks out of her.

A vertical seam appears up the front of Abi's floating body, two vertical eyelids appear to flip open and a tongue-like 'seat for one' flops out; a nice dry bit of organic lounge furniture if you're keen on 'parking it' in what appears to be someone's gaping mouth, actually someone's ribcage.

'Looks weird' doesn't even describe what's going on. You look into that gaping door-flanked grotto and you know you're in some weird Space Alien From Beyond territory, you know you've wandered into the Twilight Zone.

But if you tried it.

If you actually took a seat, took residence within that scarily floating form.

If you could just muster up the courage to take up Abi's offer, and get inside, you'd have what's known in science fictional terms as a *levitating revelation.* You'd see what happened when you took your place in the seat. You'd see how the 'screen of its fluttering body' went obscenely one-way-transparent when you're sat inside the cockpit. Inside her anatomy. Inside *it* might be a more comfortable mental frame for your mind to occupy. *In* it. Seated. Chauffeured in a see-through 240° viewing experience. You'd love it. You really would. If you were brave enough to take that first step, make that first move. To sit on someone's proffered tongue of softest velvet and be seduced back into a luxurious oxygen-giving space that can accommodate a full-sized human being.

Admit it, you're fisting yourself with excitement just thinking about it, aren't you?

There's a lovely humming sound when she moves about. Like a wasp. No, like a line of wasps. No, that's not quite it either. Imagine, in the distance, ten wasps. In a rippling line. These ten wasps are joined by ten more wasps. And on until there's a wall of ten by ten wasps, all buzzing away. Now, imagine that face of wasps rotating round to reveal five more faces; a cube of fluttering wasps. Imagine this cube of wasps buzzing around in total freedom, random impulse from communal *ouija board* agreement.

That's how her lovely humming noise sounds, in that it emanates from all sides of her.

If you were brave enough or trapped enough to be inside her cockpit, you'd see how the material she's made of can relax and contract at the cellular level, like the lens in an eye or the skin of an octopus; this trick accommodating varying degrees of either-way transparency. You could see in, or see out. You'd be so comfortable. You'd be at one with your floating taxi-cab, able to just chit-chat with the driver and sit safe in the knowledge that you'd be delivered right to the door of your destination.

Remember, Abi's still human, no matter what her anatomical representation. And there'd be no rushing through the rain with a newspaper over your head, no 'drop me off here' three-point-turn at the end of your cul-dse-sac, that's just an amateurish no no. Right. To. The. Door. Right to bed, in fact. That's what a real chauffeur like Abi would do; she'd tuck you right back under the covers and jump in beside you to keep you warm, her surface cilia softly stroking and caressing your tired body until you wander off into sleep to dream of another day in front of the corporate whore monitor of your deepest darkest nightmares.

And if you look real close at Abi's busily fluttering surface, you'd see that she's still all woman. There's nothing missing. You can seen her rudimentary legs tucked underneath her the way crabs pull in their claws, protecting her genital undercarriage. You can see how her fingers pull back the vertical eyelids that allow the tongue to flip out. You can see the ribs up the side of the 'peanut' shape, the standing skull shape. You'd see that there'd be ear-remnants and clavicle remnants and spinal column-remnants and shoulder blade-remnants all tied up into a neater package. Yes, you can see how her form has been derived from the silhouette of her elongated skull allowed to morph into a more stream-lined or aero-dynamic form.

You can understand or at least sympathise that she still has human needs, like any other living *sapiens*, while appreciating how very alien she has become. How easy it now is for her to move through the air; a hot knife slicing through butter.

"What are you?" Hennessy surfaces again, tentatively.

Abi Chopsticks, that floating peanut that she is at least, again tries to scoop up the dolphin/peregrine, nose first. How could she really hope to separate the imagined thing from its truly solid existence. Hennessy was, and always will be, part of the landscape, part of the furniture of mankind's architectural legacy, a rock in a rolling sea. Immovable, insolently embedded.

He let's her try to suck him into her insistently opening and closing, her disturbingly flicking in and out chair-tongue. But even she knows something's not right, it's like licking a marble floor or trying to bite a chunk off a concrete wall. It's like some obscure mathematical conundrum where Hennessy into Chopsticks won't go. But the contact is enough to ensure Hennessey that the in-built algaeic energy source is alive within each of her mitochondria; she's literally glowing with energy conversion.

"What are you?" Hennessy tries to get her to talk, but only receives a thrumming re-phrasing of the sound of her locomotory surfaces in response, a distinct retreat from the odd thing that he is. She turns away forlornly; gazing, it seems, to the window which, while open, is no way going to allow her egress from her prison.

Hennessy, cos he's a bright lad, understands her dilemma and does a beautiful thing. Kicking off with his dolpin-like tail, he shudders up through the floor, up the far wall and leaps right across the place where the glass of the window and the window frame itself are situated. There's a brief explosion of light and heat and noise, and rainbow-like filaments linger in the air momentarily before the hole in the wall where the window used to be is revealed.

If you could rewind this scene, and slow it right down, replaying each interlaced moment, you'd see Hennessy's tail slamming out of the building on the far side of the wall and, as he continued his leap through the physical space of the window in its frame, slamming right through the window on this side, causing the physical structure of the silica particles that compose the frozen treacle-like glass sheet to vaporise, the expanding pressure wave taking the wooden frame with it; like a red hot bullet through ballistic gel.

Time to report back to base; the simulation is now properly under way.

It's only later, as dawn breaks over Oxford and Abigail Chopsticks ventures out into the sunlit world, that she starts to understand how her embedded algae relate to the greater source of all energy. The sun. How fundamental to her locomotion, by a power generation mechanism that is something akin to photosynthesis in planets without having to go green. More based on how the cardiovascular system of a mammal might approach a solution to the conundrum of solar energy conversion. The magic of human blood cells, enhanced to burn received photons rather than relying on the limiting oxygen/carbon cycle of its 'more normal humans'.

And that is the big consideration here, Abi Chopsticks (no matter what her physical appearance) is still the same human, with the same memories and the same emotions and the same desires and fears as she had before she took the pill. You psycho-polygraph her before and after the transformation and you'll notice a Personality Profile score of 100% correlation between the two. No noticeable deviations in either state, prior or current. She'll see the world in exactly the same way, like this or how she used to look.

Except that she won't. Abi Chopsticks no longer has 'eyes', so she can't 'see'. But she can still (very vividly) make out the shapes and forms that glow before her like kaleidoscopic night-vision footage taken through a fly-eye lens of many filters. She can easily distinguish between animal and plant, male and female, friend or foe. But her 'sight' goes a whole lot deeper than that. Her senses have altered to the point where pheromones mean more to her now than they have ever meant to any human.

She comes to rest by the side of a stream, ten miles north of her cocoon location. She is thirsty. And like any organic life form, she needs to drink to stop from drying up, shrivelling into oblivion. She unleashes her tongue seat and laps at the moonlit pool. She appears to be alone. Enjoying the reflection of the sun's rays from the dusty mirror of the moon's ever-pitted surface.

Not yet aware of how her new body works, Abi wonders how she'll feed. How she'll get the proteins and vitamins she thinks, still believes, her body needs to move around as it does, burning calories like a humming bird. She doesn't realise that she's become a thing of solar-powered sucrose, a human plant, a floating peanut with a heart that will remain forever human. She starts to miss her old form, ever so briefly. Reminisces on what it means to be touched and stroked and patted on the head or hand-shaken or aroused by a mouth, a finger. What will her life be like now that she is so very different from the woman she used to be?

Downwind, across the stream, a lone deer looks up from her midnight sup, startled by the thing on the opposite bank. There is no sound but the tinkling of the stream. Both creatures gaze fixedly at each other, in their own way, sharing the moment of extreme terror and un-natural connection.

Before separating, each to their pre-ordained fates.

10
YOU THE PEOPLE
YOUR FIRST REAL TASTE

And suddenly, as if the whole first few years of your employ were just a cynical Psyche-Vertisement, you find you've been back at work for three days with no discernible break in either your work load or the closeness of the ever-impending deadline.

You've resurfaced.

You've survived.

You reside in your all-too-familiar shallow-cubicle, that gives the illusion of privacy but still allows management to *keep an eye on the soldiers*. In fact, it's the exact same one you occupied in Dusseldorf. Same pinned on memos, sketches, reference. Same single Polaroid of a girl you thought you met at a party and can't even remember the name of.

Alongside you are the exact-same bunch of work colleagues, at least those who also survived the last bout of Restructuring to pay for your Satellite's relocation to this new base, this New Jerusalem; this…Oxford.

But today is like the first time you've ever seen The (real) Industry in all its pornographic explicitness. You've tended to keep your head down, you know, slouch down in your seat, get on with your job. You haven't been allowed out to do any Captures yet. Here in Oxford, as then in Dusseldorf, you'll have just got on with your job without really saying too much; doing just enough to keep middle management off your case. You'll have attended all the requisite meetings and parties, the punishments and trappings (or vice versa) of corporate life. You'll have been a productive nobody; a greasy machine cog. Happy to just be a part of something bigger. Item arrives. You *Professionalize* it. Item moves on. Nice and smooth. Money in the bank. Job for life.

But now you can't take your eyes off it.

Them.

You've got loads of work on your plate, as ever; projects to finalise, summaries to write, plans of action to agenda-ise and set in motion – arbitrary characters to Capture once you're allowed back into the field. You're a busy bee with (suddenly) not enough hours in the working day.

Time yourself.

Go on, take out a virtual stopwatch or other means of ticking off the seconds and time how long (retrospectively) you've just spent watching Veronica(?) on reception fiddle around with her tit-strap that's just so close to pulling off the big nipple show it's literally selling tickets. You could gawp at Veronica's constant tit-strap fiddling like a dribbling dawg all day long. You forget the waste of time. You overlook the hours spent distracting yourself from the real tasks on your plate. And you've never done this before? Have you been asleep or something? Have you been on some drug-induced trip?

You're already wondering where the time went and you haven't even set your virtual stopwatch yet.

You've wandered off again.

Stop that.

Look down at your watch and note the Time. Note down exactly what time it is right now. Okay, you got it? You're ready? Now, look up.

Breathe for Christ's sake, you're going to go blue – it's not like you're out of the woods yet.

You're mesmerised by that corporate whore at work, fingering her stress-damp titty-cup strap, adjusting and resettling the fine fabric across the once talcum-powder-fresh flesh before, during and after the endless procession of calls cuts across her twitch-psyche like kitten claws on rice paper.

You remember a call-girl joke that ends, "Man with penis, holding," and a dull ache throbs through your forebrain, like you've been banging your head against a hardback copy of The Bible for three and a half hours. You wonder if you actually have a fractured skull under the frowning covering of rumpled skull skin.

She denounces oh so cutely, Veronica; cuts off oh so sweetly, transfers and derails with consummate ease like a greased ball bearing going round and round inside a hamster wheel. And all you're thinking is, "Surely soon that fucking bra strap will just snap under the intensity of her fiddling and her nipple will show," you're literally grinding your gums against your clenched fist in frustration.

And she doesn't even have large breasts. That's not even the point. We're talking the principle of the thing here. She's itchin' to just dip both hands into that bra and scoop those soft white titties out from their hiding place, displaying pink flesh buttons arcing from their gossamer sheaths like every morning's blatant, cross-eyed rising suns.

And you should be getting on with your work. You're well and truly fucked if you carry on like this. At your bi-annual appraisal, they're sure to throw the time wasting book at you, and it'll hurt, it'll hurt like hell, especially when they tell you what contract you were gonna be on, what legal repercussions you are likely to expect.

Oh, yeah, they'll lay it on thick and heavy at your Exit Interview, as that last bi-annual appraisal will rapidly descend into. Don't worry, you don't have a chance of averting the obvious. The cards are stacked against you. And all because you couldn't keep your eyes off the stupid distraction who never puts out, the eye-candy that'll prove your ultimate undoing.

Stop.

Look at the clock, right there on your computer monitor. How much time has elapsed? Did you miss your dinner hour again? Is there some important meeting you should have been in thirty-five minutes ago? You fucked up again, didn't you? It's called missing time, and it's very like what reputed alien abductees report – *It's like time itself somehow seemed irrelevant and when I woke up it was three days later.* Well, that's what happens. You get so entranced by it, by the corporate circle jerk in all its fascinating puke-value that you don't even realise it's rotting your brain. It's not even about the moral issue, whether you should or shouldn't even be interested in 'that sort of thing, with those sorts of people', it's about your head. And what's. Slowly. Dissolving. Inside it.

It's true, though you've only been in this location, in Oxford, for three days, you're already suffering from the rot. In Dusseldorf you had the impression that you could work here until you died, it was what you were destined to do. Non-fame but wealthy non-fame. Maybe it's the change of climate, or the Oxford pollen.

In quiet moments, here in Oxford, the staff'll sit there like seals sunning themselves, preening their fleshy areas of lice and ticks, there's even more of a community feel than when they're banging each others' brains out. They excel at wearing the most provocative of garments, slung loosely across pampered flesh no more than a gossamer shawl, decorated as delicately as a modern meal would be spiced by the greatest chef in the top restaurants of this fine university town.

And that's not even what you see at the Purchaser End. What you'll see is a 'transaction' or a 'credit card payment' or a 'bill payment' or a 'breathing tax payment' or a 'thinking tax payment'. You'll never get access to this level of it, the Sleaze Machine. You'll never see its split thighs revealing all the gory-putrid innards of Commerce and Money-making. You'll never see that this prostituting of the human condition, this naked raped anal free show of inner office hand fuckery and domination games is how it all works.

Human degradation, slavery and arbitration is HOW your world does what it does, it's how the wheels of Corporate Industry are oiled. If the fucking idiots you call your co-workers or work colleagues didn't ingratiate themselves so, there'd be no fatty fast food, no sugary frozen dinners, no microwaving infinite broadband uplinks and downlinks, no globally obsessive sharing of personal data with 'those who will rip you off for profit and egress to the great big financial melting pot you're slowly boiling in'.

It's You The People, yourselves, who have to understand this.

You may read this and ask, *what is The Industry, anyway?* but then you haven't *really* read it. Have you? You've not absorbed the information to a sufficient degree. You're still thinking there's salvation in a totally broken financial system where every day, millions upon millions of so-called normal people fist-fuck and ass-lick and toe-suck and vomit-fellate and multi-cock-gag and bloodshot-eye-spunk and slimy-shit-eat their way to the top, shrieking "Bless You, Bless You," at the top of their Team Pizza-rallying contralto.

"Come fuck me, boys, watch me exceed my weekly quota by a corkin' n-percent," where n is a value you can never truly attain but the carrot, always the carrot of compliance to the mob within the mob, the web of conspiracies that ensure that you'll try your damnedest, with or without suitable lubrication on any given day, to impress that amoral dumb-fuck you Hitler-salute with every lost evening behind the desk, with every spoiled weekend finishing off some report, with every after hours meeting your not scheduled to attend, with every gratuitous performance review that is designed to make you feel like a trash bag of dog turds and cat puke, so that you'll fuck yourself on air, in public, to the whole world.

Just to make a buck for The Monster, to satisfy him, sate him, Sat-an.

In truth, you haven't been the same since R³ relocated your company from Dusseldorf to Oxford. When you were based in Dusseldorf, it's like you'd reached some sort of occupational zenith. Some top-rung career ascent was upon your horizon. Everything had finally slid into the right place, properly moist and fitting, after years of toil to make it so.

Since your arrival in Oxford, things haven't been the same, it's like you've been looking in a cracked mirror. You can still see a perfect reflection in each of the shards but you're aware of the rift that's coursing across your perception. It's like you are cracked, on the inside. Like your mind is no longer your own. Like you are the cracked mirror, busy distorting the memory of your whole existence.

And you don't like it.

You don't like the way it's made you look at your fellow colleagues, your team members, those upon whom you depend for the sort of creative environment you thrive within, those who depend upon you to be on top of your game every moment you're in the office.

You don't like this totally unnatural tension that weighs heavily upon your everyday working environment like a threatening storm cloud. And it's just the little things that are mounting up. It's like your mind is being unnecessarily picky to the point of you being assaulted, day in, day out, by this new you.

Some of these office whores (as you've ashamedly started to think of them) pout so strongly for so long you start to fantasise that when they get home from a hard days corporate sucking and self-deprication, they have to unclip the plastic-covered steel dog-snarler from their over-stretched and pox blistered mouths; you know those special devices Hollywood dog-trainers pop into the mouths of Doberman Pinschers to give Magnum P.I. a scare? You've recently started looking at them more than you used to, scowling at them for hours on end, to see if any one of the corporate undead are actually wearing one of those devices, so fixed are their smiles.

Except it's not just the little things that are mounting up.

You're looking across at your co-workers, your colleagues, right now and it's like they're all on some sort of drug or fungus. Their eyes just roll about, they have this look on their faces that sorta says, *Well, fuck you mister, we know what we like and we're gonna see the world our way.* They have this accusatory look about them that you are some sort of fucking degenerate for questioning their concrete resolve. And it's like, when one of them turns their smile in your direction, there's this preceding list of other people who've also smiled. Like they're not really one person each. Like they'll willingly swap each others psychological underwear and lick it like they enjoy that shit. Like they've been schooled in how to behave, how to express this corona of themselves. A blue-print that dictates their mannerisms, their inter-official gyrations.

It's like, just looking up like this from your desk, from your choresome tasks, it's like you're walking through a mist all clogged up with the pungent musk of a million sweating underarms. This stench hangs over your office like blinkers over the nose of a race horse, and you'd notice it more if you weren't still shedding this morning's Psyche-Vertisements of Kevlar Kubitz transit.

The George H W Bush *New World Order* speech from September 10th 1990 has always been one of your favourite P.V.s. You actually ponder how the world might have been had Bush Sr not been involved in that fatal auto-accident outside a burger joint in D.C. just after delivering his 1990 speech. The shimmer of chrome left across his broken forehead from the fender of the car that was never formally identified.

What sort of world is an *'ordo ab chao'* world? Maybe we'll never know. But maybe you don't believe this lie? Maybe you think something else happened to mankind since that P.V.? That's because you are insane and are living in a mental asylum. Time for your medication, dear reader. Time to get real.

What are they offering, these salacious corporate drones, to whom, and why? They all look afraid for their jobs, even the really crafty ones who've been in their jobs for years, those who've confidently reversed themselves into the particular tick burrow of their role and seem 'set up for life'. They all have this sallow look about them. They all know the tenability of their position is wonky at best, ludicrously unstable at worst; a constant basis.

Seems that if you don't look at them, the team, if you forget what they are, some of them, and only some of them, mind, look almost human. That's why you prefer to remain plugged in most of the day, despite the obvious health risk of limitless online connection to Central.

You're thinking, *if I have one more of these shaved cunts thrust their profit projection into my face I'm gonna go postal and to hell with this career path I've been dustpan-shovelling for the last ten, twenty years*. Who really gives a fuck for Pinnacle or Highpoint or any of the other made up badge names pinned on the tit of the global call girl? You're thinking, *one day, I'm gonna go out in a blaze of split-tip semi-auto Armageddon.* But you don't. Nobody ever does.

In fact your growing obsession with this sense of instability hasn't gone unnoticed.

MIKE PHILBIN

11
THE CUSTODIANS
PPS OR PATENT PROTECTIVE SERVICES

Local time: 2343 hours.

The site of the *King's Arms* was originally an Augustinian Priory built in 1268. Following the dissolution of the monasteries in 1540, the land passed to the mayor and City of Oxford. An entry in the lease book of Oxford Council, dated 1607, *states Thomas Franklyn has license to set up an inn with the sign of the King's Arms*.

Franklyn's choice of the sign of the King refers to King James 1 (1603 - 1625) who was closely associated with the adjacent Wadham College. The King's Arms is nestled right in the lair of the dragon-lion which now hosts a gathering of the Custodians via local-to-local Skype link across the globe.

Location: the Wadham Function Room.

The lights are on, but the external French shutters are locked; external French shutters – only in Oxford. A dozen key members of the *Custodian Liberation Group of 38* are in residence. Conspicuous by his absence is Dafyd Atkins, Head of ESI or Eye Sys Industries, where this cunning plan first originated.

Holding the floor, Frank McCardle, USAF, and Damon Hoskins, BsC are two 'defectees' from their side of the Globalist Equation, namely The Military and The Oil Industry. If you can think back to the 1980's where subversive art duo Gilbert and George first found fame, you'd know what they look like. McCardle is the bald, bespectacled one. Hoskins is the other bloke. This 'double act' head up the tech side of the Custodian defense initiative against those who would sacrifice the entire human population to the god of cashmoney, the overlord of dividend, the demon of global governance huddled under the sinister shadow of the umbrella of corporate tyranny, aka profit. And breathe.

McCardle and Hoskins are human-looking, still, there had been no need to coerce these forensic investigators into a regressive, if truly beneficial, transformation from 'mere men' into Re-Wilded intelligence. Why waste energy on something inessential in the war that mankind was unwittingly engaged in, at his own expense?

McCardle and Hoskins deliver their report like a rapid-fire double act. Hoskins lays out the logic of the plan, but often-times McCardle OODA-loops in realtime and ameliorates the action with his hair-trigger wingsmanship.

"You've got to think small, to subvert big," Hoskins starts off in consummate style, ever the professional, considered, acccurate, ever-focused on the Big Picture, "One tiny change here. One tiny change there. A *piquant soupcon* of alacrity here and a cunning dispersal of silver nitrate three weeks in the past on a jet stream nobody was watching. And voila! It's raining on the White House lawn when moments ago it was sunny and the President's delightfully mad-hatteresque tea party is suddenly spoiled.

Children in fancy dress are running hither and thither in the drizzle. Security is scampering after the first lady's shrieking offspring like it's a March hare hunt, and they're the tongue lolling slaughter hounds.

"We work on the principal of infiltration. Even our Russian friends knew all about this, and they tried many ways to profit from their network of *paminyatchiki,* or *agents under deep cover*, children taught to live in America and ascend to the highest roles in Business, Defense and Government. But all the while working for Mother Russia. Well, what works for the goose, works for the gander. You see? Our friends at the Home Office...

"And our friends at the State Department..." interjected McCardle, "All our friends at the Patent Office, Goldman Sachs, JP Morgan Chase, HSBC, our friends in the military, our friends at the Evertainment Issuing Office...sorry, sorry, sorry. Mr Cheese. As you were."

"Wait a minute. News flash. Fungoidal solar energy conversion confirmed in one of our volunteers," McCardle catches the eye of a big-haired young man sat at the back looking bored, "Willemsen, you're good to go with 'the party'," and does this corny nudge-nudge wink-wink.

Willemsen salutes under-enthusiastically.

"The way we did it was this," Hoskins holds up a hand, "You don't mind if I continue, uninterrupted, for a short while?" before lumbering back into his flow without waiting for an answer, "We made millionaires of all the billions of Evertainment sockets. Just dumped a load of 'borrowed' zeros and ones into the account chip of each for only a fraction of a second. It wasn't that great an act, a ghost move on the Chess Board, if you like, to show what we could do. And very few of these corporate drone devices, these so-called humans, will even have registered to their host that there was virtually unlimited credit available for use for that fraction of time. Imagine what would have happened. Anyway, it was all smoke & mirrors. No one knew. No one suspected that they were part of the world's best heist ever performed by civilians on the Police State." Hoskins wipes a bit of spittle from the corner of his mouth with a clean white monogrammed handkerchief.

"Fewer than seven hundred dedicated individuals or 0.00001% of the human population were responsible for the tactical penetrations we made into the so-called armour of the global tyranny..." McCardle again, machine-gunning stats.

"But it would have been enough." Hoskins jumps back in, searching for the words under the intense pressure from his cohort, "In fact, in fact yes, it's exactly like the PPI or Payment Protection Insurance scam where no Consumer realised they'd already been sold this instrument as part of their load or credit facility – this ghost-move credit is still tied to each of the 'millionaire'd Evertainment accounts, for those who have the ability to query the numbers. But nobody ever does, nobody ever will. We've been 'educated' that statutory Evertainment is deducted monthly so no one really notices what's going on with payments, back and forth. It's just something that's a perk of your employ by the Overlords.

"And that's one of the R.E.A.L. problems with PPS or Patent Protective Services. It's one of the major flaws in the Fascists' centralised government, centralised corporate control structures, of the New World Order (as they used to be called, back when people still had brains to think with, back when people still had mouths to shout with and hands to fight back with) that a few people can be trusted with the security of their ambition. Centralised Services and international-front offices for Conglomeratised back office operations still gives the ability for a few loyal traitors to coordinate and kick up the joint with no real effort, any time they feel like flexing their revolutionary muscle. You *happen* across the correct codes, you have willing *martyrs* who are in position, you can unleash all the world's silos of nuclear bounty upon an unsuspecting world and *obliterate* any status quo in the name of financial money-laundering drug-running human-trafficking..."

"Or Capitalism, to give it its proper term." McCardle jumps in, leaning further forward to make his point.

"The digital trillions that we 'momentarily' moved out of centralised hands will not have gone unnoticed by the commodity markets, that was the point. Just the recorded fact of this ghost move itself will probably lead to the downfall of what we used to call The Northern Hemisphere. The markets will probably have noticed a severe breach of global trust already and will be working minute by minute to excise themselves from the amateurish business practices of the Finance Houses connected with that blip on the grid.

These de-regulated Free Market guys are ruthless, and stupid. But nothing passes them by. They'll do anything to protect their investment for their Pay Masters and we just used the adrenalin rush of thcsc cagcd attack dogs upon themselves. Of course, they'll just 'print more pretend money' to cover their losses but nobody will *stand.under* their insane game when they see the gaping flaw as noted in the fatal depreciation of their own trading accounts. Stock markets will fall in the next few hours – it's already happening. But this is nothing. It's just a cover for another more cunning take-over bid."

"But the patent swappage..." McCardle unleashes his impatience.

"Yes, because of how their Patents are stored, registered, recorded, held in separate databases all over the world. This is the perfect way to hit them where it really hurts."

"Accessed..."

"Accessable, or not in each separate paperchase, will take them upwards of three days to realise something's not right..."

"By then, of course, we'll be gone; elsewhere in the ether..."

"Elsewhere in the area..."

"No longer traceable. No longer connected to what went on and they'll have lost all their precious private equity in the form of peoples' ideas."

"In that brief window of online opportunity, we were able to totally disable the accrued wealth of the Bank of International Resettlement, registered in Bern C. H.. We only loaned the patents, though, licensed (or adopted ownership of) them for a few microseconds so that orders could be carried out with full authority. The basis for our model was the way the 9/11 operation was coordinated, from inside, from within our governmental base of operations on the day of September 11th 2001 by the use of patented technologies transferred across secure networks and code-hacked to verify authority and subvert You The People, in the name of Profit."

"Take you to the cleaners, more like," grumbles Hoskins, busy with his laptop.

McCardle substantiates his bold statement, "Using these codes and these permissions of transfer, a legally-binding Uber Patent has just passed in Congress. Everybody voted on it, whether they knew this or not. It is all there in the Abstract: *method of control for the redistribution and reassignment of all private patents to the Custodians Group LLC.* It would be next-to-impossible to make the method any more obvious. But that's it with patents; it's always about hiding the obvious in plain sight. Legalising tyranny. Formalising slavery. Brokering the planet for your own personal gain. Well, we turned that idea on its head to ensure that only the planet gains from our actions as a group of leaderless resisters."

"On a side note," Hoskins interjects a tangent, true to type, "Agents among our Chinese and Russian friends have claimed responsibility for the 'deaths of biochemists and engineers within the Oxford Wall'. It's a classic distraction. They'll be so busy exhausting themselves tail-chasing, they simply will not know what's hit them, come Saviour Day,"

Hoskins continues McCardle's patent pool dissection like nothing had happened, "I'll read you this brief corporate statement to show how, even back in 2001, nobody had any real idea how integrated the patent pool/financial instrument machine was in the running of wars of terror on this planet. This is an official press release from one of the biggest players at the time, and I quote...

We improve essential services by managing people, processes, technology and assets more effectively. We advise

*policy makers, design innovative solutions, integrate systems
and – most of all – deliver to the public. We support
governments, agencies and companies who seek a trusted
partner with a solid track record of providing assured service
excellence. Our people offer operational, management and
consulting expertise in the aviation, BPO, defence, education,
environmental services, facilities management, health, home
affairs, information and communications technology, knowledge
services, local government, science, transport, welfare to work
and the commercial sectors. We advise, define, develop,
integrate, deliver, and maintain solutions that transform how
clients achieve their missions.*

And it was at this point that Asalah Al Faghori realised she
was completely out of her depth among these guys. No one
could really tell if their involvement was a help or a hindrance, if
they were setting the Custodians up for a fall. But facts are facts,
they had control of the Patents, and that was the most important
part of their global contribution to Free Planet.

That they could, at the slightest whim, take control of the
Evertainment system, the Military Surveillance system, the
Global financial system to deliver The Custodians' stark message
of a Free Planet to an unwitting, and perhaps unwilling, global
audience was the key factor.

What they didn't realise, yet, was that all this had to come
down – all these cities the Empire had built over the centuries
had to be allowed to crumble before mankind could really live.
They don't yet realise that, one day, in the cleansed future, all the
satellites will fall from the sky and all the foundations of what
we used to call Society will have rotted away like a leprous foot.
Free Planet, as overseen by the self-appointed Custodians would
have to fail. The earth would have to learn to play its own game,
would have to live within a re-wilded homeworld.

But that's long into the future - tomorrow night at exactly
seven o'clock local time, the first edition of the Natural Lottery
Show will hack into the GES or *Global Evertainment System* to
deliver the intended message of *a Free Planet for all*.

And you know what? The more Asalah Al-Faghori thinks
about it, the more she becomes concerned that the whole
Custodian Liberation is a complete *red herring* doomed to
ultimate and embarrassing failure...

12
YOU THE PEOPLE
BLESS YOU

You can't see it yet, dear Reader, dear Slave, dear Adulant at the Retail Slaughter Temple of the God of e-Commerce. You can't really believe that that's what your so-called productive life has become. But it's only because you're screaming in a corner with your hands over your ears and your eyes screwed shut. You're screaming and kicking and making as much noise inside and outside your body as you can, so that you'll never hear or see or touch or taste the truth of your worthless fucking attack dog training.

"Bless you!" you hear her across the artificial treeline of the shallow-cubicled office. You can't tell where she is, or what she's doing. But you've seen her at it before. You've seen her take a faceload of manfat and shout, "Bless you!" at the top of her shrieking contralto, the cum still gurgling in her back throat, still diffracting an occluded eye, still inflating like a silver bubble from a dilated nostril.

Her 'office banter' consists of phrases like, "Oh, yeah, mister!" and "Fuck me, big boy!" and "Nnnngh, come on, you wimp!" and "You're in deep, baby, now do it, now, oh oh oh!" and "Miller Lights, honey, heh-heh-heh," and rallying cries of, "This bitch needs more cocks inside of her!" and "In the hole!" and the sporting like.

But it's the "Bless you!" exclamation that really grates on your nerves. And there's a laugh that accompanies it. This laugh, this insult to humanity, is like a machine gun rat-a-tat-tatting all over the office; bits of paper flying around, shattered concentrations, broken line of thought. You never heard her in Dusseldorf. Was she even an employee there? But she knows everyone. And everyone knows her, of course. Boy, does she work it hard. It's physically painful to be there, near her.

That's your job, it seems. That's what you do all day, now. Though you don't realise it. Your corporate role, in a MHM or *Machine Hive Mentality* where performance and bonuses and kicking enemies off the ladder of success is *de rigeur*, is to sit here grinding your teeth at the back and flinching whenever an appreciative "Bless you!" and a machine-gun giggle rings out, indicating yet another ingratiating slab of *sir, yes, sir!* has gone off in her facial direction.

Don't forget to breathe. Breathe! But this isn't even the extent of the torture.

Soon…soon, we're going to go deeper than you've ever gone before and it's not going to be pretty. We're going to show you what it's like to be a real person, chopped off from even this GST or *Global Sucking Teat* and you're not gonna like where your world ends. Not at first. In fact, you're going to hate it a lot, for a long time. But given patience, and enough strength of conviction on your part, you won't throw yourself under a truck or find the pavement coming up to meet you for thirty stories or slicing your forearms wide open from elbow to hand or downing gallons of bleach, sleeping tablets and really cheap red wine.

You won't need to do any of these world-lost things, as long as you can understand that things can get better for you and the seven billion inhabitants of your ruined homeworld.

"How were your first few days here? I apologise for not coming over and formally introducing you to the Oxford gang sooner. You know how it is in such a perky office."

That's what you hear a female voice say. Simple and to the point. You look up from some migraine-inducing business of the day. You unhook yourself from the psyche-soc'.

"Sorry?" you'd heard everything she'd said but decided that to have her repeat it would be the least offensive way to earn some charity Brownie points.

"How were your first few days here, in Oxford? " that's what you'd heard her say in her dulcet tones, and she repeats the exact opening phrase again. A scarily-professional smile ripples across her face like a winter chill, "Welcome," she adds. And she's fast, she can think on her feet. She shows this by enhancing her introductory spiel, adapting on the fly, "I apologise for not coming over and formally introducing myself sooner. You know how it is in such a vivacious office, post relocation."

Vivacious?

"My name's Erotica – Human Resources," she offers you her soft, white, thin hand. You think of first-year nursing students.

It's the first time anyone from Human Resources has come over to your desk and calmly delivered a personal introduction. And, everybody knows a visit from H.R. is never a good thing.

But, pathetic sap that you are, you're (momentarily, yet) genuinely crackling with excitement, aka lust. Makes the constant migraine of the last few days in your new work domicile momentarily worthwhile. You are actually sweating – though you don't realise you've been sweating like this since your Corporation crashed Oxford. You haven't noticed the chaaange.

You reach out and shake her hand. It's not a pleasant experience. Like having a small, dry shy lizard in your grasp.

"Of course, Erotica's my Industry name," she glows like a winter sun haze, "Erotica's not a name any parent would intentionally burden a child with, right?"

And you're flattered. As you should be. It's Erotica's job to flatter. To tempt with contempt, to overpower with hours, to command by coercive subterfuge. How low would this H.R. cypher go? Would she pop her soft white tits out for you so that you'd work work work ever harder on unpaid overtime for the CGM or *Corporate Grease Machine*? What is this reeking sewer that passes for a stream of consciousness? The more you think along these abstracted sex-lines, the more aroused you become. Yes, you heard it right. You are sexually aroused by Erotica's pungent proximity. There's such a gorgeous smell coming off her. Not a 'scent', a smell.

But it's the rictus grin, the soul-draining leer of blatant brinksmanship, that ginger-wigged mask upon her head, the flinch of human flesh where each line of code of her DNA seems to jump from one active process to the next in the clunk of a microswitch. That you can not (will not ever be able to) deal with. As long as you squint your eyes away from that level of definition.

She fingers a Tick on her Tablet, and moves on – delivering the exact same initial introduction to your nearest cubicle dweller.

Human Resources drones move like they're not from this planet. There's this thing about them, this crazy dance – they're dead behind the eyes but their abused bodies are jiggling around at the cellular level like they're possessed by some sort of non-Earth creatures, plural. There's some ancient curse or something tricklin' across their lips of an H.R. Drone as they gyrate, delivering orders. You look real close and you can actually see the tiny demons dancing in their dark red tribal garb. Pitchforks aloft.

Now, it's not about believing in the devil. Neither should you. But picture this crackling visual, you're in a dark room and someone turns on the light. It's a strip light, you know. A neon. The ignition tone and the subsequent low-flicker-rate buzz drill into your skull like a cackling sadist. You're being screwed right in the cerebellum by this middle management lackey, this order bringer, this tallier. That's what it's like to have her look at you, like that, all her frenzy of a job-to-be-well-done, within-budget and on-time. She's shimmering with it. Chrome is her perfume, can you see this? Can you picture someone standing there like a solid block of chrome, powdering a mist of silver scintillations that you pick up as some rare-earth perfume? Can you feel it yet? Can you taste it? Can you smell it? Is your tongue tingling? Are your nipples hardening? Are you even still conscious enough to discern the lie from the global truth?

You're thinking, if you're gonna sit there looking like nothing more than a fuckable twat at least look like you're enjoying yourself, you Industry Drone, get some goddamn light in the eyes, show some fucking trait. This isn't just your 9-5 job, this is your life, you should live and breathe and sleep this dream job – it's the only thing you're worth, the only thing you're capable of, you're a corporate toy, a clique child. Who cares if the pressure breaks you? Shut the fuck up and show me more, X-rate my motivational interest, for fuck's sake.

You can see that most of them are just doing their job, their sucking and blowing the way nature intended, see them fingering themselves with manufactured pride in a task well done. Some, even though they're taking part in the office game, don't seem too excited by the daily grind, in fact, they look close to sleep. Elsewhere some snooze off their hardcore early morning gang bang, power napping for an afternoon of complicit corporate rape. And you look again, and that one fuck monkey catches your eye; there's something about the way she grinds their hips. They do it so that you'll notice them, so that they mean something. Why do they care who they fuck with, they just wanna be seen to be actively taking part in the fuck play and hoping that at some point in the dull-as-ditch-water day you'll wanna pick up your keyboard, smash it across your neighbour's sneering face and rip the over-tailored business suit from them before shoving the shared telephone handset into their still-gaping maw like the android did to Ripley in Alien, shove that filthy fucking porn rag of horror sounds down her worthless fucking wolfshit throat.

Still others are career ass fuckers, career cock suckers, career hand jobbers, career whores and thugs and criminals existing on the fringe of legality while the newcomers just get drawn into the mire, inch by fist-fucking inch.

Some of those corporate covert bitches really know how to milk the crowd, draw the eye of the unsuspecting colleague, blowing kisses across the office and fiddling with their hair like they've got all the time in the world and their schedules stretch out into infinity like a parade of cock pecking geese, honking with glee at their prostitutional revelry.

Some of them are chewing gum, for God's sake. You don't find out until much later that it's not gum, it's a hardened wad of cum middle management's allowed them to cud on, post gurgitation. A large throaty accumulation like a living off-white cancer that grows in the mouth and rolls sourly around the tongue with each now completed task, the tally of horror mounting as the day proceeds. The gob-stopper in reverse.

"Yes, I have toys," Bless You breathes in your ear, in passing.

Then, she's on your desk, her pock-marked white thighs split; a sheet of hot white lightning across a glum sky. Her suppurating-cunt hair peeking out from the sides of the skankiest string you've ever witnessed. She's gyrating her under-guts at you like you're about to stretch up with a Giger-alien second mouth on a stalk and take a fucking big bite out of her rancid pie. You'd end up choking on crusty chunks and spitting out hazel nut clusters, so best not go there. Her face is like this climax-mask of restitution, locked in lust; a gummy grimace. You smell rancid yellow olive oil leaking out of her pores.

Everyone knows that engaging with these career rutters like Bless You, until you're broken in, means you'll suffer a very uncomfortable evening of vomit and weeks of moral regret having taken the bait without the necessary prophylactic precautions.

Many of Bless You's sort can type real fast, that's maybe the only way they get so much work done and still spend all day, or so it seems, in the middle of some wild orgy of the manicured flesh. You look around, nervously. Are there cameras actually filming this confrontation between you and her? Is upper management in on the game, jacking off to the free show? Is every aspect of this office being broadcast across Eli-X's porn universe right now, live and direct to slum housing units across the developing world for a first down payment of $14.99 and a monthly interest rate to rival any loan shark?

Some just seem to be stuck, on a constant loop of absent-mindedly fingering themselves and rubbing their damp clitorises and the inside of their smooth white thighs and their belly buttons and then returning again and again via the long skin circuit of kitten claws on rice paper to the spiky expectation of one nipple after another, round and round they go like fucking circus horses. They aren't even doing it for any specific hierarchic audience or bonus, they're just unable to stop fondling their breasts, exposing their genitalia, or waiting, mouth open like a starving chick, waiting for cum to land on their face and slime into their mouths, cum across their teeth, cum across a fluttering eyelash. They're prisoners to their own insatiable ladder climb. Many of them are pierced by their slavery to the chore, the daily grind. Where or when do these girls get off?

And the guys are no better, 'priapic trolls' would be the alchemist's way to describe these chest-high erectile beasts pounding into shaved gashes like they're the leading cyclist in the *peloton* of the Tour De Fucking Machecoul, out in the heat of the countryside, pumping and thrusting up a mountain of open cunt.

You're sure to get reprimanded for squandering valuable office resources and not taking part in the family feel of office life, contributing to the gormless Nerf war of the otherwise dull grey working environment. You realise that two weeks into your Oxford employ, you're gonna have to put out or ship out. You have to prove yourself reaaaaaal soon or it's a summary dismissal without pay or in-lieu remuneration.

13
THE CUSTODIANS
FOR THE GOOD OF FREE PLANET

Local Time: 2359 hours and fifty nine seconds.
Guest Parade begins to play: *The Oxford Boat Song.*
Announcer, "Welcome to the most prestigious PGS-event ever!"

When you're tired of winning
When you get tired of fame
Or when your head is spinning
And you've drunk all the best champagne

Then we'll all sing together
To Diversity we'll be true
Then we'll all sing together
Diversity waits for you...

...thus advises the choral accompaniment, courtesy of several freelancing baritones from CCC or *Christchurch Cathedral Choir.*

The announcer is one James H Willemsen, a surname of Nordic derivation, no doubt.

Willemsen had proven himself to be an Oxford-fanatic, having indulged in his fair share of *Bullingdon* japes in local restaurants and such. He already had one degree in Ancient French History under his belt, his published thesis focussed on the 15th century Burgundian era under Charles VII; a time during the Hundred Years War when Paris fell under English rule.

Willemsen has a sycophantic fascination with Gilles de Rais of House Montmorency-Laval, virgin-heroine Jeanne Romee's Marshall of France, a highly-religious nobleman with an unhealthy interest in the Occult (or hidden) Art of Alchemy or turning base metal into Gold, and ritualistic child murder.

Willemsen is the charming ring-leader for tonight's social occasion, having been unanimously elected *Trooper in Chief* by the other eleven members of this term's PGS or *Piers Gaveston Society*: a less-than-innocent cos-play group limited to twelve key members that has a truly despicable corporate blackmail agenda that stretches through the career of most people who will study at Oxford.

A reputation the Custodians are about to turn on its head in the most spectacular fashion.

Forget the Prime Ministers, the London Mayors and the Heads of Business & Opinion who've been Trooper in Chief of this audacious clique, this year's Piers Gaveston Society has among its members one key figure who no one suspects would betray the 'club' to the masses. The ring-leader himself, his royal righteousness, James H Willemsen is this very night going to split the legendary peach of decadence wide open in full sight of a public that will reel back in nausea, aghast. Nothing you've ever seen, no story you've ever heard, no matter how lurid will prepare you for tonight's slanderflesh excesses.

You'll be a changed populace when you see how far humanity has *cum* to deliver the message of a *Free Planet for all,* how unbelievable is the power resident within all humans in the seven billion strong army behind The Custodians; that's you lot out there reading this.

You'll all be mentally scarred by this next bit, and it's for your own good. A shocking wake-up that's long overdue. For too long have you looked away – tonight you will stare at this unseemly act and you will understand your role in a real world, all the simulational polygony will shatter, and pure-simple life will confront you in your most defenceless moment.

You will see a rarely-revealed world of social manipulation that has existed for centuries.

But tonight's (*ahem*) debauch is signatured not in Satanic Sacrifice but in the low-key refrain from the Oxford Boat Song as riffed in variation by Christchurch's resident period quartet playing on period instruments that are usually kept behind glass on floor four of the *Ashmolean Museum* on Beaumont Street. Merry music to accompany the Bolly and the Caviar and the cunt-licking and the cock-sucking to come. A nice warming up session for the unseen horror that will befall these feckless Libertines; these hee-hawing lackeys of The Corporate War Machine.

You'll want to take a drink; everybody's drinking tonight – that's the rule of PGS.

Six large punch bowls and seventy-two AGHs or *Anonymous Guests Honourable* are allowed to clash in any experimental configuration, that's the whole idea of these intimate soirées. But tonight you'll only return to ONE of the punch bowls, again and again, before the third-hour chime of Great Tom. That's the way it'll go tonight, whether you like it or not. As chosen for you by The Custodians, your saviours, tee hee. Bunch of mischievous fucks.

The Venetian masks everyone's wearing tonight have also been chosen by The Custodians, your saviours and mischief makers. Handed to all guests as they passed through the Meadow Building entrance into the legendary Tom Quad, each mask has been DNA-matched to each Honourable Guest in the guise of a 'secret blood ritual' held a couple of weeks in advance of this event. Matched and enhanced. The masks have been sprayed with a pheromone part-primer that, in association with the specific (gene-spiked) punch bowls, will ensure flocking of the DNA-map toward tonight's ultimate goal.

And, of course, everybody is oblivious, as per the design of the Need To Know game which (even here) is troublesome to shuffle off. They're just 'having a good time,' God bless them. And by 'having a good time' of course we're talking about drinking, finger fooding and, well, let's call it 'getting to know the other members of their *specified social grouping* networking.' They've no idea what this 'networking'll lead to – how could they?

But soon they'll discover the relevance of six on top and six on the bottom. They'll work out a way for water to be processed. Methods to dispose of waste products and gases will be worked out among them, too. There'll be a way to keep an eye on any of their 'residents;' the eyes and ears'll face inward as well as outward.

You've no idea what's going on, do you?

And that's part of the design, part of the horrible game, part of the deception.

It's not like anyone would really rebel against the concept were they to discover the real reason for tonight's event. They had been specifically chosen, after all, after submitting their name, their blood. But not for this, maybe. Not for this solution. They'd been chosen genetically, as a short list of those hundreds of Oxford students who'd submitted to the 'secret blood ritual'. Call it Darwinian Competition and everybody loves a competition, right? This lot do, anyway. They're the most adventurous, the most ambitious of Oxford's illegitimate bastards and this, whether they realise it or not, is what they were all destined to do, destined to be.

In the early stages of preparation for the spectacular climax to the night's proceedings, the meandering ruleset that dictated such 'scholarly flirtations' was in residence; as if fate herself was in amongst them, introducing him to her and so on.

Soon, however, biochemical order starts to assert itself upon the social chaos. Six groups of twelve attendees each are getting on like a house on fire and each of the six groups are equidistant from each other, separated across Tom Quad. In fact, it's going so swelteringly well there's a floating (18) certificate stamped all over the action. In double-fact, much of this footage will end up on the cutting room floor or be spliced into a sabotaged project as happened with Tinto Brass's *Caligula* film.

But first some anatomical facts:

A flayed adult human being will only give you about two square meters of usable surface area, but if you extrapolate that sorry total to the volumetric potential of a dozen human beings, you're talking about a six-sided cylindrical volume that could occupy an entire family, or two. You could accommodate the non-uniform scaling of bones like rafters across a ceiling. You could appreciate the potential of twenty-four retinas covering the inner and outer surfaces of every wall. You could visualise the complex and volumetric mass of the upper and lower bowels where all the fruit trees, vegetable patches and fungus could grow. Water (in the form of rain flow or direct cloud harvesting) could trickle in from expanded pores in the cornea-like windows and roof of such a floating home. Energy could be drawn from the sun and pushed through agglomerated capillaries, flying surfaces could take all sorts of forms; there are many ways to get a mass of organic matter into the air.

But we're giving away too many suggestions; that's not how this should go.

No one suspects that the sound system has been spiked with liberal amounts of subsonics, causing a curious groin-loading affect among the attendees, adding to the gravid state of their loins, spurring on their fervour; their need for each other. Standing waves are being set up such that structural blueprints can be orchestrated around the subsonic three-dimensional forms.

Tribal Foundation, that's where we'll leave the slathering pornography of this party's climax. We're going to interrupt the sleaze with a final announcement and here, finally, is the big cheese himself James H Willemsen to ring the closing chorus.

At the height of the party's sexual zenith, an opulent pollen-like musk smogging six distinct genetic groupings de- Sadeing in their respective areas of the Christchurch courtyard, Willemsen gets back on the mic, coughing for attention before firing up his freelance baritones and encouraging the Guests Honourable to take note of the motion for a second, trying to get some sort of unity going, some sort of knee-jerk spontaneity.

Some may call us sinners
Be thankful that's all they'll say
Some may call us sinners
It's done with such restraint

And we'll all sing together
To Diversity we'll be true
And we'll all sing together
Diversity waits for you

"For the good of free planet," PGS host Willemsen suggests, sloshing his half-empty glass in the air. People look up from their cock-sucking, their clit licking, their anal pumping, their titty twisting, their eyeball cumming, their vaginal fingering. It is like the communal eye of some amazingly complicated sea creature looks up from oil raping itself, tentacles here and there, filter feeders leap out all over the shivering beast's crenelated outer carapace, octopus-like skin rumples and cuttlefish-like cycling light shows explode under faces glowing with unbridled lust. The roving eye of this beast is dilated as fuck, like it is on the most mind-fuck psychedelic mankind had ever invented. It barely focusses on our man, aura-spotlit in something like a block of coldest white crystal.

Willemsen bullies the tempo of his wassail until everyone joins in, until everyone believes, until everyone is 'of one mind'.

Then we'll all sing together
To Diversity we'll be true
Then we'll all sing together
Diversity waits for you

"For the good of free planet," Willemsen reminds them again, cos that's his job.

For the good of free planet, they all echo at the top of their stupid useless drunken bloodshot ejaculating facial orifices. Roars and screams and gasps and shouts of "God" ring out. Climax, climax, climax as sexual unions are fixed in space, stood stock still in time. Cum is gulped down throats and smeared in hair. Cum is shared from mouth to mouth and splattered on breasts. Cum explodes in all directions, soaking everything and everybody. Mixing with sweat and vaginal juice and anal cream and all the other man-made lubricants of the human body's glandular system.

One by one, the way fertilisation happens in the womb, the way a wriggling sperm penetrates the shell of an ova; a vast peristaltic shock wave pours through the six groups.

Over the course of the next few thousandths of a second, each of the six distinct groups of exactly twelve partying sex-freaks explodes like organic fireworks. It's not a uniform explosion, either. Each of the twelve elements explode in their own specific furry way, one after the other; slotting into biochemical and architectural roles within the already-floating core matrix, shuffling into position with the quivering levitating mass, flourishing like a bloom of tiny living corals that solidify into the calcified beams and spaces of resultant coral reef structures. Faces are thrown back. Spines are split and stretched. Arms are flung out in the epicentre of the blast, blood exploding and solidifying into ducting and wiring. Eyeballs empty of their vitreous humor and flatten themselves into position, pulled tight as drums.

Some members buckle down, some soar in rainbow arcs, some delay their bodily ejaculation, some prematurely insistent.

Notice all the air vents and cilia and flapping membranes of the living surfaces of gold-leaf levitation taking control of the air, churning and channelling it through the internal maze of these living hexagonal lifeforms. It happens so fast, it's like some cheap magic trick. You feel conned by the efficiency and the speed of it all. One blink and it's done.

Six living abodes ascend into a ring formation, each locking into place with its partner, that might prompt a science student to think of a basic Benzene molecule. The ring of six carbon atoms. The basis building blocks of all organic life on Earth. The potential for more complex configurations should be obvious; residential growth of each Diversity can easily be accommodated using this organic chemistry template.

And still no sign of Dafyd Atkins, head of ESI - maybe something's up?

Two new Oxford gargoyles perched against the silhouette of Tom Tower had gone unnoticed all through the victuals of the proceedings. One resembles a big bird. One resembles a big dog. They exchange a brief glance of satisfaction before moving off into the barely-breaking dawn like thieves, scallywags, classical mischief makers modelling the monochrome arrows or stripes of *ye olde prisone garbe*.

MIKE PHILBIN

14
YOU THE PEOPLE
YOUR FUNERAL, BUDDY

Two very bizarre things happen this morning:

1. You have to clear a human turd off your desk. Not a toy one. Not some practical joke piece of moulded plastic. This is a real human turd. Someone would have had to squat down, right there on your desk before you got in, to lay this length of steaming brown pipe. You can even see where the anus muscle has crimped off the tail of it, begging like a clever puppy, its front-paw in the air.

2. The email flag pops up cheerily and it's a collection for your funeral. Enough money has already been pledged to buy quite a nice casket. Seriously, that is not right.

You've been summoned to The Monster's transparent-walled office at the far corner of the open-plan space at 12:00 noon exactly. Today. This way he can be assured that, even with fake-FlexiTime, the office is jam-packed full of sleazy industry. Every employee will notice your *Dead-Man-Walking*, see how you fidget and twitch as you approach the Inquisitor's Cabin. He loves this, your boss, The Monster. He loves the power game. Crystal glass corner office, furniture made of chrome that shines a little too sexily. You gotta love his theatrical panache.

Your unexpected sense of corporate dread and co-worker curiosity since your arrival in Oxford had obviously not gone unnoticed.

"New off-shore...ahem, Satellite. New contract," says The Monster, having called you in to 'tear you a new asshole' or 'motivate your productivity', or 'use whatever phrase you want'. That's what all the old inertia-addled employees call him, The Monster.

"And it's not just you."

He sits there, with his archaic mic-set on his head, like he's some sort of Grand Controller, some Intranet D.J.. If he was on his feet, you'd see that he was tall and thin and has the kind of physique that can only be described as possessing 'wiry strength'. In fact, your eye's have wandered over to his side of the office on several occasions and you've never seen him stood up, it's like he's welded to that chair. In fact, you've never seen him move, never mind leave the office and (perish the thought) have a random chat with an employee. The Monster's like this malevolent 'permanent fixture' at the end of the office, where the real light comes in. Permanently scamming some New Deal at his level of The Industry.

A prisoner of his own glass cage.

"So, we're no longer in Dusseldorf, *Dorothy,*" he has this strong northern accent and a right cunt of an attitude to go with it.

He doesn't ask you to sit down. He just sits there, slouching back, chewing on a pencil. Looking up at you like he's no older than a teenager, "Don't look at me like I've just shat in your throat. We didn't just 'Relocate to Oxford'. An old hand like you. You realise this, I'm sure. We're a totally new legal offshoot of the old octopus, my lover. New Rules," he claps his damp palms together, "We have updated everyone's NDA that's *Non Disclosure Agreement* – you know nobody ever reads that shit, to their eternal damnation. We've altered the details of everyone's employment contract to reflect our arrival in this new 'Land of Opportunity;'" he makes the sign for speech marks. *"Everybody...* and that means *you*, little worm. Little worms!" he shouts insanely at the glass wall overlooking the workers, hammering on the glass with a fist, "That means you, and all your discontented sort."

You start to say something in your defence but...

"You're in The Industry, lad; The Industry. How long did you think you could suck on the teet? I mean, none of us is getting any younger, right?"

He wedges his pencil in his mic-set, just above his right ear.

"Sit. Sit, you look ill."

You sit, right on the edge of the seat.

"This is just a courtesy call," the inquisition grinds on, "A way for New Management, that's me, to meet the New Staff, that's you. And that's what you ALL are..." his arm sweeps out like a sail in a gust of wind to indicate the entire workforce visible through the transparent walls of his office, "New staff. You've all had your liabilities reset; you're all on three months' probation as of now. And that's just the way I like it. Back in control. Power regained."

He adjusts his position; a quick flinch pinches his face, "Way I see it, where there's mugs, there's brass. All right? Promise them the earth with the rallying cry and then shit on them from as high as possible when they start thinking they deserve a bigger bonus or a better wage or working conditions," he finger-quotes again – 'working conditions' this time.

On the H.R. or *Human Resources* side, the bane of any corporation is the Long Term Employee. They're paid generally much more than the new graduate and are (legally) much harder to get rid of. So, the corporation came up with this excellent solution to their problem, Periodic Relocation. That's where the company gets the equivalent of a bank holiday, it can reset its liabilities i.e. you, and Bob's your Uncle.

In the corner of The Monster's office is a tall cylinder of chrome, like a modern shower cubicle. Your boss presses a button under the lip of his desk and the cylinder flips inside out with a soft pop of sphincteral air. You jerk your head to one side, instinctively. It's all you can do, confronted with the retching gust of arse stink and the sight that now confronts you. Can it be true? Can your boss really have his own chrome toilet in his corner office? You've never seen him use it. And it's fair to say that, occupying as he does a totally transparent office, anyone in the open-plan office could at any time witness the urination and defecation of their boss. But that no-one has makes this intimate sight even more embarrassing.

Part of the information gathering mechanism in The Industry is the communal toilet. As corporations quickly understood that all the greatest (most valuable) thoughts happen on the toilet, that was the obvious choice to develop appraisal strategies for – your DNA is not your friend.

"It's a giver, this one. Not a taker." that's what's he tells you. You don't understand. A giver? Not a taker? Is he talking about you? Is he talking about The Industry? You shrug. Because what he's said is just too inappropriate for the location and the circumstance of a standard Dead Man Walking bullied-boy situation.

"This toilet," he chimes like a lovely church bell you can see via psyche-plug on your micro breaks, "Just like the one in the communal lavies, you think?"

This just gets worse and worse. Is your boss really asking you whether this toilet is different from the other ones? What's the *giver/taker* question anyway? You really haven't twigged.

"Have a good long hard look, my lad."

The Monster gets up from his lovely, ornate chrome chair. In all honesty, you've never seen him do this. You've only ever seen him installed in his crystal box, the feedout from his holo-network shimmering across his expressionless features before you arrive in the morning until after you've left in the evening. You've never seen how difficult it might be for him to actually get himself up. Standing up, you'd imagine, just couldn't be this difficult.

And then you see maybe why – you only see it for an instant before your mind cuts off the connection, revolted.

The pulsating chrome extrusion pouring up from the centre of the seat like a lubricated dildo; a direct sphincteral data uplink. The top two thirds of the thrumming tower are covered in a dull, green excreta like baby poo. Something sinister like that can only hint at the crucifying lifestyle and cancerous diet of these ultra execs. Over time you see how the green poo is absorbed into the mirror-surfaced dildo. Maybe management psyche-plugs just have this wider girth for bandwidth reasons? Maybe they have a lot more data to digest? Is this how the upper echelon *really* communicate their higher orders to their immediate subordinates? Is this how they gather their webs of information. Your knees feel weak.

"There are numerous managerial weapons in the corporate arena, never forget that," says your boss, "One of the most useful ones our engineers have ever concocted is the Appraisal Toilet. It's like a normal toilet but, as I've already alluded, this toilet is a giver, not a taker. Do you understand what that might mean?"

You get a ball-shrivelling inkling into what the giver part of the Appraisal Toilet might imply and you hope you're not 'next in line'.

"Well, yes..." you begin to illustrate for your boss why he should fire you rather than concrete your employ with a permanent contract, rates of pay and dismissal procedures pending; stammer, state obvious, "It gives, rather than receives?" You're wondering whether you'll have to endure anal rape from this arcane contraption and you're considering your legal position.

"Well, done," he grins, waddling over to the Appraisal Toilet like John Wayne after a three-state cattle drive. He depresses the toilet's chrome flusher. The bowl fills up with a strange Technicolor soup. Your boss turns to you, a terrifying grin on his face, "Come on, have a look at it, now that it's primed."

He waves you out of your chair to join him for a good close look into it, "It's really a genius piece of kit."

As you're creeping to within target of the bowl you witness The Monster dip his cupped, white hand into the psychedelic soup in the bowl and slurp it into his gaping mouth like an expert wine taster. You gag. You're close to throwing up your breakfast. You turn away momentarily and reach for his desk. You hear him gargle appreciatively then gulp, not spit. Too much strangeness to not puke but amazingly you hold onto the contents of your stomach. Crazy shit-ass world this is.

"What you gonna do?" he asks, "Find another job? When you're blacklisted? I have all you lot under my thumb. I own you fuckers. So, Dear Disgruntled Three Monther with no severance arrangement, go apply elsewhere. Spend even more time in those Psyche-Vertisement-sponsored Kevlar Kubitzzzzz." he waves his hand around, agitatedly, buzzing like a wasp, "Could you imagine a commute to a more distant employ? Another Territorial Centre? Another Global Territory? Could you imagine all those stacked up Psyche-Vertisements cancelling out lethargically throughout the working week. Unknowable as a bad record until the home-time whistle blows and you have to once again submit your consciousness, your sanity, to the the the barrage of Kevlar Kubitz PVs once again? Don't make me laugh, little person, you'll be staying here with US – your new family – for a good long time. And you'll fucking learn to like it."

The Monster shows you some video footage of some screaming woman being tortured to death. There's blood and guts and bones and wires and broken teeth and eyes gouged out with meat forks and you're thinking is this like a faux-video nasty or did this really happen? Was someone really murdered in this slow painful way as an example to all who might think of outing the game? Unmasking the real face of The Industry. Is this one of those legendary snuff films you hear they blackmail all the Top Executives with? Will the torturer pull his mask off and it'll be the sweating, panting face of The Monster? It could happen. Could be You under the mask. Ask yourself. Are you a Top Executive, in disguise? Under cover?

"This is what happens when you dare to break your NDA. This is the way I'm paid, in kind. In results. Any praise, the buck stops with me. Any complaint, it goes right down to you. And, as you can see, I don't like rats. Rats, do you hear me?"

You're thinking, *Yep, this is real snuff. This is an official warning; first, last and only...*

The Monster thinks long and hard before he says his next bit, "I'm sure you got my *little gift*, this morning. I want you to sort yourself out, lad. Start earning your crust. Get out and about, again. Get back into the real world. I know you're up for it, despite the reports. Get back on the streets like first thing, tomorrow morning. Get me some real Captures, lad. Or you're history. Are you with me?"

You smile because you'd thought this chewing out was gonna be a lot worse.

"Now, fuck off, eh," he adds sweeping back to his chair as you move to leave. He resumes his seat a little too angrily, continues his intranetworking like you never happened.

15
THE CUSTODIANS
BULLINGDON WOODS

Local Time: 0532 hours.

A generous clearing in a dense patch of wooded hillage, somewhere to the west of Oxford, like a secret mushroom risen upon the rural horizon. A place of ancient significance, and a location few people ever visit – especially this early in the morning.

Human and hybrid creatures, several of which we've yet to be introduced to, have gathered in this opening on this tree-ringed lump of land. To the south, were one to venture to the edge of the woods, one could just make out the village of Wootton. If you look real close, you might be able to make out a tiny finger smear low on the horizon – that's a troop-carrying Chinook helicopter on regular military drill into and out of Brize Norton Air Base.

Within the clearing, horizontal rays of sunrise pour through foliage as a pair of stragglers arrive to hear the words of Asalah Al Faghori, self-appointed spokesperson of the Custodian Liberation. Beside her, her trusty side-kick, lover, body-guard Rotimi Ogunjobi. Above the sound of early-morning bird tweets and leaf rustlings, comes a buzzing noise like a million wasps. There's a tension in the air, anxiety among the assembled crowd concerned about attack from the above.

Something insistent, and furtive, like a squirrel but man-sized, leaps from tree to tree, pseudo-human hands gripping, nose twitching, long flat feathery tail flitting about in balancing sympathy.

"Relax, my creatures; my Re-Wilded friends and colleagues..." Asalah smirks, opens and refolds her wings, herself slightly on edge, sensing the general apprehension about this meeting, fighting the irrational urge to flee.

Suddenly, breaking the tree line from the east, literally buzzing from the photonic ministrations of the rising sun, explodes a golden song brighter and gayer than any church choir's soaring lament. It seems to come at you, this insect-like vibrato from all directions at once. And there's barely a downdraft, as there, hanging low in the sky, occupying much of the view, hangs a massive doughnut-like structure, slowly turning around its central axis – think Benzene ring and you'll start to wise up.

The six separate hexagonal elements of the ring break formation and flutter down to the ground, landing equidistant from each other at the periphery of the clearing. This really is an odd place; a ring of trees in the middle of nowhere, surrounding a Neolithic-fort-like plateau atop a gentle hill. A spiritual space, some might say. A haunted place.

This is the first meeting of the New Bullingdon Club for the Trinity semester, topic for discussion The Custodians plan of action for the coming days, weeks, months. The Piers Gaveston party was a total success; a success beyond anyone's expectation. In fact, the Custodian Liberation is all going far too smoothly.

"We are gathered here, today, in a secret location known only as Bullingdon Woods to the select members of our new Diversity," Asalah begins her introduction, "It is nice to see so many who have already adopted the Custodian way, and so many who have shown commitment to such in a future iteration, are all present at this inauguration of the official Campaign for a Free Planet. I'd like you to raise your glasses, beaks, muzzles, funny-shaped back things, your too many arms, your communal living spaces to the cause we've committed our physical and intellectual lives to."

"You know this is really gonna hurt, don't ya?" one dissenting voice from the back mutters.

"We are…yes, we will have to make the ultimate sacrifice for our fellow man. But this is something we are all aware of. No negative voices are to be allowed to 'sway our resolve'. Tonight, is the first live insertion into the Evertainment system of our *Natural Lottery* programme. We have activated all the correct Uber Patents and Command & Control Disablers with a three day delay to avoid suspicion in the early weeks of the show. We intend to take this show to the entire world, at the same time every night. We aim that every living person on Planet Earth will hear our message. Like a new record no one likes on first hearing, we will repeat and replay our message of a Free Planet for all the world to hear, until people finally get it. Until the world starts to wake up from its ridiculous monetary nightmare. Until people *under.stand*."

"What if it doesn't work?" the voice again, from the quivering underbrush, the one dissenting voice of reason.

Asalah herself had started to worry about such, but decides to bluster forward with her counter-attack, "Who said that? Why would you even bother to attend such a meeting and consider such a thing? Can't you see the simple logic that hesitancy itself is the key to man's downfall? Can't you see that prompt physicality is the only way forward?"

A smile creeps into her eyes, "I'm tempted to re-cite my 'Ninety Billion Souls' epitaph at you'all again, merely for suggesting that Free Planet might be somehow flawed or fractured. It's a pure thing, like a crystal or a pearl or a snowflake. It's just that our brains have been brought up to compete and conflict with one another, constantly, for personal gain. Our minds are a busy jumble of words and dialects and phrases and theologies and prejudices and disrespect of our world in the name of Success and Competition and Lottery for the poor."

"Poppycock," coughs the voice of reason, the hidden voice no one can put a body to, the voice that seems to slither around the darker parts of Bullingdon Woods like a spirit of Christmas Past or portent of insomnia for a world in the throes of a terrible dream, "Portent of insomnia."

"What utter nonsense are you talking? And why not show yourself? Are we that infiltrated that we can't even show our enemies? Are we that lost to The Game the world has been playing for centuries?" Asalah fluffs up her feathers into electrified attention. It's strange to think that during all this time, a bird-girl has been dictating to a bunch of genetic freaks in a clearing in an unnamed wood. How insane our world has gone, how uncocked the gun.

"Surely, it can't succeed," again the voice of reason, the ever-in-motion stalker, "Surely, they'll have factored this into their game plan for the world; *their* world. They'll have con-tin-gen-cies?"

"Contingencies..." yes, she's thought this through, over and over again.

"Who cares?" Asalah sticks to her guns, "By then, we'll have opened up the entire planet to an ethical future of Creativity, Passion and Kinship for everyone. A new world of Re-Wilded nowness. Not some hopeless subsistence of prison gruel, punishment TV and global lockdowns."

"Not true," again the voice of dissent peels out.

"By the time they think about reacting, their whole MIRC (that's their *Military Industrial Religious Complex,)* will have been disarmed, dismembered, in the name of Free Planet. And we will be honoured by our Galactic Friends. We will make Earth a beautiful tourist destination for millions upon millions of the Universe's diverse cultures and travelling alien species who've always been averse to sharing their message with a war-monger'd race like us. Our planet will be reclaimed as the true Garden of Eden it has always been prophesied as being. We will once again know God (a real living God) in the plants and the animals and the Future Humans we thought we'd lost to Drone Existence in some Borg Machine of Death and Devaluation."

"You're living in a dream world that can no more support itself than a house of cards in a hurricane..."

"You say that. From your shadows. You claim that. But no one ever asked you. No one has ever tried this before. And we must try, as we have never tried *anything* before!" and amazingly, her last statement conjures up a group cheer from the genetic freaks of the Bullingdon Gathering. A breakthrough in command and control has (somehow) broken through the public conflict of dissent vs. dogmatism.

Asalah Al Faghori has become the leader of the Custodians, as was always her plan, her mortal fate if you like. For this day has marked Asalah Al Faghori as the enemy, the embodiment of what it means to give one's soul for the betterment of mankind, the act she's just performed has ensured that the term *Martyr* will be applied to her name some decades into the future once those who rewrite the history books have had a chance to reconsider and reassess their profane summaries of How the World Was Pulled Back from the brink of disaster by the actions of a few useless eaters.

"You're a monster," comes the final pronouncement of the only dissenting voice among the Custodians, tonnes of resignation in the murmured declaration.

No one takes up the appeal, everybody else is 100% fixed on the goal of a Free Planet for all, and the cost will be commensurate with the post and the tasks in hand.

"Correct, we are monsters, in their eyes..." Asalah is about to launch into another of her speeches.

"Incoming!" a snake-man hybrid, with the Michelin Man-like lateral body ridges of an earthworm and stubby arms, wriggles frantically onto the edge of the clearing, dead leaves sticking to his slimy surface.

With the C4ISR or *Command Control Communications Computers Intelligence Surveillance and Reconnaissance* grid still in active orbit around the Earth, the initial thought is of a military strike from black helicopters and/or remote drones, suicide robots filled with thermobaric weapons to eviscerate this iteration of the Custodian Liberation even before a trace memory of such could infect mankind, the real powerhouse of Corporate (War) Governance.

The group freezes as one unit of mutual terror, each aware that to move might mean to reveal one's self.

Breaking the tree line from the west, however, flies a lone peanut taxi. This is the one who asks to be called Abi. She hovers around the clearing, does a full circle, then seems to sniff at one of the hexagonal floating homes, before landing nearby and disgorging her charge.

A male human being, totally naked, hairy and bearded, tumbles out, scrambles to his feet, rushes about, seeing where he is, not understanding, what all these people, these creatures, these strange organic structures, can mean. He turns this way and that, looking for an exit. But in no time he is scooped up again by the floating peanut that is Abi. Her surface flickers through various levels of translucency, and you can see the peppered silhouette of the man, trapped inside her, screaming, hammering at the 'door' to be let out.

Abi slams into the floating mobile home she'd earlier sniffed at, right on the corner where a soft knuckle splits to allow here to slam her front aspect into it, lock on. The whole 'ship' burps into life, bio-luminescent 'lights' go on in the dwelling as the man runs from room to room, shrieking for his life, shouting for his wife, wondering what next will happen to him. What horrors? What torture?

As if on cue, more Peanut Taxis of various aviationary design pour over the tree line, thrusting their human contents into the floating homes they're deemed genetically suited to occupy.

"Let us out, this is an abuse of our Civil Rights!" the human members of this new Diversity shriek words to this effect. But they don't understand…it's time to re-educate them in the Free Planet way. When you're married to your Peanut Taxi it fuses with your DNA before sniffing out your 'family tree' in neighbouring Diversities, allowing you access to only that geneline.

Asalah punctuates this traumatic ritual with, "The Natural Lottery show is all ready to go, it is built into our game, we've licensed ownership of the Patent Process that controls both the genetic matrix and controls Evertainment, we are inextricably linked to Going Live. Free Planet for real. Finally, people will see the world with all the drapes pulled down. All the gory details of political life explicitly on show."

Ensure that the meeting is being filmed – it's all about Documentary Evidence.

16
YOU THE PEOPLE
KICKING THE INDUSTRY HABIT

The Industry (obviously) isn't what it used to be.

You no longer sit there hacking triangulated meshes from the nonsense of virtual 3D space. That was ten years ago, man. You had to do everything by hand. Back in the day they called the 2D guys *pixel pushers*, because that's what they did. And the 3D guys like yourself they called *vertex butchers*, because one always had to crop and trim to the demands of the RTE or *Real Time Engine*. You don't have to laboriously hand-animate the individual matrices any more – that's what burned out a lot of the old guys.

The thing that really changed it all was a product called Symbiosis™.

Symbiosis™ was the shelf name for the software package of the Symbiosis company you were the *Functionality Tester* for (as a freelancer,) when the start-tomorrow deal-of-the-century Dusseldorf job offer came in. Symbiosis had a few new ideas, one of which was a unique user interface that negated all the manual input and pre/post-production tedium of its 'competitors' at the time. It took a lot of the other firms to court on copyright/patent grounds, won, closed down its competition and the rest is history – they played a clever legal game. How could you know, back then, that Symbiosis would *become* The Industry, in all ways and to all levels of the corporate game?

But how does Symbiosis™ work and how did you (without a degree in Computer Science) get a gold-dust job in The Industry in the first place. You may have 'no qualifications' but you have one essential thing The Industry respected back then and encourages in their employees today: the desire to get shafted in the ass at every opportunity. There's no Union in The Industry so they can get away with murder for their art.

That's what you do. It's your natural talent. How come you didn't get it earlier? How come you didn't suss that out? You stand out like a sore thumb. You're the wrong age. You always felt like the granddad among the grandkids even ten years ago. Today's kids feel a whole lot differently about the pioneer spirit of the early days of The Industry – of course they do, what else is there in their cored-out skulls to think?

But it still has the same sharks preying on the hapless individuals – both employees and customers. They didn't even need to interview you for the job, that's how easy it was. They had a file on you already. They must have been waiting to headhunt your sort of lunatic. You attract flies like shit, that's how 'reputation' works. When history looks back on it, they'll see you in the same light that they saw the grave robbers of old.

During the last four hundred years of the life of Oxford jail, on the site of the 11th century Norman castle on New Road, those who were hanged by the neck until they died for their petty crimes would be submitted to an even more hideous eternal torment of having their slipped-off mortal coil dissected for medical purposes. But even back then there were never enough corpses to cut up. So they employed grave robbers to go and dig up the dead. Obviously you had to have an eye open, as a grave robber – there was no point delivering rotting corpses to the medical schools via the back door. They wanted cadavers that were fresh, well, fresh in the sense that but for the coldness of the flesh and the lack of social graces one could imagine that they could, in the very next instance, sit up from their mortuary slumber and shout "I'll do anything, just please don't Y-cut my beautiful torso!"

It's the same with the Symbiosis™ software.

Originally, you had actors who would interface with the Symbiosis™ software via a few dermal clip-ons and a braincap. The routines would run; the data would be taken. It was nothing clever. It just went through the random probabilities of movement from electromagnetic muscular stimulation. It worked out all the geometry from surface tension projections, it worked out the joint limitations from muscular spasming and based on melanin cross-matching and skin resistance it built its own fully dynamic, fully textured characters for use in PIE or *Popular Interactive Entertainment*. But you know how it is. Everybody gets sick of the same old actors in the same old games. Even in a different skin, you go "Gah, that's just the guy from *Infinite Fighter 112 ®*" or "That's the same dance girl they used in *Pole Dancer 56 ®*".

These 'actors' were paid well for their service to the art of locomotion – they were downloading not their souls, but their physical acuity into the Symbiosis software. Symbiosis was stealing their lives while retaining their souls so that a Purgatory of eternal torture of button presses could befall them. The general game-buying public knew too much, and they remember everything thanks to what used to be called *The Internet*.

They're eternally sugar-hungry, *Consumers* – it's an integral part of their skittish garb. They crave variety every waking second. Shiny new things must jingle in front of them at every opportunity; think colourful mobiles for babies. You remember, those plastic hanging toys that rotated while playing soothing tunes that kept babies from crying before Evertainment did all those jobs parents don't like.

That's what you are – a body snatcher. It began as *Reality TV* but then the temptation for variety became too great. No one cared about 'the professionalism of the actor' any more, they just wanted New Flesh every flick of the cursor or click of a button. Imagine an androgynous entity stood before you flickering through a vast array of sexual, facial and body types – that's what really turned the industry into the mega drug that we know today – all human identity mulched together into a thickly gnarled paste of lowest common denominator. You're not a physical body snatcher or grave robber, there's no digging in your job. You collect the necessary "Variety," using the commercial Hollywoodised term. It's a fact that there are never enough Captures, never enough Variety, to satisfy the consumer's desire for constant change, so you're unlikely to be out of work any time soon. And who really cares if the capturing process is fatal in about 1 in 33 non-professional captures?

Don't you just love the corruption of the corporate mindset?

Anyway, back to today's first three jobs: a fat politician, a gangly youth and a mother. It's for use in an ISE or *Interactive Soap Engine*. That's the real BIG thing now – Interactive Soap. Everybody got real sick of TV soaps; they had just saturated the market. Then some clever boffin came up with this algorithm where you could actually be a part of the scripted action. It was mostly online gaming by this time with a lovely *Thinky-Cap*™ interface. The entire world got the addiction. Everyone effectively became anonymous within the strict confines of their online envelope. It was all the rage. The ultimate cross-dressing.

The fat politician and the gangly youth you've already 'captured' – that's what they call it - *Character Capture™*. There's no abduction involved. It's not that kind of criminal act. No bodies are snatched, other than the data of their living selves. That's all the companies need; the data of the character and how it moves – that's the essence of your trade, recording 'motivation': trapping the vital essence of 'performance'. You'd never go back to the old days knowing you could do it this way. It's so much simpler for all concerned.

Then she approaches you.

Well, she's not approaching *you*, she's just walking down the street. But she's walking down the street in your direction. There's certainly some *urban* edge there to her kinky little street strut. Pushing a sports buggy in which a fat mixed-race child lies at a funny angle, stone cold sleeping; maybe drugged – you know what these young estate mothers are like, they'll do anything for a bit of peace and quiet. She's got these retro-70's lurid shades on and her head's held high, she's about to pass you by. She has this great (what would you call it?) Attitude. She's known for the whole length of the street that she's been in your scope. Maybe she's looking for Talent Scouts like you to impress. Maybe she dreams of having her jittering screaming trembling auto-motive system captured for fleeting digital immortality, if that's not a massive contradiction of terms.

She screams 'mother', or at least this generation's degraded definition of the term.

"I'll have what he's having," you open the gambit with a gormless grin, right there in the street, hands on your hips so she'll stop and chat.

"He's zonked," she fingers the long brown fringe out of her eyes, she even moves like an ingame character, "He's been connected to *Paedo Play Party* all morning. Look at him, the little skallywag. He's all chomped out," this proud estate mother puts her weight onto her right leg and tilts her head sympathetically, a natural catch for The Industry. She looks over her shades. She has glorious hazel eyes – maybe mahogany – really rich brown with golden specks that *actually* sparkled. You don't even see that she was *Trying Too Hard*™. You're what they call *Oblivious*™ or *Spellbound*™

She's a good looking young girl. You just about wangle your way into her place for 'coffee' and it's the simplest thing to spike hers, while she's distracted by the critter, with the correct dose of *Dozey*™ (the regulation somnolent all the respectable Satelliters were using) and soon she's prepped and ready for Capture.

It's a pokey little apartment – more a living room with a big sofa bed along the back wall, to one side a kitchen area and a shower area. Smells of sour baby stuff. Proper little single mother's apartment she probably scavenged off the council when her mom threw her out of the family home in disgrace or some such sob story. Let's not be judgemental – let him who casts the first stone...and all'a that.

She reacts very well to the Dozey™ and just for added effect (though it wasn't in the manual) you strip the young girl down to her cream-coloured cotton-effect knickers so that her breasts will flail around when she's in the throes of a Symbiosis™ capture; a sleazy job like this has to have its perks, right? You put the rubber gag in her mouth so she won't chew the enamel off her teeth and switch on the Symbiosis™ interface. Her kid had started screaming in the pram where she'd left it.

She'd actually asked you what was in your briefcase with a wry smile on her face as she opened the door to her pungent apartment. Like she knew who you were; that you worked for The Industry. Like she knew exactly what she was doing. You were so tempted to spill the beans and just let her off with a cautionary warning about her parental posture in public. But you couldn't. Looking down at her, you realise that she's perfect for the role. And it'd impress the boss – the precautionary *Sword of Damocles* hanging over you.

You flick the Capture switch and her body starts rattling through the upper-dermis emulation; the tingling calm before the storm of her joint calibration. You bend over her to smell the sweat lifting off her jittering breasts like a greasy smear of light. Her child is still screaming in its buggy. Never mix business and pleasure, that's the golden rule – or *should* have been. Her eyes flit open. She reaches up and zaps you with this thing on her ring finger. Stings like hell.

That's when her 'disguise' falls off – must have been the electrostatic discharge through your system, and it's 'Bless You' looming over you.

"You!" you scream at her through the disabling jaw-vice of pain.

Bless You stands over you like a fiery mirage all smiles and peer appreciation – she'd already showered and dressed. There was a very fresh smell to her. The baby isn't crying any more. Was the baby even real? You didn't check, did you? She seems very proud of something, nodding to herself in approval. Your body feels numb, chilled, but you sense the Symbiosis™ dermal clip-ons and braincap have been applied to the correct parts of your still-tingling body.

"I couldn't believe it when I saw you coming toward me in the street," she says. You could see how she'd already spent her sizable commission as you watched her hazel eyes, "I knew it was you. I couldn't believe they'd let you out of the office so early. You just screamed *disgruntled employee*. Perfect for the I.S. I'm working on. Two birds with one stone," she says and smiles one more time, flicking the switch to capture.

17
THE CUSTODIANS
NATURAL LOTTERY, ONE

Local time: 1903 hours:

A little girl runs into her mommy's bedroom, obvlious to what mommy might be doing in there, and with whom.

She bounces on mommy's bed like a cat-nipped kitten, "Mommy, mommy, did you see it? Did you see the talking birdy?"

"What's that honey?" mommy was 'doing business' for her Corporate Overlords; you know, connected into her office account which is a white-noise access level where Evertaiment is strictly forbidden among the workers, not allowed to intrude.

Mommy is groggy; battling the snap-out whiplash.

Mommy checks her petulant flame of anger at being 'ripped from the real' in such a careless manner.

"The talking birdy on the TV, mommy," the little girl points to the bio-socket at the back of her head where Evertainment lives, 24/7/365. The light in her eyes is literally a rippling supernova, "I was watching Purple Bear and this talking birdy burst into my head, mommy. I don't know what the talking birdy means by *Natchel Lotty*. Talky-bird talks stupid mommy, and it's stealing all my fun."

She folds her arms and makes her face pull this big sulk.

"What?" Mommy shakes her head, reaches for her glasses, struggles to unhook the arms from each other, rotates them so that they're the right way up, puts them on, inhales, "Now, what are you saying?"

"Check the TV, mommy." the hyper-active child indicates mommy's bio-socket with a flick of her head, "Do it mommy, before the talking birdy flies away."

"Access 32/15/90," mommy *ThinkTiVate*™s her neural connection to the Evertainment Grid, "What channel did you say it was on, Purple Bear?"

"Mommy, it's on every channel," the kid's face falls in like this massive gawp of awe and wonder. What's it mean, mommy?"

"Wait a minute, sweet peaches; this shouldn't be up yet, there's been a mistake, let me see," but there it is, invading the

pine cone of the Pituitary Gland like some sort of fluoride bullet
– *Natural Lottery*.

Centre-mind, is the 'talking TV bird' everyone in the know
recognises as Asalah Al Faghori, once-promising biochemistry
post-grad at Oxford University. To anyone else, there's no
discerning between a Symbiosis-faked persona or a real girl-bird
hybrid. Everyone believes everything Evertainment tells them,
as a rule; that's the only real power The Industry has. The
mommy grinds her back teeth furiously as she vidies the owl-
like thing rattling on in its decaying orbit spiel of gormless
naivety.

Asalah chirps, already well into her Creativity spiel...

"...I mean, what in the name of all that is holy, unholy or
atheistic are you doing, going to work 12 hours a day, 48 weeks
a year just to earn money to pay for food and water and
accommodation from some global slum landlord and prison
thug? Just what are you doing?

I mean, look at me – I'm a genetic chimera. I'm not even
religious. I don't even believe in a God, a Creator, a Prime
Mover. Hell, I'm not even a fan of the Creationist science-drug
Big Bang Theory. And even I know that working like a slave
with whipmarks on your back in the form of your credit record is
not the life *any* god intended for us. I'm not even playing Devil's
advocate, because as you can surmise, I don't dig on no Satan
flesh or Dark Lord meat, neither."

To me, it makes no sense that You The People should still be
whipping yourselves on the back all the time in the name of *The
Conglomerate Empire*. Tell them to "get lost!" Let them invent
clever droids that will liberate our lives so that we can all just do
whatever takes our creative fancy. Tell them their game sucks.

Maybe even some of us will understand that death is better
than the life of a gladiatorial slave – plus it stops the elitist
freaks enjoying your suffering. Deny them that and their sick
and twisted corporate world comes crumbling down around their
ears. At last. Finally.

Where am I going with this? Well, as per my arbitrary-
mood-swing mentality, I am going to say something that is both
extremely stupid and extremely profound. Ready?

Creativity.

Creativity is what makes the sun – out nearest star – affect the earth. Yes, is it not obvious? We're in the same gravity, well within that which our parent star first ignited. We are made of the same stuff, forged by the same stellar processes. Of course we're still affected by the movements of our parent, we're still connected to the solar umbilical chord. We are more than stardust. We are S*unMind*.

Yeah, Creativity. And SunMind.

I think there's also a way to communicate our SunMindness to the mother, like the hunger parasites in a meat-eater's body, we can influence how that great ball of fire treats us. I think we can avoid a global cataclysm by worshiping the sun like those old idiotic indigenous people used to. Maybe that way humankind might see the odd burning bush or singing lake every now and then.

Maybe that way real Creativity, real Passion and real Kinship can be returned to the affairs of the people of this barren homeworld..."

Suddenly, in centre-mind, 3D footage of a clearing in a wooded area.

Sounds natural and unnatural saturate the minds of the viewers, all connected to the Evertainment Grid, every channel infiltrated by the activity of Custodian Liberation.

Without warning, a wobbly-doughnut-like UFO is shown breaking the tree line. This strange entity comes into full view so that the viewers can examine the electromagnetic anti-gravity effect that is keeping it aloft. The viewers see how each of the six floating homes can attach and detach from the body of the Diversity, and living space can be shared between the occupants. The viewers see the separate elements of this Diversity land in the clearing, one by one.

Asalah describes the footage...

"This is the first successful landing of the *Cumulo Diversity* arriving and splitting off at Bullingdon Woods."

She smiles then, at the mention of Bullingdon Woods, like it was some sort of in-joke.

The mommy knows what 'Bullingdon Woods' means but it only makes her sad, sad and angry at the slaughter to come.

Asalah grows serious once again, and footage of the attempted assassination by military rocket attack of the Custodians ensues while she continues her spiel...

"Luckily, as you can see, this unprovoked attack did not eradicate the Custodian Liberation, as was the aim of The Chess Players. A cynical armed response will never eradicate mankind's Creativity, his Passion and his Kinship. These floating-home diversities will ensure that the living surface area of Free Planet can remain untouched, be properly ReWilded/restocked and kept beautiful forever."

Now, because you were there, you know that no alleged military rocket attack ever took place. You know that these floating homes didn't look like this, they were far more organic. You remember how the Peanut Taxis fed stolen humans into these floating prisons made of twelve genetically fused individuals. You remember that, right? Let's witness the next viscid extrusion from the Lies & Deceit Machine.

Asalah goes on...

"Based on the latest technological advances, these Floating Homes are self-repairing. Each floating housing unit will have space for living and space for hydroponic cultivation and also six docking modules, to which Peanut transport taxis or other housing units etc can be docked. There will be space in between each floating housing unit Diversity, as part of the grand design, so that that all-important sunlight can get through to the ground below.

Using the 4-valent connectivity of an atom like Carbon makes sense in that it has been proven to allow both connectivity and free-flowing association of other atoms into and out of the mix. So, each carbon housing unit will have FOUR utility ports for those who want to remain self reliant; you can connect anything you want to this like another hydroponic, water/sewage or transport unit. You can also convert each of these into 'connectivity ports' were you to want to join a group of these floating housing units and make a community.

A single housing unit may travel faster and with more maneuverability than a Diversity of linked housing units. One of the advantages of connecting/traveling with others is that it takes 'your' nav-computer offline thus saving your energy for some other purpose. You join the group. You are adopted. You belong."

At least *this* section rings true. She goes on...

"You elect to become a permanent part of any Diversity you join by giving up all your docking modules to attach your housing unit permanently into the communal molecule...you would come to a communal agreement on the external transport modules, sewage/water and hydroponic modules so you can still have mobility external to your agreed impermanent floating unity.

One aspect of the Diversity that can't be shown here is that the connected living units might incorporate to form cathedrals in the air. But this is for a future edition of *The Natural Lottery Show*. To a time when mankind will be ready to under.stand.

For now, let it be known that You The People are the future of mankind's liberation from slavery. Only by actively supporting the Custodians can we all hope to escape the stalemate of Fascist Commercialism You may pledge your involvement at the conclusion of this first broadcast. A wonderful future awaits you all, on a Free Planet."

Asalah bows her feathery head, ruffles her feathery wings.

The Custodians restore control of the Evertainment grid to The Controllers; the Times Roman E.T. or EverTainment logo refocuses in back of your medulla oblongata.

"Mommy, the talking birdy makes my head hurt. Why is she saying that we should all be free," whines the worry-crazed little girl, "Why's the talking birdy saying we should rebel against our programming? Mommy, what does she mean?"

"Nothing, honey. It's just a silly TV bird. It's like Purple Bear or something; I don't know. Maybe some mischief makers are just goofing around, you know, trying to make people laugh or something, you know how mischievous big brothers can be my little petal angel. You know what it's like to be an innocent little potato, cooking in the oven," mommy says.

"Mommy, what's the matter with your eye?" she places a little finger on the heavy wetness brimming on mommy's lower eyelid.

"I'm crying for the TV bird, honey," and a sob actually catches in her throat, she blushes involuntarily, as if caught in some intimate act, before steadying herself, checking her emotions, "I'm crying for the TV bird, darling, and all her little TV friends who are going to die real soon,"

She takes the little girl into her arms and hugs her, rocking her slowly as she continues, "All adults know the talking TV bird is a game that will never play out. We should prepare ourselves for whatever may come once that happens."

Mommy holds the confused child by the shoulders at arms length, "We should *all* get ready for what may come," she pulls her back into her softly-sobbing embrace.

"Mommy, I love you," the girl gurgles as a line of snot snails over her upper lip, onto mommy's shoulder.

"I love you too, sweetheart, but the world is an insane apple with a nasty stinking worm wriggling out of it."

18
YOU THE PEOPLE
CARFAX CAROUSEL

Carfax Tower is all that remains of the 13th century Church of St Martin's. It is considered the centre of what used to be the old walled town of Oxford. It sits on the *carrefour*, (hence "Carfax") i.e. crossroads, of the four major roads that make up the cardinal spokes of old Oxford: St Aldate's from the south, Cornmarket from the north, Queen Street from the west and the High Street from the east.

Up the centre of Carfax Tower spirals a time-worn stone staircase that allows access to the flat roof where millions of tourists from all points of the compass have come to take pictures and enjoy the panoramic views of Oxford's 'dreaming spires'.

But that's not why you're here, today.

You're not here to 'see the sights', though in many ways you don't yet understand this is exactly why you're here. Its been hours already, and the stifling heat has soaked your shirt to your back. You can barely breathe in this sweltering tourist chimney that winds and winds and winds to the top of the Carfax Tower like a gun barrel. You have to be here, today; it's your destiny. Your final stand against the forces of evil upon this planet, or so you think. Your best gesture, at least.

You'd made it here, as if in a day dream…just walking along with your head bowed, your step heavy, your gait all sorts of unbalanced, your breathing laborious, like you were pushing through cerebral sludge. Ya know, just like how most pedestrian mall-zombies look on a daily basis.

You don't know how long you'd been out here – feels like days, but it could have just been hours. You'd not even cared to look for food, not like it would have done you any good as most dumpsters out back of restaurants and supermarkets are DNA-locked against such 'free loading'. As far as they've always been concerned, you're a Corporate Drone or a Sheep-eyed consumer, or you're just dead. No profit-making entity is in the business of giving handouts, as attested by all the death camp-like skeleton claws being thrust out at you as you made your way here. Penny for the night shelter, sir or madam.

You know that phrase, *they only come out at night*? – well, flip it for the living dead, the de-commissioned of the corporate workforce; the redundant: the restructured masses who only come out during the daylight hours to empty your pockets with their economic inactivity.

This is *so* not like you. Even hungry, you'd have fought back, robbed some store, robbed some shopper. Anything to survive. This, this letting yourself decay from the inside. That's *not* you. But you're not listening, not even to that inner voice you've relied upon to get you this far in your oh-so-short-and-meaningless career, this life of slavery to the Invented Persona, to The Industry.

Here you are, poor victim – you even got in the queue as far back as Cornmarket, that's how important your final stand had become. Like you were here to take part in some product launch or mall opening or film premier or anything to take your mind off 'that which had to be done'.

As you communally shuffled round the corner, there was the Carfax Tower clock. You'd just missed the little marionette show on the hour. Yeah, you didn't even get that right today. Do you even feel like yourself any more? Where's your fucking human spirit gone? Where's your spunk, goddammit?

Why aren't you thinking about the people you'll leave behind?

Why aren't you thinking about the great things you've done as a human being?

Why aren't you thinking about the way you can make this world a better place before you leave?

Oh...maybe you're thinking this is your *Leave The Planet A Better Place,* your 'Do right by *Free Planet*' gesture. Self-eradicate your virus-like germ-like cancer-like effect on the gorgeous Global Game. Are you sure you're not working on auto-pilot? Are you sure you're not being controlled to self-destruct in some way? Are you sure that there's nothing further you can do while you still have breath in your lungs and blood in your veins?

But you don't know what 'Do right by *Free Planet*' means yet; you haven't seen the Natural Lottery broadcast. Maybe you'll never know.

You're now barely even halfway up the ancient tower, and it's starting to smell real nasty as a river of piss pours down the stone sewer between your feet. Everyone lets loose when they're faced with their own mortality. And nothing stinks worse than human piss and human shit accruing under your feet in what amounts to a mortuary chimney. You put your hand on the old stone wall and it's nothing but tremulous slime. And you can't tell what that slime is made of. You hear far ahead near the top of the staircase a young couple fucking. It's like death is some sort of sexual rush for these idiots, but this is a renowned phenomenon. And besides, there'll be no witnesses to their 'crime'. No witnesses who are going to spill the beans on the identity of the 'sexual deviants' once this ascent is over.

Under your feet, the age-rounded stone steps seem ambivalent to the weight of far too many serially-ascending visitors moving one communal step forward at a time. There's a signal there – it's just that you can't see it. Not yet. You still have to go through the fire, emerge out the other side. And you still paid to get up here, you actually authorised One Entrance Fee for ascent on this terminal journey. It's not like Carfax Tower management don't really know what's going on outside their own premises. Sure, they don't have a clean-up contract with 'private contractors' to shift the rotting carcases and fly-buzzing effluent, once the inevitable has taken place. And it's happening more and more each day as everyone who's not sponsoring the Great Global Gamble seems to be on a collision course with their own mortality. There'll be a reason, there's always a reason. But it's an evasive one as of this moment in your short history.

Make money by any act of servitude, that's the golden rule – make money for the already rich. To them, you're just one of the faithful, at this point. One of the flock. One of the bleating lambs in the ever-constricting pen. About to be slaughtered in the name of Induced Miasma on a global scale. Imagine this scenario taking place in any number of Tourist Towns across the earth; Madrid, Hong Kong, Brisbane, Brasilia. Imagine thousands of people per minute pouring over the edge of a tall building and crashing to the ground, their faces grinning in exultation as they give themselves to the greater cause, this mass exodus into oblivion. Payouts made. Debts settled.

It took you no time at all to realise that there was no point living on such a tainted cheese, such a poisoned well, such a shattered crystal of a planet, once you'd been Captured. How could anyone aspire to bring an innocent child into this insane world of corporate espionage and death camps and indentured servitude?

You'd seen it all, and you'd thought that was the way the world worked. But no more.

The line of people takes a communal step forward; one laboured step up the chilling spiral staircase. By the time you get to the top, you'll have all made one hundred and twenty four steps. But the hundred and twenty fifth step is the most important, for you and your series friends, your partners in doom. And you'll all discover what that means in a few minutes time.

And no one's talking.

You're all just standing there. You all know why you're here. You all know what you're gonna do. Like, what would be the point of 'conversation' this late in the endgame, right? What you gonna ask? What are you gonna share with already dead people? What would be the point, when all answers are like a fatal move on the chess board? Check-mate in three…two…one...

And there's the final destination. The final chapter of this book you called your life. The green metal staircase that leads to the final exit where your maker and you are about to get *Real Intimate*™.

This groaning, swaying, green metal staircase spirals to the top of Carfax Tower where wind swept acolytes of the self-murder culture prepare themselves to pay the ultimate price for their enslavement to some ludicrous arbitrary doctrine.

And everyone who's made it this far has their breath grasped from them. Like their last gasp has been robbed out of their lungs. It's not like they're gonna need it.

You stand there, with the chill wind ripping through whatever clothes you have on, tugging away at your hair, making your eyes water. There's no real smell of death up here, which is the one good bit of news. In front of you, the queue of doom spreads out and approaches the edge of the tower top like lemmings under some sort of spell; the word *voodoo* comes to mind, but you don't even flinch from your programming. You're really nothing but a drone, like the rest of these insane fuckers, giving their actual lives for the corporation.

'A nice clean simple death is all you deserve, for your sins of disrespect, your crime of neglect' goes the script.

You take a big deep breath, the last breath you'll ever take, and prepare yourself for the obvious. You gird your loins, thrust out your arms like all before you had done, you look up to the sky like all before you had done, walk out toward the short wall surrounding the tower, put your foot on the low rampart.

In your defense, you don't cry out to a lost mother/daughter/lover like almost everyone before you had done. For you this is a personal moment not for sharing, and your silence at this time is its own mark of your heroism, script script. Your final solution to the enigmatic phrase 'Do right by Free Planet' that you've yet to understand the meaning of, but the script, clever script. It just seems like the right thing to do, this offloading, this cleansing of the world by your ultimate gift to the world. A clever end game of your own personal creation.

You push off with your forward leg, looking up at the soft grey chemtrail shimmer of Oxford's sky as you start to teeter up and out, leaning forward to your own demise...and no one is going to rush up and save you. You can be guaranteed of that. This is your last moment. This is the end, my friend.

Don't even bother to breathe.

Hold your breath all the way down...

It's only as you're plummeting to your death, with the wind blowing through your hair, face and clothing, that you remember the instructions from the starred small print in the footer of your PCCM or *Professional Character Capture Manual* that states in barely readable 8 point, *"In 4.5% of all Captures there's a side-effect of suicidal tendencies; observation for a minimum period of six hours is advisable if not recommended. Seek medical help, if symptoms persist."* Of course, no capture professional worth his salt has six hours to waste mothering some 'actor' through his post-Capture sulky-wulkies. That's like Unpaid Overtime, and you already do enough of that every Crunch Time. No thank you, Dear Overlords and Masters.

Can all these plummeting suicides be suffering from *Post Capture Depression*, is the Industry really that necrotic?

Just as the red-settling slaughter scene at pavement level finally slams up to meet you do you remember a face dematerialising before your eyes to reveal 'Bless You' in all her leering glory; what did she actually say? Where was this? What was it you screamed – 'Disgruntled Employee?' Was she sent to off you? Were you sent out on your last mission to be captured yourself?

Your last memory is her painted fingernail flirting with the Capture button. You see her hand flickering like a nasty z-sort bug in the code, like when companies used to spend years developing their own glitch-ridden engines, prior to the global take-over by Symbiosis™.

Then the flash of light, the bone-crunching slap of impact.

19
THE CUSTODIANS
NATURAL LOTTERY, TWO

Local Time: 1900 hours precisely.

E.T. or EverTainment Logo shatters in your back brain like a mega-come-down from the most delicious drug ever invented; you start to shiver, instantly.

ANNOUNCER (in over enthusiastic intro-mode): *if it's seven p.m. It must be time for another edition of The... Natural... Lottery!*

BAN "PRISON" NOW
BAN "GOVERNMENT" NOW
BAN "ORGANISED RELIGION" NOW
BAN "COUNTRY" NOW
BAN "EMPIRE" NOW
BAN "WAR" NOW

That's how every episode of the Natural Lottery Show starts, a font-shuffling holo-dimensional 3D signature that scrapes around inside the braindance like some sort of high-friction amulet in a cracked chalice, like some abrasive scouring pad for a burned milk pan, like some vague scolding denunciation from a once-proud parent, scorching but ever so easy to take. Logo flicking, switching, *ever-taining...*

No pain at all real-ly. Far too easy to under.stand. Far too compelling to not be-lieve. No resistance to the message at all. Just another Psyche-Vertisement hit of Total and Utter Compliance. Mankind is so impressively gullible. It's all about presentation and style over any valid content.

It won't even take that long to totally indoctrinate the slaves of planet earth into Custodian new-think, this new-liberation of their Selves™. They're primed now, primed by successive governmental shock therapies like 9/11 and Gulf of Tonkin and Iraq invasion and...it's a very long list in a very long entrenched warfare against YMCA or *Your Maternal Critical Acuity*.

Mankind is ready to accept any old story, any old alien invasion, any old Al Qaeda or invented bogey man. That's where and how Natural Lottery slots neatly into their worthless lives, like a silk cushion for their state-generated fears.

Natural Lottery is their salvation, and it's all gauged by how much they wanna believe it can be so. Mankind has been gutter-trained to acquiesce to any number of mind games – he has no idea what's real and what's not. And that's the really good thing about these End Times. This is the time to strike, while the iron's hot, while the powder's primed and the flints are cocked ready to unleash the rallying cry.

Do right by Free Planet.

Feathery front woman Asalah Al Faghori's at it again, trilling her puerile message of genetic mutations as a means to fixing the global schism, at exactly 7 p.m.

Tonight's subject – "Passion."

Here's how she lays it down, after a brief twitch of feathery preening...

"A King would never let down his People.

"This is how people used to think. A King is put into power by You The People so that His Office can protect yourselves, your women, and your children from harm. Within the Kingdom, the people are free to express their hopes and grievances to their King and he will do what he can - to the best of his abilities. Even if you don't like the idea of a king, the basic concept is well-intentioned enough. The King of an ancient tribe was like a hierarchic father figure; he would be the first into battle when conflict arose, he had the passion of his convictions that no one should harm his people, and was more than willing to show the enemy that the name of his tribe would continue on through history as long as there was blood in his veins, breath in his lungs and passion in his heart.

A King would never let down his people.

But that King, that benevolent philanthropist – however tyrannical or individual or despotic his methods of rule – is all but dead. He has been sold out by his people, by the lure of profit. After many centuries of border negotiation and inter-marriage with neighbouring tribes, the king finds a new mercantile plague within his lands promising his people true freedom and riches beyond their wildest dreams if they were to abandon the king and come and work for them in their stateless company.

"these mercenary companies grew and grew, soaking up skilled workers and apprentices from all over the tribes of the world, enslaving their people by financial reward. There are now mercenary companies and conglomerate associations for every trade you can think of, basically prisons of commerce. The King has been robbed of his greatest asset – his people. And some would say this is a really good thing – King's are nought but egotists with a Messiah complex. But you're missing the point.

Passion has been transplanted with Profit.

Yet, the old tribal borders brokered over decades of bartering with neighbouring tribes still remain, and the mercenary companies like it like that. This gives them insurance value, future accountability and power over life and death, every option to manage their profit. These old borders make You The People think that your freedoms are exactly the same as they were under your protective King. But you have no protection. You are an employee of a corporation. You pay rent to a corporation. You pay for your utilities to a corporation. You help repaint and replaster the walls of the corporation halls in the name of image and marketing.

"You The People are slaves within this global corporate structure - you have none of the freedoms you thought you had, worst of all you are now the enemy of the corporation. Your increased standard of living threatens their profit margin and their annual report is dotted with black marks.

Solution? Global meltdown; conglomerate restructuring it's called. Coming to a village, town or city near you. And the streets of your village, town or city will run red with the blood of dignified people torn to pieces by the ruthless mercenary gangs who lied to you you in the name of riches you could never retain.

The only one who loses is you, the people...unless...*unless* you wake up, *unless* you put down the toys of corporate war and grow up.

Unless you go, *yeah, this should be a Free Planet. We should live within, and carefully manage, our limited global resources. We should use once-patented technologies so that local solutions can be found for empire overspend.* Until we all have this over-riding passion for our homeworld and are pro-active and competitive in replacing, rejuvenating and revitalising this poisoned earth, we will remain nothing but dull-witted slaves of a self-destructive abstract, the profit/loss account, the ledger."

At this point in episode two of The Natural Lottery, we cut to a head and shoulders shot of Asalah Al Faghori. As she was before her transformation. This is the footage of a healthy young woman. You can see her naturally dark skin. You can hear her words.

Sweat is pouring off our young heroine. Shivers sword-swipe through her body in chaotic choreography. The skin actually seems to twitch jaggedly, one wonders if it won't rip or tear. Remember those images from childhood where someone in a science lab touches the electrostatic generator and their hair billows out?

"The physical world. A mathematical expression. Of man's intent," she gasps, gulping hard, rapid air.

"But it's...not just this. There are animals. Computers. With *neurones*. That process. Energy convers..." that last word raised into a shrill shriek – "...tion!"

"It's a...rapidly soul-stripped earth and there's no stopping. The onslaught. The nightmare. The drowning!" she part-shouts, part-sobs, blurting out the last word like it was the most important thing she'd ever say in her life.

"I can't...," blood issues from her lips in a pink spray where she's tried to bite off the scream, imprison the pain, retain the agony, her gumline reddened; vampiric.

Without warning, while you're looking right at her, she soft-explodes with a barely-audible thud and what remains is like a festering apple caught in the last frame of a time-lapse-movie documenting its rapid rot. Poof, in the blink of an eye, Asalah Al Faghori is nothing more than a multi-coloured fur ball on the too clean carpet of her room. A vaguely human silhouette and palette, no sharp definition. No movement. No final exaltation or disclaimer. Just this pile of dried fibres, like wind-blown grass, settling, finally relaxing, released from its gusty turmoil.

Cut back to the girl-bird, in-studio...

"We must have Passion for Free Planet to exist, and sustain. Without Passion we'll have no enthusiasm for chaaange. Three long A's. Real long-term Change. Not some promised political insult of change, right? You realise what I'm saying. *Chaaange.*

Even though I sound like a bleating lamb, I am a real wolf. I am a living moment about to be shared with you. A grain of sand embedding itself under your collective eyelid to become a pearl. And by that I mean an end to War and an end to Slavery. And a protectionist or *Custodian* future for mankind where we put the Planet first and the planet will do right by us."

Her face lights up with the total confidence of child-like glee.

"That's all we really need. Creativity. Passion. And we'll talk about Kinship in tomorrow's show. For now, that's it. Think *Free Planet*. Think *Custodian*. Think *End To Empire*."

The E.T. Logo reforms from fluttering butterflies co-mingling on two suitable-cropped patches of lavender.

Surely there's no-one out there in Evertainmentland who'll sign up for this ridiculous Natural Lottery and offer their genetic lineage to Free Planet so that seven billion can be Free, so that the planet can Re-Wild. That's anarchy, and there's just no way they'll allow that, right?

But you'd be surprised how many desperate people are out there in the mainstream, keeping schtum and doing nothing that would draw attention to themselves, until it's time to act. Watchers. Learners. Schemers.

And watch and learn and scheme they did; in their hundreds of thousands.

Within the last hour of Episode Two, two point four million humans from all over the world have DNA-signed away their lives 'for the Good of Free Planet'.

It was like some insane Mexican Wave of bleating sheople – Chaaange-Maaania – that sliced through the Collective Conscience of the Evertainment audience, an oily flame tossed onto bone-dry tinder.

MIKE PHILBIN

20
YOU THE PEOPLE
GOD BLESS, EROTICA

You look back and you're being dragged from the mound of bodies at the foot of Carfax Tower, piled up by the derelict casings of three public phone boxes and an old concrete bin. For an instant the image of the receding public phone boxes and bin, smeared with gore of human deceleration, flip-form into the three pillars and the one cup of freemasonic ritual, flip-form once again into the three towers and the ceremonial crater left by the slaughter at the World Trade Centre complex at some point in history Evertainment has been telling you to forget since you became a corporate drone.

You see your life literally turning to dust, filling your mind to a depth of several nano-meters.

You see groups of people dragging bodies from the pile and dragging them away, to do what with you don't want to know. Likewise, fervent hands are pulling at your body, tearing at your clothes, making you naked in the middle of Queen Street. You can see where you landed, your soft-bodied landing. You can see the smear of blood that leads underneath you. And the streaks of others similarly removed from the scene. You have a panic attack; you can't work out if the blood is yours or just something that you've been dragged through. Either way, there's a slaughterhouse stink that clings to you like you're already dead. You stink of other people's death. That may be more figurative than you think.

Your manly scrum pulls your near-naked body roughly down a side street. You won't have heard the stories of people moving suicide victims from the centre of town to barter/sell off for fresh meat on the black market. You might be on someone's dinner plate without even knowing what happened.

"That's it, that's it, get all the clothes off him. It's all bugged," shouts some woman in command, "Yes, even the underwear. Oh, my god, yes. And any jewellery you find. Any special connections and ports, you find, let me know."

"I've been Captured," that's the first thing you spit out of your gotta-be broken jaw in a splutter of blood and enamel shards.

"You what? You're not supposed to be out of the office," the woman moves (has the attitude of) the Human Resources drone who welcomed you to the Oxford office, but the voice is off, and she looks nothing like her; a bad-guess sketch of humanity rather than a living breathing rendition. Like looking at a refraction. Or a cardboard cutout.

"Erotica?" you realise this is not the body of that HR drone, as she presented herself to you several days after your groggy arrival in Oxford, in the office. You don't recognise her, but you 'know' her. Everything about her is identical, except the face, the voice.

"Oh, this?" she points at herself with both hands, "You're not supposed to know about this. Does that help?" and she's more like you remember her, sounds right.

Before you can answer, the teen mob who are helping drag you to safety are confirming, "Teacher, we're seeing fibres all over this man. What has he done?"

And, "Teacher, we've never seen such an infestation."

Additionally, details reveal, "Teacher, he's weighed down with accelerometer fibres, so many life-signs transmitters, so much baud rate dedicated to his..."

"Is he still broadcasting?" Erotica, at least this morphic simulacra of that HR drone, has to make sure they've got everything before moving you to a Safe House.

"Teacher, he's been cleaned. But he'll ache like fuck tomorrow. It's like we've just pulled all the nerves in his teeth out of his head and the adrenalin rush is still withholding this bad news from him. If he survives tomorrow, he's made of sterner stuff than I think I am," one student said.

"He's made of ninety billion bits of sterner stuff than you ever will be, sonny. You really don't know who this is, do you?"

"Teacher?" you ask, and then you realise your forearm is totally shattered, literally hanging at an awkward angle like you have a second elbow and the pain suddenly hits you. You black out like the pathetic spaz that you are. You hadn't even felt the cold, as they were stripping you of every single nano-surveillance device known to The Industry. You dumb fuck. You missed it all, the whole sensoreal spectrum passed you by. Oblivious. Dud.

*   *   *

You awaken in some bar, somewhere high on planet Earth's concrete and steel antiseptic architectural mallscape. The first thing you do is grasp your forearm. But nothing is broken. You check the rest of your body. You're in a business suit. Grey pin, single breasted. Nice shoes.

You have a *subliminal* message in your head...

...Look for Floor 18...

Through the wide-sweeping transparent wall on one side of the bar, you can discern that you're in some open-plan corporate-lobby-style multi-storey temple that reminds you of London City Hall, but you could be anywhere in the corporate beehive. Hugely ascending spiral walkways rise and fall through the shot, seeming to span the entire inner volume of the building. Offices and businesses sprout off the spokes of a central elevator (drop points) with escalators criss-crossing, spiralling up and around.

And this is the weird part.

You are in this too-famliar building, not knowing why you're here, but in your head is a second subliminal...

...JuJo...

A name that you believe relates to a corporation (there once was a game corporation called KuJu but don't think they're any relation) where you're supposed to be by now. You know you're late already. You got lost thinking of the Japanese for nineteen, got 'confused'. You ended up on floor 19. You're wondering whether this is some sort of test to see if you can actually master some as-yet-unrevealed interface connected to a Symbiosis module – and we all know you're real good with interfaces.

You're a cunning fucker, and even now you're looking for 'tells' in the design of the complexity, in the layout of dread within your addled brain. Even bad interfaces have some plus points, you remind yourself. At least with an interface, no matter how crude, you're offered seemingly valid series of procedures, some tactile purchase on the task in hand. Otherwise, you're lost in a ruthless diceworld of 0 or 1 – and that's a minefield taking children's arms and legs and souls back to Hell to be doused in gallons of Napalm, Rocket Fuel and Agent Orange.

You remember the elevators.

You can still taste them, their odd scent or taste. You've ridden in one of those commercial null-zones to get this high. But you have no idea what you could be doing in this obviously-corporate building. And you know you won't have 'walked through any door into a gleaming lobby' – there are no such things as 'doors' on modern buildings such as this. Security is too tight. You'll have merged with the front security surface of the building and, if you passed some series of arbitrary DNA-checks, you'd have been allowed through like chemical osmosis.

You got this far, for a reason.

The best thing, for you, would be get up from your stool, walk out of this bar right now and never come back. If you know what's good for you. Just walk as fast, and far away from this haunted place, as you possibly can. Never come back.

You've attracted the attention of the barman, just some lad straight out of school in a pair of dark pants and t-shirt, "Have you ever heard of a company called..." you look around, furtively "...JuJo?"

"You've missed your stop, mister. You'll wanna head back to the elevator and press 18. That'll take you where you want to go. Then he does the oddest thing, he winks at you. And you're like, *what the fuck?*

"Cheers," you mutter.

"No worries," the barman moves to take the order of some gentleman sitting down the other side of the bar as you crawl off your bar stool and make to leave.

It's only when you get inside the elevator that you realise what's happening.

There is no floor 18 marked on the sporadic non-series list of buttons projecting from the dull-grey metal of the control panel. You read them out loud, "One, two, three… seven... twelve... fourteen... seventeen... nineteen... thirty-six," and that's it. Seven buttons on a space that could be filled all the way up through a four by ten grid. What sort of legitimate company building has so many missing floors?

So, it's not on floor nineteen. You press seventeen and the doors of the elevator shut. There's no discernible movement up or down. The doors open. Floor seventeen. You find the floor 18 mezzanine is accessed by a sliding walkway just off to your left. It's actually marked *Floor Eighteen.*

You feel a little groggy, somehow, having stepped out of the elevator – you were never good with elevators.

You end up in this lovely smoke-glass corporate waiting area with long flat leather sofas, awaiting somebody. You're lying back on this one sofa when your interviewer comes in. At this moment you realise you have on a very old business jacket and you have no C.V. or portfolio to 'show your potential' or 'reinforce your credentials.' You're not even sure if these 'industry essentials' will be relevant here. Wherever or whatever here is. In all honesty, the matter is never brought up throughout the very strange interview.

Instantly, you realise that something very weird is going on 'electromagnetically' or 'psychologically' in this waiting room. You lie there like it's the most natural thing in the world, all the while concentrating on controlling your right hand which was shaking quite badly. It hung there, in the air, in front of you like some limp claw. Quivering, visibly. The interviewer (who never introduced themselves, or seemed to enter the room) points out your shaking hand, in passing, and you seem to be able to bring it under control. Half way through your interview, you sit up into a seated position, having spent at least a half an hour on your back on this leather sofa in this waiting area.

Has the interview begun yet, you wonder?

Then these tech guys arrive. Again, no more than teens – jeans, t-shirts. One of them carries something under their armpit like a folded up newspaper. He takes it out and unfolds a super-high-resolution monitor in front of you. Just unfolds it like it's the most natural thing in the world, living pixels. You are shown a selection of 'transforming gold characters' or 'assets' that you're supposed to 'help in making', whatever all that means. They tell you that you'll be using Houdini (a package they know you hate, on the principal that the 'interface' is a blank code window) and all seems well.

Everybody seems very happy with your 'responses'.

"He's all done, Teacher," one of the tech guys folds his monitor up again and tucks it under his armpit.

Erotica breathes, "You made it then, virus free. Good. Very good. Welcome to Prodigy," she says, and holds out her slim hand like it's the first time you've both met.

You shake her hand, looking around all the time at the faces of the hackers who've just put you on the rack, run you through their system.

"Teacher?" one of the young hackers begs leave.

"Yes, yes. Leave us," she dismisses them. "Come, we have a lot to discuss, you and I."

She leads you into the bowels of the operation and you neither recognise anything nor can you seem to remember anything you're shown in the brief journey from Waiting Room to Briefing Room.

It's like as fast as you can see it, the image slips from your memory and you're just looking at something fresh. This sensation happens no matter how long you stare at any one thing, trying to retain a memory of it. A chair. A table. A coffee cup. A white, cylindrical capsule popped onto a receptionist's tongue. As quickly as they appear on the list of your cerebral inventory, they're slipping off into Oblivion (there's that word again) like so much cat-pushed crockery. Down down down like falling leaves, crushed underfoot, swept away. Dust. Ashes. Wind.

"I guess it's time to give you your first 'legitimate' assignment out in the real world, now that you've familiarised yourself with 'how Oxford works,'" she opens her gambit.

"I don't remember any building in Oxford being more than a few stories high," you tell her.

She makes a note on a notepad, with a 2B pencil. She smiles then. Looking directly at you, "Your first mission will be to Capture someone. Someone special. In fact, your mission is to capture someone so special that there's only really one of them in the whole world."

"I accept the mission," that's all you say. No hesitation. You're still a fucking robot, a mind-controlled killing machine, after all. And you don't even realise it. If you understood your true potential, this story of global tyranny and mass manipulation, this Covert World in the name of profit, would be over already.

21
THE CUSTODIANS
NATURAL LOTTERY, THREE

Local Time: 1900 hours.

Seven p.m. local time rushes round again like some demanding brat, intent on getting his/her way no matter what the intrusion.

E.T. Logo melts like butter in the sun, white-noises to bubbling ant shells.

ANNOUNCER: *if it's seven p.m. It must be time for another edition of The... Natural... Lottery!*

BAN "WAR" NOW
BAN "PRISON" NOW
BAN "GOVERNMENT" NOW
BAN "EMPIRE" NOW
BAN "COUNTRY" NOW
BAN "ORGANISED RELIGION" NOW

Flip-flopping graphical to avian facial morph as Asalah Al Faghori is back in the mid-brain, regular as a clockwork owl, seven o'clock on the dot, tick tock.

Evertainment sluices off its corporate salesman cloak and this grinning thing, this fake feather render, this puppet, chirps and burbles its aggravating message to the masses. Every night so far this week. Here's what she has to say on Day Three. Woo, woo!

"Kinship;" are you ready?" Her presence in your head seems to be oscillating, the way *Queen* used cheap stereo tricks on their early work.

"Kinship is not about Brotherly Love or some hippy-like Kumbaya hugging thing... except that it is, via patents."

Left brain bias.

"What?" you ask. Right brain bias. "Patents?" left brain cut. "You mean those pieces of paper that assign ownership to ideas?" Right brain cut.

"Sure," left brain cut. "Patents," centre brain, dull aching sensation streams out across the Evertainment network: fingers tingle, hair stands up on the backs of arms, nipples erect...

Asalah continues...

"It's time we realise that all of mankind's intelligence is ours to share; all. Of. It. Seriously. On a Free Planet, there's no longer any need to make profit or enslave others to do so. The world is free, from one God handed down to every single one of the seven billion sovereign individuals on this homeworld.

Why don't you realise this?

Why haven't you clicked that you're not supposed to be at war with the need to generate finance? You're not supposed to live or die at some slave driver's behest. You're not supposed to owe your life to some overlord. You're not supposed to pay some self-appointed prince to live on his land.

This is your Free Planet.

Kinship – where does that tie in then, where there are 'pack leaders' and 'minions'? Well, simple human society, as we've been spoon fed it, tells us *that's just the way it is*.

"Well, fuck that. And I'll address this to a small collective of several thousand money-makers who think they own this planet. Fuck you. Seven billion sovereign individuals are beginning to wake up to your corporate tyranny, beginning to realise that this state of affairs has existed before in recent history.

The 'commoners' forced to live in destitution.

The 'aristocracy' don't pay any taxes.

The connection lost between reality and the game that the 'elite' are playing.

Sound familiar? It should. It's the exact set of circumstances that led to the 'marie antoinette eats cake' french revolution with its guillotining of the royal families and sub-families of France. Okay, it took a lot, it always takes a lot to push You The People to start to stand up for yourselves, that's the way of a beleaguered public majority who've been schooled in the curriculum of *Corporate Compliance*.

But this is coming to an end, this is the real revolution, this year, on a global scale, real kinship will bond together those who thought they owned the place with the real owners of the place i.e. *everybody else*. The patents will be released from their private prisons. The elite haven't even taken this outcome into account; they're the ones that are truly asleep to the potential of mankind and the power of Kinship.

Get ready, it is going to be a memorable ride."

And another five million people have already pledged their genetic vote to the cause. This is going much better than she, or the Custodian Liberation could have hoped for after just three days. In fact, its been all too easy.

"Do you know?" Asalah addresses her captive Evertainment audience again, "They say that only a handful of private individuals own planet earth."

Due to conquering armies.

Due to intermarriage among tribal family heads.

Due to exploitation of the world's resources.

Due to murder plots, assassination plots and company take-over plots.

Due to ancient languages foisted upon the conquered.

Due to downright amoral empire building.

Due to nuclear weapons and the threat of global annihilation.

Due to profit.

Due to terrorism.

Due to prisons.

Due to taxation.

Due to laws.

Due to money.

Due to country.

Due to organised religion.

Due to campaigns of racial prejudice and ethnic cleansing.

Due to water rationing.

Due to food and seed manipulation by huge corporations.

Due to land lords and heads of state and royalty.

Due to the the prostitution of clever individuals among their number drafted in to help enslave the less-well-educated and dupe the more vulnerable members of our global society, only a handful of private individuals own planet earth.

Or to put it more bluntly – no they fucking don't! This is *not their* planet. This is *not their* country. This is *not their* religion. This is *not their* people. This is *not their* oil. This is *not their* wealth. This is *not their* accounting chart. This is *not their* battle ground. This is *not their* mindset. This is *not their* GAME. I mean, who the fuck do these deluded imbeciles think they are?

Big business, Patent privacy, Corporate government, Espionage and Assassination, Empire, Taxation, Trespass, Communism, Capitalism, Socialism, Zionism, Fundamentalism, TV-Evangelism, Creationism, Big-Bang-ism, Atomism, LHC-ism, Doom-ism, Facebook-ism have failed you. All these blockages to your Creativity, your Passion and your Kinship have broken your soul.

Planet Earth is the 'property' of all seven billion individuals and, as Custodians, it is *your* job to protect it," she screams into your mid-brain with such vehemence that it's like a tiny earthquake is happening somewhere in the world, like all the R³s are moving at once. And maybe they are, fleeing the inevitable.

Asalah turns to a chrome-finished bird waterer, where she takes a long bubbling gulp on the pipe, satisfying her intense thirst before continuing on.

"All empires fail."

She slides her beak through her wing feathers momentarily.

"We all know this. Empires fail for all sorts of reasons. But they all follow a similar curve, a bell curve.

Look back through history at the Egyptians, the Babylonians, the Romans, the Viking, the Nazis, the Commonwealth, Soviet Russia and today's modern empire The Corporations. There's a juvenile thrrrust when opportunity arises, a middle-age spread when inertia sets in and an often-rapid decline into morbidity due to some conflict of interest that leads to total cancerous failure of the system.

On a long enough timeline, all empires fail.

So, why do you keep funding an.oth.er des.pot's empire dreams with your communal subscription?

They will fail.

But where does this fit in to our initial mention of structured anarchy, localised Diversity and, ultimately, a Free Planet.

I think the guiding premise of 'protect your planet under any circumstance' will always, ALWAYS, trump any self-preservationary Empire's defenses. But what does this actually mean? Would it mean bringing down the population of the planet over time?

It should.

It makes sense that if there are fewer of us to feed, we can probably feed those who remain better and easier - and this can be done over time, with care for our planet and how we restock what we take. To do this we have to mercilessly crucify the for profit financial model that has ruled this earth since time immemorial.

In fact, if you look at the bell curve for human existence, we're just about at the point, right now, where we're accelerating up to the zenith of the bell curve, which can mean only one thing. The descent. And this may be a gradual or catastrophic decline in numbers. But it'll be okay.

As long as we don't allow Big Government to dictate and Big Pharma to decide who should live and who should die. As long as we ban all large-scale corporate vaccination programmes and educate the general public in the vast area of the bell curve that you just can't have all the kids you want.

You don't even need all those kids.

I suspect that if we the seven billion inhabitants of this planet just locally, together or as individuals, just understand that we can't keep trying to build the Human Empire to the detriment of the other balancing factors on this planet – the flora and the fauna – we can effectively nullify the human race bell curve. And by this I mean we can take ourselves, our very race, off the catastrophic failure curve, for ever. We will succeed because we are taking care of Free Planet like it is a new-born baby. We will succeed because mankind is becoming aware of the balances on both sides of the life equation.

Though self-important frontal-lobed mankind thought he could, he can *not* have it all," she said, gently. Softly. See how the scream became the whisper?

"Empire after empire has proven this, nothing will change until we break the feudal empire bell curve and support the anarchic-seeming structure of ruler-less rule-less yet-benevolent planetary existence alongside our fellow man.

Death to war. Death to profit. Death to boundaries. Long live a Free Planet of Creativity, Passion and Kinship;" she suddenly looks very weary – how can one bird find this much to talk about, night after night? She once again takes a drink from her bird watering machine. Her thin pink tongue sending wet-spray of vibrating trillings into a joyous frenzy. Like watching a sparkler do its fatal sparkle-curve.

Sated, she adds, "Tomorrow night will be the first of our Prize Givings. The first winners of The Natural Lottery will be receiving their access code to a future many of you have never even dreamed of since you became Consumers, dead meat for the Fascist sausage maker. Not long now, and then your Free Planet will phoenix-rise from the stubborn ashes of this ruined world."

E.T. Logo returns in all its corporate glory.

22
YOU THE PEOPLE
TO KILL A MOCKING BIRD

"And you're sure you have no next of kin?" Teacher asks you.

"You sound like I'm on a One Way mission," as you say this, your Yellow Bus conveys you through The Wall, heading north out of Oxford. They look like those Yellow School Buses that used to transport kids to school before Kevlar Kubitz ensured 100% attendance. It's not painful but it's just the way they seem to 'blend' through the Oxford Wall like either it or you didn't exist, both merging with you and opening around you, maybe at the electrostatic level of your atoms, down to the astrophysical roots of your genesis. Your shuttle drove on through into the walled city like it wasn't there. You can feel a full-body tingle, but it doesn't last long, and it's not much of a tingle, if truth be told.

"All Cities have these 'force fields'. Well, shall we say 'cities' in inverted commas. The old 'build a cathedral, call it a city' scam. York, Cambridge..."

You have no idea what Teacher's rattling on about; nothing new there then. Your Yellow Bus takes the left fork of two on St Giles, Woodstock Road.

"They're not really 'force fields'," she continues, "They're technically genetic disruptors. You don't have the right code. You're not on the right bus. Zap, you don't feel right for a couple of minutes. Some company called..."

"Yeah, **ESI.** I was in The Industry, remember. 'From Dream to Real in the Blink of an Eye,' or some crap. I probably even have a t-shirt somewhere..." you say.

"Once you're in The Industry, you never leave The Industry," she pats you on the inside of your thigh, condescendingly.

You can't work out if she's trying to make a joke. You look at her, study her eyes. But she's giving nothing away. Her eyes are just passive planes of reflection; you get back nothing you don't put in. Your Yellow Bus commutes slowly up Woodstock Road, letting professors, students and maintenance staff of Oxford University on and off at assigned stops. You pass a church on the right, a big important-looking church with an impressive spire and its own burial grounds – imagine the real estate cost to this economy.

"Where we going?" you ask, but it's like she's either ignoring you or pretending not to hear your question. The tree-lined sub-urban streets of north Oxford roll by in their ancient design; red-brick, bay window, moss on roofs, exclusive private vehicles parked in gravel driveways. This is a special place, where the Controllers of Global Finance live. It's just that obvious. Everything has, and always will focus around Oxford. Maybe there's something in the water.

She presses the *Request Stop* bell and you alight on Woodstock Road, cross to the other side. A building with a plaque on the garden wall hails *Columbia State University*. Teacher puts a hand to the detector and an ancient gate more moss than wood swings open on creaking hinges. You squeeze through after her as the gate continues to open, obviously making way for some sort of private transport. There's no A.I. in this gate, it's just a rotting wooden structure on a motorised hinge, a timeless relic.

"And no next of kin," she looks at you, "You're sticking by that?"

"Can we just get this over and done with?" you turn around as a door creaks open.

The front door of the private residence is opened by a ghost.

Well, not a ghost, more like a reflection. Of you.

"A-Washington!" the woman shrieks and leaps forward to hug you. She pulls back and holds you by the shoulders, taking a long hard look at you. She's acting like you're her long-lost brother or something. Thing is, she looks exactly like you. In every single way.

"Guys, guys, he's here!" she shrieks back into the hallway.

Another 'you' comes to the door to greet you, shaking hands, pulling you into a hug. You look okay in a beard, you've lost weight.

"Well, well, well," comes a third, balding, heavier-set you.

Let me do the introductions, "A-Washington, we all know you," Teacher is addressing you, "This is C-Jefferson," the female you, "G-Roosevelt," the skinnier you, "T-Lincoln," the heavier you.

"It's like a mobile Mount Rushmore," you quip but nobody seems to get the joke.

"Go in, go in, we have such work to do," Teacher closes the front door after you. It's just a normal front door.

* * *

In a dusty, musty, eye-tingling drawing room on the first floor is a very strange creature, part-woman part-owl, an actual girl-sized, bird-like thing. Her wingspan easily nine feet. Her taloned feet look lethal.

"This is Miss Asalah Al Faghori; you won't know anything about her, yet, you lucky soul," Teacher says. The other three 'yous standing nearby chuckle among themselves, nodding and smiling. Damn these infuriating in-jokes at your expense.

"Asalah, tell our new friend why we're all here, on this Earth..." Teacher addresses the bird-thing.

The bird-thing speaks, "First Age Of Man: back when mankind was a baby, historically, he was a manic animal, forever pumped up on adrenalin, looking for every and any way to not get killed by every living thing that snarled in his general direction. Man was like one of his neighbourhood of wild animals; untamed, spontaneous, alive..."

You look at Teacher, incredulously, as the twittering continues. Teacher flicks her eyebrows, just once; barely perceptibly. You hear a tiny pneumatic hissing sound in Al Faghori's speech, like a tiny drill powering various vowels.

"...There were less than a few million 'humans' worldwide – made up of the diametrically opposed tribes of the Cro Magnon and the Neanderthal among others – and we've come to call this age of man the hunter gatherers, because they hunted – and hoarded – like their lives depended on it. They gathered fruits and berries and herbs to fill their bellies. They were AT WAR with each other and with nature."

And you wonder where this is going, when will it end. She twitters on still...

"Second Age Of Man: approximately nine thousand years ago, in 'Jericho', man learned how to cultivate crops and domesticate some breeds of wild animal. This is known as the beginnings of the Farming Age. Communities evolved around the products and owners told workers, imported or drafted, what to do. Now, most historians will tell you that the next Great Age of Man was the Industrial Revolution when time and motion studies, new materials and automated methods of manufacture greatly sped up our evolution, as a race..."

You're all watching, waiting. No one mentions that 'Jericho' is just round the corner, here in Oxford. No one's moving.

"...The Farming Age never ended, it just went global."

...chirp chirp, twitch twitch...

"What happened was this; intellectuals noticed that the farming idea worked so well, coercing innocent animals that grazing was good until they were wholesale slaughtered for the benefit of the few, that it was ordained as a way to control Empire. In an Empire, man is disposable, chattle – a slave to industry. Either entertainment for the elite or a foot soldier in some Corporate War Machine.

The Farming Age never ended, but now we are the domesticated cattle who earn the crust for the wealthy landowner. They give us TV and sports and fast food and beer so that we'll shut the fuck up and do as we're told. We'll pay our taxes, and like it. We've grown flabby, both physically and mentally. We've lost our ancient edge. We're cornered in. We're ready for the wholesale slaughter that World Wars periodically bring upon the herd to benefit the profit-hungry banking houses.

The Farming Age now contains seven billion sheople, worldwide, members of the farmed flock. Oh, as I missed to point out earlier on, the hunter gatherers never really died out; they became the hunter gatherers of humans. They became the slave drivers and the debt collectors, the jailers, the secret agents. Government and industry interviews and employs these aggressive psychopaths every day to manage the flock, as 'Jesus' called it – 'religion' being a brilliant master-stroke in the forced compliance of mankind to the hunter-gatherer dictat of the Farming Age..."

And you're hoping there's a conclusion on its way, sometime soon.

What *is* this? You look around the room at the assembled crew, you times three, Teacher, bird chirper. You're wondering when this will end. But it doesn't. It just continues on. Never-ending trilling litany to no audience. And the funny thing is, you can't work out whether this scene is taking place in linear time or not. Something's slipped out of synch.

Let's listen some more to the chirping birdy...

"....The Third Age Of Man: forget spiritualism, forget salvation - surely Auschwitz and Dachau and Bergen-Belsen taught you that." Asalah Al Faghori feather-shudders with a rare mix of glee and total mind trauma.

"You can pray and pray and pray to any God you want, you can pray until your eyes bleed and strange little sores appear on your inner thigh. And it won't matter. You 'victims of the global religious campaign' out there, you Jews, you Christians, you Buddhists, you Sikhs, you Muslims, you 'Aquarians' fighting the belief war, you 'believers' are a really good reason why this whole planet is so eternally fucked up. You're told to Turn the Other Cheek and other such nonsense. Remember Vatican City is the richest place on earth outside the banking/financial world. You all fell for the con.

Custodianism is about immediate purge.

Just like the Inquisition. But instead of it being for some religious purpose of control of the masses, it's about the revitalising and re-wilding of a Real Planet that industry – the by-product of the Farming Age under the auspices of the Hunter Gatherer Age – has allowed, due to unethical military-industrial-congressional-complex practises umbrellad by anti-lawful non-disclosure agreements and National Security, to ruin. Well, near ruin. And I'm not talking about a world full of zoos here. We've had enough of them. For both the animals and the humans – prisons or corporate sweat shops.

We need to take back this planet, as our own. We are the Designated Custodians of this world. You, me and everyone in your social network. It's our responsibility to purge, literally strip, this world of poisonous thinking, poisonous technology, poisonous political policy. It's time that the new age, the third age, the Age of the Custodian allowed this planet to heal, to rebuild from the ground up, to re-nature-ise our homeworld for the benefit of all our children's children.

And what about the original hunter gatherers of Industry? I'd be tempted to say they be re-assigned the task of helping us tear down the walls of Empire. I'm tempted to say they be re-assigned the task of clearing out the wild beasts from our societies, pitting them against each other so that fewer of them exist. But I'd be wrong."

"Had enough yet?" Teacher asks you.

"Is this, a test or something?" you ask, looking about.

You'd recognised the capture equipment attached to the girl-sized bird as soon as you walked in and wondered why nobody just stepped forward to activate it. You look around. All faces are pointing at you, like this is your role, your job alone. Everybody expects you to do the deed; no one else is prepared to execute it. And still you can't work out the timeline in this chicken-egg situation. Was Asalah Al Faghori real before you do this, or was your doing this the act that made her real?

"Remember, as the Second Age – Farming – lives in us, so does the First Age – HunterGathering – live on in us; as evidence by our forward facing eyes. None of these 'supposedly separate' ages ever ended, they just became something else, some other mindset, some other global movement; within us, of us. And it can happen again. We can use our inherited farming and hunter-gathering skillsets, our heritage, to advance a new era for mankind; a Third Age – Custodianism – where a Free Planet of ..."

All moral debate aside, it's a simple act to flick the Capture switch on this rattling, prattling chatter bird.

23
THE CUSTODIANS
NATURAL LOTTERY, FOUR

Local time: 1900 hours.

ANNOUNCER: *SevPM! NatLot!*

> *BAN"EMP"NOW*
> *BAN"COU"NOW*
> *BAN"ORG-REL"NOW*
> *BAN"WAR"NOW*
> *BAN"PRI"NOW*
> *BAN"GOV"NOW*

Day Four of the Natural Lottery incursion into the Evertainment Grid is as before, E.T. Logo slippy-flips from form to form, spelling out the petty demands of the Custodian Liberation. Ban this, ban that. Hail the new elite, etc. But it's all far too fast, far too urgent, too panicked; too curt, too impolite, too speed-freakish.

Feathers ruffle, water drank, girl-bird squawks and burbles...

"I get loads of people going, 'Asalah, my dear...' – that's what they call me, you know..." a glib trill escapes her chuckling bird-throat, her raised head swaggers, "...if we close all the prisons, dear heart. If we let all the sexual freaks and psychopathic weirdos out. What are we going to do-ooooo with them?

To this I normally say R.E.I.N.T.E.G.R.A.T.I.O.N. and I spell it out, laboriously, like a snail clambering over strewn hay. Every valuable member of the human race, every individual born to this world, should have a place in it. A good place. A warm and loving place. Soft and slow, like molasses over a gauntlet.

Welcome to my Free Planet. Welcome to my Custodian lifestyle. Welcome to a place that no one's experienced for over two thousand years. Anything goes. Life is for living, not for fear and doubt. Not for repression or slavery," she takes a couple of burbling gulps of water from her chrome-plated bird tube.

"Not only have we not experienced a Free Planet since before the Roman, Norman, Viking Invasions and Conquests that raped and pillaged tribal life into a pre-industrial hell-hole aka City Life, but we've been made to feel guilty for every single thing that we are ever since.

Original Sin, nice flash car; d.u.m.b. children.

Loaded down with debt by finance, loaded down with doubt by psychology, loaded down with fear by government propaganda.

We've been at war with our Global Controllers for nigh on two thousand years, who want it all for themselves, and fuck all for you. It's time they know that we know how life should be lived on a Free Planet. No more meters. No more taxes. Free energy. Free food, water, shelter.

It is time to release prisoners from all jails, zoos and factories. It is time to re-integrate all 'criminals' and 'animals' and 'workers' back into real life. No point punishing the elites, or their attack dogs – the thugs of private armies and politics – they are nothing more than victims of a profit-based arbitrary-rules Empire game of R.I.S.K.. These 'game players,' as insidious as their crimes may be, deserve re-integration back into the Diversities that will sprout from a Free Planet birth..."

Back brain fades to black, hiss of static overload, getting louder, resonating threateningly.

"We interrupt tonight's broadcast of the Natural Lottery to bring you this vital message from our sponsors."

And the voice-over artist has changed, has a much more sinister tone...

"Due to the vagaries of this so-called 38-member *coalition of the willing* The Custodian Liberation will not be 'freeing the planet from tyranny' any time this century. The tyranny of an all encompassing Prison Planet is way too big to fail, way too big to go to trial..."

And for a second, you're taken aback. Is that your voice on the voice-over?

"The Custodians will, instead, all die horrible slow deaths – like this..."

Sounds a lot like you. You nearly shit yourself; that's a really good simulation of how you sound. No, that's bullshit. But the announcement continues, in your voice...

"This message will self-destruct from your Evertainment backlog before you can understand what's happened, you fucking fucks. Tomorrow, you will witness A New Dawn that signifies the demise of the Free Planet and reinforces, yes reinforces, why you will Always be Slaves to The Industry. Play the fucking footage, Harry, I'm belittled by the game..."

Every Evertainment channel that's showing the Natural Lottery show broadcasts a view of a hillside overlooking a lake. It could be the Lake District in England. It could be a view from somewhere in Zurich or Berne in Switzerland.

Cut to a small pine-finished winter cabin overlooking the same lake. You've definitely never been there before, but it's really familiar. Inside the room, just within the boundary of the bay window, the bird-girl Asalah Al Faghori is captured to death and then left in a pool of her own blood, bright yellow puss and seeds spattering out of her beak as she thrashes around on the floor, defenceless. But that's not the weird bit.

You're there, projected into the scene, somehow.

You, or at least someone who looks *a lot* like you, jump up and down on Asalah Al Faghori's thrashing body, stamping the life out of her fragile bird frame, laughing like a lunatic; the forehead that looks exactly like yours would were you doing this is all sweated up as if you're on some massive drug rush, like you're not yourself. And you're not. You're not even watching this broadcast, but that revelation's for later.

For now, the person on the screen who looks and sounds a lot like you races around the pine-dressed room like an angry wasp. You're wearing big military boots and you use these to stamp on the face of Asalah Al Faghori, literally kicking up a storm of feather down. She actually lifts up off the floor, as you lay into her, kicking the bag of feathers around the room. In your eyes is the most horrifying manic glare. You race up to the camera, a bubbling froth of white foam at the corners of your mouth, your bloodied fist clenched in front of your snarling face.

"Killed the fucking birdy!" you chant, "Killed the fucking birdy!"

Bird blood spatters up onto the bay window, dotting the depth of view and forcing the backbrain rendition into razor-sharp foreground focus.

You're back on top of her as she feebly tries to defend herself from your rabid onslaught. You hands reach in and pull out a handful of feathers and blood. You reach in again as the flapping of broken wings flounders in the raging mania. You're ripping out handfuls of chest feathers, flight feathers, ripping off tail feathers. The lethal-looking talons scrape ineffectually at your bare forearms like you're made of steel or something. A light knick, a red line, a suggestion of epidermal discolouration for the camera but no lasting damage.

Meanwhile you turn to the camera, a mouthful of feathers splutter from between bared teeth. You're in some sort of *Attack Fugue*™ and nothing's gonna stop you until you're finished with the assassination; you are, after all, nothing more than a lackey for the Corporate War Machine and that's it. Fact. You dog. You monster.

You're reaching around inside the throat/chest area shouting, "Wish bone! Wish bone!"

You hammer and smash down with your blood spattered fists onto the already dead bird once called Asalah Al Faghori and rant and rave and raise your voice in a pitiful whine of ecstatic exaltation. You're on your knees, but occasionally, with a sexual rhythm, you're pounding up and down on your toes, too. Up and down, as you hammer the bird's carcase to little shattered bits of bone and gristle and worthlessness.

Inscribed across your sweating, blood-dripping forehead are two words you can't make out, some slogan, some mantra that ought to be readable. F-something E-something. Damn, this should be readable.

But you're not here. You're not even watching this broadcast. It can't really dawn on you that this isn't the cosy room on Woodstock Road where you actually met the real Asalah Al Faghori. You were always good with names, and stories.

What you can't agree with is the rest of the footage...you're panicking, you're running about breathlessly, that scribble on your sweaty brow. The destroyed body of girl-bird. The brutal removal by elite military personnel the size of radiated Hulks of your ranting self from 'the crime scene'. Could anyone really survive such a rifle whipping?

With your knowledge of the Capture process and the vagaries of organic motion capture, you (a technician after all) would be able see the mini-tells of non-real motion. As good as any physics/skeletal system gets, there's always tiny pass-throughs and tiny mis-calcs at the atomic level. It's not easy to break down into language you'll understand but it goes something like this, *if you know what's real, you can always tell what isn't real* and this is a much more fundamental statement than it at first seems.

You see it on your forehead then, swirling like families of bacteria among the glistening beads of sweat. The phrase FUCK EARTH carved into your own flesh; the tell that unveils your role in the stage play; your subordination to End Game, another BFFO or *Blatant False Flag Operation* upon the people of this planet.

Finally, another person rushes into the footage like a ballet dancer performing *Swan Lake* and melodramatically discovers the dead girl-bird. A sharply-inhaled shriek, hands over mouth, a horrified glance to camera. Orchestral crescendo.

Mind goes blank...

The Natural Lottery show (defunct) is replaced by a Global Psyche-Vertisement with about as much subtlety as a fist-fucked battery hen.

The people – let's call them the seven billion indentured slaves – of Prison Planet, are in uproar because We Want Our Custodians. They still don't get it but they'll still go on the rampage for the return of their precious little distraction, their soap on a rope.

* * *

The girl runs into her mommy's room, but she is not there.

"Mommy, where are you?" she runs about the house, opening doors.

"Mommy, where's the birdy show?" she finds mommy in a back room, cloaked in shadow, her face in her hands.

"I told you this is the way it would go. Honey, it's just a Show, it's just *Programming*."

"What's *programming*, mommy?" the girl heavy blinks with utmost cuteness, crouching down beside her mommy. And a lone, lonesome, tear rolls out of mommy's eye.

"You're so cute, peaches," she takes her by her tiny little chin, "Come here and let mommy give you a big hug."

The pair embrace. At the door a hammering starts. Gasps of fear. Tightened embraces.

* * *

Tonight, everything that you've taken for granted in the corporate opium den will fail, you'll have no more anything. Tonight, planet Earth starts the long slow painful process of re-wilding, restructuring and replenishment that will be the living penance everyone will have to pay for their Crime of Consumerism.

Tonight, all the corporate clocks stop. Everything changes.

24
YOU THE PEOPLE
SEVEN BILLION TURRRISTS

The hypnotic Samba drums of born-again Tribalism ring out across Oxford like a baby released from the womb by the birthing pains, released to a better world. It's like a Carnival, somewhere to the north, maybe in University Park, maybe somewhere up toward Summertown, maybe they're clogging up the traffic on the Banbury Road.

Maybe multiple streams of jazzing, dancing, jigging, celebration are headed this way, to experience real (not imagined) freedom in the town from whence GCD or *Global Conglomerated Domination* has been folded into the mix for the last few centuries like poisoned egg whites. Except that there's nothing to protest. Or maybe there is. No one is speaking here. No one has any agenda here. Not yet. It's just a march of the subscribers, those who pledged their DNA to the Natural Lottery over the last four days, with drum-banging accompaniment. A natural conglomeration of rational people, who might be a little pissed off that their lives were just as they'd been before, not realising their luck to have found themselves spared the fate of the rest. Those billions of people who didn't pledge, those too busy to see.

And it's getting closer every minute, this procession of the freed.

Soon, Oxford will spill over with the spontaneous and joyous celebration of Creativity, Passion and Kinship that is yet to truly take hold of the hearts and minds of those who find their lives forever changed. The party is headed this way, people, be sure of that truth.

The world no longer has money dragging it down to the bottom of the ocean. Patents have been freed up from Private Control. Borders to human creativity have been dragged down. The earth is our ally in the war against slavery. There's a whole world of ideas no longer restrained by commercial profit-based concerns. It's going to be a soft, slow change for sure but that's why we're all here, witnessing it, sharing it, living it, moment by moment.

There's no government left to appeal to. There's no Police Force to hold you back. There are no prisons left to incarcerate you, neither factories nor zoos nor state penitentiaries.

People from all walks of life have physically unplugged from the dud Evertainment dream machine and staggered out into the invigorating sunlight to join in this rally of the masses. This is happening in all the world's Prison Cities and all the world's Urban Universities of Crime, Suffering and Punishment.

And that's all it really is, You The People getting together and doing what your collective heart desires. Maybe for one day only, but significant all the same. This is where the better world you'll leave for your children's children might germinate. That is, once you've understood what is soon to hatch from the remnants of the Evertainment monopoly, what truly horrendous future awaits mankind.

For now, there seems to be light after the ending of the corporate tunnel. Suddenly, everyone wants to share being Kings of the World or at least pretend being Custodians of Planet Earth.

Many of the self-appointed and ambitious and egotistical and greedy Kings of Industry would have liked to keep hold of their stolen wealth, their stolen land, their stolen castles, pawns and strategy of the great Global Chess Game they've all invested so much of your effort in. They would protect their investment at all costs. They would kill their own kids so that their stolen world can't be stolen back from them, reclaimed.

But it's over. That's the final verdict. It's finished already. It's now just a case of accepting what has happened and realising, that like the rest of humanity, the world is now a shared place and it will be better for that – better than it has ever been under any fake-Empire of me me me.

The drums grow louder. More jubilant with every freed second.

* * *

Bless You, the rival *Character Capturer* who ruthlessly evicted you from The Industry in the name of her *'disgruntled employee'* assignment, comes up behind you in a crowded street in the centre of Oxford. You're just standing there with your hands in your pockets, at the junction of the four cardinal roads of the old city, squinting up at the the clockface of Carfax

Tower. Waiting for the hour to strike, with your mouth open like some common dullard. She raises her arm to the back of your head like she has a gun. She stands there, like that, counting breaths; one, two, three...

"You were never very good at Trade Craft," she says to you, before making a *kapow* noise and blowing your imaginary brains out through your gawping face.

You flinch and spin around, uttering a muffled croak of shock, "What the fucking fuck?" People look in your direction suddenly like you've just popped up on their radar, like you're the enemy.

"Criminals always return to the scene of their crime," she has her open palms out in front of her, defensively. On her face, that same magic wand flutter of mischief you'd been exposed to so many times in your last few days in The Industry when Bless You ruled the sexual roost. She looks you up and down, right there under the Carfax clock tower in the centre of Oxford, "Businessman, eh? Not much of a disguise for a covert operative."

"I'm not in hiding," you don't understand what she's saying, or why. "I'm not covert, as you put it," you try to make her understand.

"You didn't catch last night's Evertainment?" she asks you.

"Of what?" you ask, unsure where this is going.

"You actually can't tell, to be honest," she gives you a long slow look of appraisal, "Your face looks nothing like that maniac with the tattooed forehead."

You move away from her, sneering in confusion, your hands still in your pockets, "You've lost me."

"You're the Killer Of The Custodians. You're the one everyone's talking about. Word of mouth, can you believe that after all these years? People are talking again," she tells you what you already should know, "But you'd not be stood here, if you knew, right?"

"At some point, you're going to start making sense, I'll put money on it," you look around, suddenly aware that passers by are overhearing this public conversation, taking notice.

"Can you hear the drumbeats getting closer and closer?" she asks.

Up above, some random ragdoll lands at the foot of Carfax Tower on this eastern side. You race to help, as you were helped from your unsuccessful suicide attempt by "Teacher" and her yoof-brigade. But this one's already gone, her face crushed on the pavement side, her neck smashed into an oblique angle. Fingers, wrists, forearms broken like twigs. Sharp fractures poking through flesh. Shoulders dislocated, legs akimbo. A black fluid runs from her cracked skull where the greying brain bulges.

"You can't save any of these people. Nobody can help them," Bless You puts a hand on your shoulder as you crouch down beside the girl, brushing the blood-matted hair out of her good eye. Well, her visible eye, bloodshot and misaligned in its socket. You look into that eye for answers to questions you haven't even formed yet.

"Why are you haunting me?" you ask her.

"Watch out!" she pulls you out of harm's way as yet another corporate suicide victim smashes to the ground just a few feet away, their doppler-shifted scream cut off abruptly by the dull thud of impact. People rush in to remove the still settling bodies, to do what with you don't ask.

   *   *   *

You both take the Yellow Bus to get you back out of town, pushing out through The Wall at its western extent. Yellow Bus number four, heading up the Botley Road. And neither of you are suspicious that the buses should no longer be running, that Oxford Wall should have been deactivated.

Moments later, at a secret location just west of Oxford on the Hincksey Industrial Estate, you realise Bless You is still talking, "It's like the end of the world, isn't it? And in many ways, that's the best way to describe what happened last night. It all started on a show called The Natural Lottery that everyone was tuned into. And I mean everyone on the planet. It was on all channels, in all territories. Literally millions and millions of people pledged their ruined DNA in some sort of gameshow or pact or whatever and then *BOOM*, the world as we knew it just stopped. Like someone had just flipped a switch. Some stuff still works, but for how long?"

"Why are we here in the shit-end of nowhere?" you ask her, pulling the collar of your flimsy single-breasted jacket up around your ears to stave off what you can of the biting northerly breeze.

"We're clearly here so I can blow your brains out and dump the evidence in one of these *industrial waste* skips," she jokes.

You don't laugh at her murder humour.

She apologises, after a beat, mouthing the word 'sorry' with a fake-shame look pulling the corners of her mouth down. She punches you on the arm, "Come on, Mr Serious, Mr Can't-take-a-joke, Mr...."

"We get the idea," you pull up the collar of your single-breasted jacket even higher.

*   *   *

You arrive at a warehouse in the maze-like bowels of the business estate.

"Have you never realised that in the industry, you know, when you're at work, you never open your mouth when you speak, air never passes across your lips. And it's true, when you think about it, it's like that reading voice we all have in our heads, that one you're using right now to 'hear' these words. It's what the Grid offers, not thought communication as such but, targeted Wifi transmission. You start to wonder if you can rig up some sort of Global Wifi transmitter. You wonder if you're the first person to have thought of such a thing," she smiles then, enigmatically, like you understand exactly what she's talking about, "You start to wonder, looking around at the mindless masses and their desperate outflow of credit accrued, whether you're the first Consumer to think of anything other than Consuming; whether you're the first bred Buyer to think of anything other than Buying." she pauses so you can take it all in; like you have the capacity for that.

"Being 'at work' refers to a store-room or warehouse where Kevlar Kubitz are parked, all day long." she explains, once the corrugated steel double doors have rolled back.

You are looking at row upon row of parked Kevlar Kubitz stacked three four five high, god knows how many deep. You can even see the bodies still trapped in situ like mosquitoes in amber.

"Are they still alive like that?" you ask.

But Bless You is in full swing and she continues her spiel, the illustrational reason she's brought you here, "There's an auto-eject mechanism built into The Industry...Are you listening to me?"

"How can they all just be there, like that?" you ask.

"You break the Corporate Code or otherwise try to alter the functions of the war machine in any way that conflicts with its strict financial principles, you're out on the streets, trying to survive among the masses. De-striped, un-badged, black-listed into poverty and *No Future*™.

Literally, as they can compute it with their quantum computers no one's ever seen outside of a mainframe facility, no future will ever meet & greet anyone who's been kicked out of The Industry. There's a data-smell about them, employers and insurers can smell it on you like a stink, your C.V. is literally dripping with the filth and grease of the shame of rejection from The Industry.

"Corporate rejects, unwanted workers, will do anything to plug themselves back into The Industry Wifi Hell, even though it's totally no good for their cells, no good at all. And some of them are really brilliant, making them real geniuses of self-deception, eh? Of course. That's how they got into The Industry in the first place. They just don't get it. They've awakened. They're tainted meat. They'd be a cancer within any GIO or *Global Industrial Organism*. They have to be rejected, so coldly, so brutally, so inhumanely, like this, for their own good and for the continued health of The Industry. They are OUTed forever, they are always LET GO, for their and the Industry's own good.

"But yesterday The Industry haemorrhaged staff," she clicks her fingers, "Like that. And global finance has hit rock bottom, overnight. One night! Total collapse! Sure, the elite have their physical assets; their gold and their territories and their title but that's it, really. The Industry underwent Critical Colony Collapse, to use an apiaristic term," she looks at you, "Bees. Apiary. Colony. Geddit?" She nudges you repeatedly with her elbow.

"I'm just waiting for the good stuff," you sigh.

"The Custodian Liberation – which you've never heard of – were a way to stem that flow, offset that collapse, halt the rot. By giving the workers Faith that someone was working in their interest, gave them Hope that things were gonna be okay and

Liberation was just around the corner. Sorta like you with your Mr Disgruntled Employee act...

"Turrrists, that's what 43rd US President-elect George W Bush called them. The enemies of capitalism, 'the terrorists'. That's what he said shortly after September 11th 2001, *'You're either with us, or you're with the Turrrists,'* remember? No? 9/11, whatever that was. When they were still blaming their ally Al Qaeda for demolishing three financial buildings in downtown Manhattan," she finally shuts up, seeming to have confused herself.

"In your interpretation of what my mind's become, I'm nothing more than a recovering Corporate Drone ousted from the hive. This is not a rhetorical question."

She punches your upper arm, "Exactly!"

You look at her like she's just put on a clown mask, "I can't see how what you're saying has any relevance to the way the world should be, might be, you know? If what you're saying is true, my life's been a total lie. I can't subscribe to that. I know what reality is. I've been there. I'm not, like you, just some corporate whore who's still working for the other side. You do realise that, right, Bless You, or whatever your 'real name' is, you do realise you're still working for T.H.E.M., right?"

You take out a white cotton handkerchief from a breast pocket you didn't even know it was there, you unfold it and you see the Prodigy logo in the top-right corner of it, shimmering like it's some sort of chameleon skin. Is this really all part of the dream, still? You take the hanky, bring it up to your nose, and blow. You finish by wiping and replacing the hanky in your trouser pocket. You give her that look, again, that one that says, *counter that, bitch*.

"You grinning corporate Psyche-Vertisement freaks really piss me off," she knocks you, perhaps a little too hard, on your forehead with the dainty knuckles of her right hand...

MIKE PHILBIN

25
THE CUSTODIANS
ACGT NOMADIX UNVEILED

"Are you enjoying your box?" it's a voice you think you've heard before. You 'recognise' it, but you can't put a face to it. The voice seems to come at you from all sides, like you are in a box. You have a sudden panic attack, realising you're back where you started. Wondering if all the events of the last few days, weeks, months, (how long has it been since...) have been merely a glitch in the Evertainment system during R³ relocation. Are you still a lowly Capture artist in The Industry? Are you still in Dusseldorf? Don't you still have a wife, a child, a family in Germany? Don't you still speak German? But that get out clause'd be a narrative cheap-shot and life's never that cut and dry. Life is dirty. Life is complicated. Life is utterly unfathomable.

You look around and you're back in The City; realm of empires; V*atican, DC, London.*

Back in the box where mundane reality pulsates with eager dread.

The floor is different; no more grass, no more Lamby.

But there are still faces at the glass. Your face. Three of you. You try not to recognise them, slam your eyes shut like a wind tunnel on full revs, like this'll help undo the hurt, like this'll roll back the millennia or somehow protect you from what has to happen to Earth for Free Planet to truly become the Land of Milk and Honey, the place where Creativity, Passion and Kinship will flourish once again, as it did so very very long ago before human history had a chance to be re-written by beguilers and thieves.

No more wars.

No more shame.

No more secrets.

"You can open your eyes now," it is said like this so that, even if you kept your eyes closed for a million years (and this is something you can do, but more of that later) you'd still awaken and you'd still see the three faces at the glass, you'd still be a Glimpser.

"Yes, this is something you've always known but somehow chose to ignore," and it has come to the point where you can no longer remember what 'being a Glimpser' means. You've denied-you-thrice as the parable goes.

"You are our brother, our sister. You are the reason we survive, as a species, the ninety billion reasons why," one of you says, like you've really ever thought of yourself as someone's *sister*.

"This is insanity," you press your hands against your ears, roaring, your eyelids screwed tight, like your entire forehead is folding down over a boiling migraine the way a blast shield pours down treacly from the skull cap, the helmet of disdain.

"Say the word," another you whispers, as if close up to your ear.

Your eyes come open, door after door after door, layers of security, levers uncogging and unwinding, mind unfolding, awakening like a summer dawn, like a shooting star, like a supernova in super super super slow motion.

You stand there, in some form of terror-induced stasis counting hundreds of thousands of millions of living heartbeats. A ticking sound like an old grandfather clock. Finally, one word comes out of your cracked lips; its been so long since you've spoken, like the striking of the third hour, "Y. E. S."

That's all they want to know. That's all they need to hear. The spoken letters of the code word they need to release you. Or allow yourself to be released. This is the word you gave them, all those aeons ago. This simple de-cypher – *Yes*.

"Done," says the third you, or rather, the third aspect of you, your tertiary reflection, that other aspect of your cube, your 'dimension'.

A flood of chrome roars through your flesh like has not happened in all your incarnations, in all your past lives. And suddenly, you remember a Global Mission. You remember why you're here. The ACGT Nomadix from a trans-dimensional place where no distance and no time exist have had their fun with mankind and now it's time to fulfill one's four-fold promise to the star who spawned you, your Sun.

"Let's do this," you resolve, despite your fear of what's to come.

And you're suddenly in a room. The room is just a normal room. Look around. Scruffy old wallpaper hanging off in the corners. Rough old carpet. There's a window, where you sense you came in, floated in, flew in; it's a white-wood-framed window, four small panels of glass by three. It's a window that has never been cleaned, but outside you can see a main road, and then a tall old stone wall, the sort of wall that looks like its been there for ages, and it has.

There are eight people arranged on a ring of chairs in this room, and they're old, but super-old, like all the flesh has rotted off their bones time and time again so that only a whisper of flesh remains, but remain it does.

They all face an old brick fireplace, in which the embers of a fire still glow. Their eyes filled with stars, dully shining, slightly sparkling. In fact, were you to look inside their rheumy eyes you'd see the entire universe from eight distinct and equidistant points in space-time as described by the opposing corners of a cube. And suddenly it starts to make sense why you're here.

You, you, you, and you are stood behind them, stood behind the row of chairs and their spectral occupants. All your four aspects present since before mankind split off from his ape lineage, since his big brain started to swell. Since the spark of the Glimpser was placed within his ancestral echo. But you have questions.

"The ninety billion has come full circle," those are the words you receive, in your head, like a message from the god of meditation. The eight seated crumblies, have turned round to face you and you and you and you all at once, like you're some in-folded batter mix, like you're four of one; all for one, like the Musketeers.

"And one for all," you laugh at the lunacy of this phrase, plucked from your mind.

These wrinklies, these rotted old stumps riddled with fungal threads, open their toothless maws and this holocaust of everything pours out of them, into your face, blowing back the hair and reminding you of every evil stench that can spill from the human bowel or the compost heap, or the taste of love scorned, or the anger and regret of conquest, or the whole human experience since we jumped down from the trees and braved the ferocity of the plains.

Running, always running.

You've dislocated again, split four-ways by this anti-siren of revelation.

A-Washington.

C-Jefferson.

G-Roosevelt.

T-Lincoln, reporting for service. You salute, all of you, all four of you now, in micro-delayed military synchrony, like young recruits on the barracks square; unified and released from petty mortal concerns. You'd always know these four sides of yourself, you'd always realised that there was a special something, a shimmering presence buried deep within you you you you like child abuse or night terrors. You'd always suspected some horrible act had been done on you, when you yourselves were the act. You, all four of you, were the answer to your own chrome legacy.

What is this chrome that's invaded your thoughts for so long? And what is the relevance of the ninety billion souls?

Well, isn't it obvious?

Four of you are missing.

The way the universe normally works is there are eight corners to to every cube. But here, on Earth, an accident in human history has happened. And there are only four corners to the human cube, as represented by the A, the C, the G and the T of the genetic double helix. A land locked plane of existence rather than a spatial volume. But what's really needed for Earth to elope its Flatland Existence is another DNA strand altogether, made up of four different kinds of base pair allele. Think of the intertwined snakes symbol used by Modern Medicine – the caduceus – how mankind was so close to the truth all along.

That four of the letters of life are missing here on Earth is irrelevant, it's what they've been transposed by, exchanged for, that's causing all the problems.

"You know that mantra, *never no more, never no less, than ninety billion sparks of night?*" hisses the old crones, guttering up stink-wind from the back of beyond, back back back in time and out out out into space like no one's ever journeyed. And it's a gut-wrenching thing to discover that you're supposed to be this 'mobile' in all dimensions. This, in itself, is where human corruption comes from, this virtual wellspring of multidimensionality dried around our base need for profit. This crossing of the Rubicon, in the name of profit and asset and war for territory and religion and dogma and all the other human sickness that's brought the most fertile planet in the universe to near-ruin and almost total and utter collapse such that the very structure of the planet and its sun were crumbling under the psychic onslaught, the minds of tortured souls, millennia after millennia in a constant grinding down of the fabric of space and time.

A soul death was about to happen on planet Earth.

This is where YOU come in.

And you'll have to do some really horrible things to really innocent people to correct the imbalance, restore the upper face of the cube.

The dual aspect of male and female need reweaving into the matrix, that's the only way this can be solved. And with all alchemical solutions, a sacrifice has to be made. A sacrifice of the innocent.

"With what happened via the Custodians bizarre and insane plan of corporate re-rule a-la *ordo ab chao,* it's fair to say that there will soon be only six billion people alive on planet earth," one aspect of you says.

Another aspect chips in, "And we all know the optimum is a five level inception for any ascending race. It's unfortunate we missed the six billion point a few years ago. The planet sent out the signal. It just went unheard. Something had broken somewhere. I mean, it's what we were all waiting for."

"The magic six billion," another you adds, as if for effect, as if you've forgotten.

"What's this ninety billion souls?" you're asking when you're interrupted.

"Asalah Al Faghori appears to be the only one of you who got that bit right. Maybe she was Virgo. Virgos are always the smartest."

Communal-of-four groan for your female self's obvious astrological put down.

"It's true. She saw the madness, if not the method."

"Five levels?" you prompt, keen to get to the good stuff.

"Five, four, three, two, one…all the dimensions laid out in ascending hierarchy. Each 'human', though this is not what they are, each Custodian, let's call them. Each saviour of this near-totally destroyed delicate homeworld. Are we happier if we just call them 'humans'?"

Nods of agreement

"Even though that's not what they are, in essence, it'll be suitable, just barely."

You're thinking *get on with it* and you're not the only one.

"Fifteen 'souls' arrange themselves within the multidimensional space-time field of a 'human'. Currently, each human has his one soul. But this is not enough. Asalah saw the connection, ninety billion souls, ninety billion neurones in the human brain. But how to make sense of it? You can't. It's outside your ability to understand. It involves the rest of the dimensions. And you can't see that from where you are. Not even math can see it. The axes are all wrong, in fact the term 'axis' is so misleading and should never have been allowed. The five human land locked senses are the first layer of the multi-dimensional pyramid..."

"Triangle..." you jump in, because you're not that thick.

"We call it a Pyramid because it's the layers of dimensionality. These things don't exist on the same timeline or spaceline, but they're all interconnected. You see?"

You don't, and you're the only one. The other three aspects of you see this all too clearly and, quite frankly, are more than a bit ashamed you're having to be talked down to like this. It's embarrassing for all the millennia of reasons. You're better than this.

"The four nodes of your genetic existence are the next layer. Then the three sexes. Then the Here and the There. Then the Sun."

You're looking at her like she's some sort of nut, which she is (by comparison with normal humans who possess only one soul).

"These are the fifteen souls of a human being. And such a warlike race is humanity that the magic number, of six billion population comes around only every twenty five thousand years or so. You gotta be real patient. Wait, and wait and then, POW. You deliver the missing fourteen souls to who's resident."

She's looking at you.

"I am getting through to you, right?"

"Look," says the fat beardy version of you, "I'm you, you're me, we're...well, separate, yet one," he shakes his head in self-inflicted confusion, "The math is stupid but the basic concept is sound. Us four, together, only happens when six billion humans manifest. This has always been the way. Think of it as a calling. There's something about that number which makes us arrive. We're here. And there's something fundamentally important that we have to do, or else mankind is fucked."

"Geddit now?" your skinnier other you chips in, for effect.

"Yeah," you say, but you don't get it, "I can hear your words, and you really sound like you know what's expected. Like maybe some of you've done this before..."

"We've all done this before!" the other three yous chant in unison.

"Hundreds of times before. On hundreds of worlds. You were there," they add, in turn.

The vision fades with the unmistakable IED or *Intermittent Evertainment Dislocation* corporate ident, and you suspect this irrational world of parallel species and super-connectivity of the humans souls is all a flashback from the Corporate Hell you used to be employed by.

MIKE PHILBIN

26
YOU THE PEOPLE
WAR WERE DECLARED

...and that's exactly how it happened. With that blasé rap of Bless You's knuckles on your forehead. *War Were Declared.* It's like a signal had been given, a signal the freak-world-to-be had been waiting for. Bless You's knuckles against your forehead. Plan roars into action.

But that would be a fallacy, an illusion.

War Were Declared on Day One of the Natural Lottery's obfuscating transmission, though nobody was really taking any notice. At that point, the Natural Lottery was just an ungracious incursion into Evertainment ubiquity; a wasp at a picnic.

People just waited for it to go away.

There were a few who momentarily 'woke up' to the message on Day One, but they (like yourself) have been promptly dealt with by the Appraisal Process. These were the unfortunate fools who eventually found themselves banging drums on the streets or banging their face into the street from altitude. A weak or strong reaction to Release from Contract, permanent non-compliance to NDA.

Are you still breathing in; breathing out?

Long slow breaths please.

That's it, relax.

Try not to panic.

Can you tell if *Reality*™ has been restored yet?

The majority of you, the mindless drones of corporate programming, are ticking along on the intellectual equivalent of the 'muzak' they used to play in elevators. Nothing untoward had happened yet, allegedly. Your 'consciousness', like that themeless meandering music expressly delivered to shield you from the ascent or descent of these hundreds of floors of high-rise living, has yet to release you from your egg-bound slumber. A soothing placebo is still soothing away the worry and paranoia of the journey. You're still smugly unaware of the vast change that's already working its way through the human genome, one hydroxyl bond at a time.

That's what most people did on Day One, turned off their minds – swirled around in a holding pattern – awaited landing instruction.

Day Two came along and more people appeared to bob up to the surface, 'take notice' of a change in the weather. This was when the first batch of pledges started to come in, a mere trickle of people too bored with their Consumering lives to see any other way out of their inherent slavery to the petrodollar to the eurodollar to the yuan or gold or silver, to the slavery of ownership by a foreign corporation and off-shore thief of their existence, some global vampire. Some brave-or-foolish idiots will do anything to just get away from the dental drilling noise of their every waking moment in corporate hell.

Day Three, more and more people pledge their lives, their genetic legacy to the Custodian Liberation.

Day Four, armageddon and the brutal murder of Asalah Al Faghori, at your hands. You utter ruthless bastard. You corporate tool. You killer.

But you know this is not *really* the way it went. You shouldn't be so hard on yourself. It's not like you had any choice in the matter. Not really. You were just one of those pawns The Game likes to sacrifice to complete a strategy of counter attack or opening up the enemy to further slaughter or ultimate endgame. You were useful within the limited remit of your role, but you're expendable like the others. Another monkey for the organ grinder.

You can see the evidence of this deceit for yourself.

You didn't hear it coming, this thing. It had wings, like an owl, stretched out all fluffy and silent, yet pearlescent, catching the light; its drooling maw hanging open the way a whaleshark trawls for plankton at the surface of the ocean. Mouth agape, closing in for the kill. You've watched Bless You be scooped up into one of those weird things, those flying toilets, those thieving coffins of some intergalactic necromancer.

You were walking back into town from the North Hinksey Business Park having been waiting for what seemed like forever for the Yellow Bus that never arrived. What had happened to your Corporate Planet? Where was the so-called Order?

You didn't realise that a series of moves on the chess board had taken place under cover of marketing, under cover of insurgency, under cover of the promise of a Free Planet.

You didn't realise that, right now, all around the world, furry cocoons of beasts-to-be and taxis-to-flee were brooding their brutal offspring and soon these freaks would be preying on those who were unlucky enough not to have been protected by the Kevlar Kubitz in-transit to jolly-old work work work.

You didn't realise that only a select number of sovereign individuals, no more than a quarter of the indentured global workforce were at work (or in transit to and from work) and not logged into their Evertainment accounts when the first mega-wave of transmutational patent-licensing shattered their geneline into a million gazillion tiny datastreams, leaving the Grand Chess Game wide open to full gametal assault over the course of the next trio of conversations between You The People and the Custodian Liberation's ulterior motive for planetary routing.

You're a victim, still. Even with the promise of a Free Planet slithering across the faces of the devout like a solemn prayer. All across the world, people like you, people who have survived the first stage of the rejuvenation of Natural Earth, are experiencing the same sudden thrill of what it actually means to be alive.

First came the Re-Wilded, those genetic freaks who were taken on a historical journey through their genetic legacy and shat out the other end a day later looking like frogs and pigeons and fish and dogs and terrapins and sloths and back, back through time, looking like all sorts of strange lizards, reptiles and dinosaurs from a world long forgotten. These hungry beasts prowled the land, leapt out of rivers and oceans or descended from the skies looking for human sustenance; the weak, the elderly, the young. Anything was fair game. Worthy protein for the furnace in their bellies.

Then came the Solos that stole suitable human carriage off the streets, bonded with their DNA and transported them to Foster Homes of already conglomerated genetic material formed by Dirty Dozens from all over the world.

Then came the Flockers, these zombie-like lust-monsters or *centipedes* who were looking for one thing only, a brutal fuck with eleven other flockers. Great sexual gatherings of these mind-scraped marauders happened in towns and cities all over

Free Planet. Many of them abortive attempts, failed ruttings, waning threesomes and bored orgies. But they were persistent, if they could sustain themselves long enough in partial transformation, limping along, distorted by their own lust; for food was the furthest thing from their tinied minds.

In time, leagues of these Dirty Dozen floating homes, more like floating prisons, were being slammed into by Solos disgorging their stolen content in-house and scooting off to do even more damage to that thing once called Humanity.

You saw none of that. Neither did one quarter of the eligible global workforce who were not logged into their work accounts during the Natural Lottery's four-day gene-fuck. You are the lucky ones. You and your only friends in the world were away from their Evertainment nodes at 'just the right time' during all four of the Natural Lottery broadcasts not to be caught up in the global harvest.

Rest assured, the bankers, the accountants, the traders, the heads of business, the judges, the police commissioners, the online marketeers, the freelancers, the samaritans and counsellors, the heads of councils, cities, countries and states, the heads of the military – those inveterate Evertainment abusers, those addicts to the online dictat and the adherence to the rule of law, the news hungry, the gossips, the shepherds of the global flock, were all subversively connected and irreparable re-wired by the four-day assault of the Custodians uber-patented end game.

And it was a beautiful game, truly. A thing to behold and worship.

Well, perhaps not worship. It was after all a flawed game, as are all such claims on ultimate control and 'final solution'. Everybody who ever has ambition to Chaaange the world in this way or that always forgets the most important part of life on planet earth, that people just want to be left alone.

They might not enjoy their office jobs or their sanitation jobs or their clerical jobs or their managerial jobs or their trade union jobs or their trainee jobs, their apprenticeship to the worshipful guilds, but by just 'getting on with their jobs' they don't have to think too hard about where they're gonna be in five or ten or thirty years time. They don't have to confuse themselves with 'ambition'. They don't have to 'project'. They can almost deny their own mortality, and perks like Evertainment intentionally reinforce that belief system for them so that they don't even feel the pain of slave living, they exist (subsist) but it suits them just fine. They're happy with their lot, if you can believe this. They really are born to be cannon fodder and no one should ever try to chaaange that, or them. It won't work, the reprogramming won't stick.

People will be unhappy with Chaaange no matter how it's delivered to them.

* * *

The (elitist) Custodian Liberation's bizarre insistence that liberty through patent-legal time-scaled genetic-nostalgia was the real way forward for mankind was no less insane or ruthless than any other Eugenics agenda orchestrated by any number of tyrannical despots and administrations before them.

But all that is academic – the die has been cast and You The People have to find some way to live with what reality became.

You were once cannon fodder for corporate war for asset, profit and dividend. Now, you're cannon fodder for outrageously primaeval creatures of mankind's psychological liberation run amok, for gannets who'll steal you away and betray you to a life of genetic modification inside the living space of a dozen mind-fucked morons. You are the target, now as then. Only this time, there are no comforting 'rules of engagement' and it's every man for himself.

Will this catastrophe be the cement that finally bonds the remaining humans to each other in a tribal pledge of fealty that's been absent from human society since before the Industrial Revolution?

* * *

You see the skies filling with new types of clouds, like perforated layers of carbon atoms all aligned in crystalline formation, and you know (because Bless You told you) that these are the new floating Diversities with such names as Strato and Cumulo and Nimbo, Alto, Cirro, Arco – you get the cloud-themed idea.

You also know that elsewhere in the skies are Diversities known as Guanine or Adenine or Cytozyne, Naphthalo, Xanthone and on it goes – the geeks live there, probably.

There are all sorts of other flocks of these connected mobile (well, floating) homes; some live in the mountains, some live in the sea, some underground – imagine living underground, *forever*.

And the point of all this?

Well, mankind has sinned – yes, as Asalah Al Faghori would put it, *literally* sinned by their mis-use of the planet for profit-based gain, for nest-feathering (pun not intended), for laundering ill-gotten gains through your OBN or *Old Boy Network*. Yep, this happened on Your Watch, humanity, and it's time you paid your penance.

And what a life it'll be, re-activated, re-wilded, re-assessed (admittedly, for you) by your superiors, your betters.

Mankind on the run. And believe this phrase, "Mankind on the run," as it perfectly illustrates daily existence now that the Rule of Law has been ripped up and thrown in the trash with all your fake constitutions in the name of this or that now-forgotten ideology. Death to Idealogy, that's the Custodian Way. 'Do right by Free Planet' is the only rule – if only they knew how that simple phrase would cause such a routing of mankind, such a literal holocaust.

Barrow boys, lawyers, agents, middle managers, town councillors and the like – i.e. exactly the right driven ambitious amoral sell-your-own-mother to make a sale types – were the ones who were now building the re-wilded future for mankind. It's irony, or maybe it's not, but you couldn't hope for a better outcome had you written it in a book. There's just no real way it would have worked. The pledgers had to be discarded. You'd have had your sympathisers, your do-gooders, your supposedly-re-wilded world run by the can't-kill-the-chicken to make a meal delicate constitution mob – a recipe for continued global apathy and eventual ruin.

This, as horrific as it seems to you, yes You on the run from these genetic freaks who move much faster than you and have much more stamina than you and are much hungrier than you in all respects, as bad as that seems, from your petty perspective, it's the best world. Or, rather, it's a world that has the healthiest chance of reflourishing in a beautiful and organic way.

27
THE CUSTODIANS
FREE PLANET HAS AWAKENED

The Corporate War Machine has been disemboweled.

C4ISR military networks have been crippled.

Fiat financial mechanisms are defunct.

Country is no longer a valid term.

Royalty means nothing.

Money has no function.

Prisons (and prisoners) are no longer a part of the human condition.

Roads will rot.

Buildings will crumble.

The justice system (and the judges who ran it) are no more; legal documentation flutters inoperably in the breeze of jurisdictional nostalgia; overnight.

*   *   *

There have been months of intense Role Modelling by some of the brightest minds in academia to accommodate the diverse cultures or Diversities the six billion remaining people of Free Planet can align themselves with for their own educational/social benefit.

The whole idea of the Free Planet movement was to dislodge the evil claws of the feudalistic corporate evil that has been throttling the life out of this once beautiful planet in the name of profit.

In coming months, by order of The Custodian Manifesto, as laid out by the members of that revolutionary hit squad who turned the tables on Eye Sys Industries and all their corporate cronies worldwide, this is how it will be:

The de-chained people are well informed.

The slave cities are being cleared away.

The monolithic corporations have been dissolved.

The programmes of Re-Wilding are well under way.

The patents have been returned to You The People.

The local energy, heating, sanitation solutions work.

The floating mobile homes are aloft.

The hydroponic growing systems productive.

DNA taxis chauffeur people safely from point A to point B.

Six billion human beings will soon be fully exploring their (inner and outer) homespace for the first time in thousands of years. The Custodians' intention? To keep Free Planet as beautifully fruitful and culturally Diverse as its never been before this time. Oh, and to have fun while they're alive, rather than working on a chain gang for a ruthless prison guard until they die.

But, of course, that's not how Corporate Governance of planet Earth will be handed over by The Power Elite, by The Industry, to the undisciplined masses, to You The People.

It's like when Communism 'collapsed' at the end of the Cold War; it's not like anything has changed for normal Russians since then. The people are still suffering under a brutal regime of coercion and corruption. Putins engineer themselves another six years in office by cleverly eliminating the decent opposition candidates early on in the re-election process, there will really only ever be one choice for President. If you don't know how the chess game works, you'll never understand what any move on the board means.

The Custodians are a scapegoat, marketed as a group of fanatical radicals akin to the *Weather Underground*, who are no less insane than the insane governors who had trodden the boards of the Global Stage before them. Sure, the Uber Patent has shifted control of the Creativity, Passion and Kinship into the hands of six billion sovereign individuals. But the masses don't necessarily know this yet, they're many steps behind, still to suffer Evertainment cold-turkey, when all they wanna do is be entrained to accept some complete and utter lie in the name of Corporate Governance, to suck on their drenched sucking blanket. Their nice soft pillow of lies that keeps them from going insane in the GG or *Global Gulag*. Nobody wants to see the cold damp concrete walls of their reality, no one.

The Corporate War Machine has been dealt a terrible blow by the incursion of the Natural Lottery Show into the Evertainment System. Human Beings are going to have to think for themselves without the yoke of Psyche-Vertisement propaganda bearing down upon their cognitive functionality.

However, this naïve promise of a Free Planet would appear to be far from decided.

The facts are these, The Custodians have been (temporarily) cut out of the loop of their own Free Planet. All efforts are being made to track down the ring-leaders and bring them all to justice like common criminals tried in New Courts of Law. All known, traceable members of The Custodian Liberation have been Listed and Public Enemy Number One, and has been attached to any residual Evertainment presence. Mankind has been set back a couple of decades in its Trans-humanist quest for profit in the face of individual planet-saving. You the people are likely to be punished (in the coming months and years) to the legal extent of the rebooted judicial system, as it will be rewritten to take into account the so-called liberation of mankind by recent events. You The People will pay as you always have paid, pay as you've never paid before, once you're all legally back in the hands of the rulers and the landlords and the chess players; once you've re-signed away your lives.

What will happen, over the course of the next few weeks, is that all those remaining Conglomerate Yes-men who stood idly by while profit was being made in their Masters' names – the Bankers, the heads of The Industry, their lawyers, their accountants, the appointed heads of Major Media Corporations, the Police Chiefs, the Utilities directors - all living executives who held 'significant position' with what used to be called Global Governance will be marched in front of the TV cameras and made to publicly repent for their sin. Some of them will have been tortured – but we all know that torture is only to insert information, not extract it.

It'll be like killing rabid dogs.

Mankind will rejoice, for he has been a part of a Global Revolution to get the corporations off his back and return the planet he has always loved to the galactic paradise it always should have been. Peaceful and in balance.

But it'll be just another show, just more re-programming of You The People. This is always how Chaaange happens. This is always how crises are exploited. This is always how the few survive, with fanfares and with rejoicing and with ticker tape parades. The masters of the Grand Chess Game will be working behind the scenes like beavers trying to reinstate the Old Order even under the guise of a lawless and leaderless New Order as offered by the birth of a Free Planet.

They wait decades for some bunch of clever-clogs to execute their maneuvers for them, it's just a waiting game, an update to the bullet that's already, always, loaded into the gun. It's how these sick fucks get their kicks, turning any attempt at reality to their image-readied advantage. And You The People will believe it, as you've believed Organised Religion and all the burning-bush son-of-God virgin-birth ascension crap and rampant money laundering that's accompanied it like Shakespeare's Shylock for millennia.

You The People were born to lose, born to suffer, born to fund (with your blood, your sweat, your tears) the luxurious retirements of those who played you into the ground, rubbed your worthless faces in your own soiled underwear. Bettered you. Daddied you.

In this amended endgame of corporate tyranny, just another in a long list of possible outcomes that are part of the fun of the game, ninety five percent of you will die so that this Power Elite (who we've never seen in public, who we never read about in the newspapers, who we never see with their pants down, never see doing dodgy deals, never see with a cocaine moustache) will always remain the bosses of this band of idiots. And those secret psychopaths will make The Custodian Liberation the enemy.

Those who broke the GSG or *Global Surveillance Grid* will allow all sorts of enemies of freedom to wage war against the west and invade and usurp and terrorise the populace of 'no countries' as if the War Of Terror had never ended; 1984 infinitely replayed with new enemies at every door. They will engineer the media circus around their plot and You The People (because none of you really think) will lap it up like kittens under the proverbial cow udder. Beg for protection.

Lap, lap; lap.

Even with the subversive revelations from Congressional minutes, Parliamentary war cabinets and Secret Service collusion. There's always too much data. And besides, mankind's off the leash, enjoying himself. Having fun. But not these fuckers. They're working hard still, always eager to make the best of a bad situation. Always keen to get you back under their thumbs and erase the exposure of their game and their lives to You The People.

So, enjoy it while you can. Enjoy your 'free planet'. That's the message. For later, maybe a few years from now, you'll be on your knees in front of merciless judges and insane legislators. It won't be a pretty sight. It will be the death of the memory of mankind, and the victors as always will get to write how that Great Chaaange was affected – how they helped Planet Earth survive anarchy, against all odds, facing all opposition – being heroes, and still making a profit.

But that's not the Free Planet that we're seeing hatch right now. Not the soft, slow metamorphosis from fertility to maturity that the Custodian Liberation's global chess breaking assault has kick-started. There is another story to tell yet; and in all good mysteries, there's always another story that's worth telling. Especially to You The People. In fact, there are certain stories that are never topical, can never be told.

And this is one of them.

This reality of what the Custodians have unleashed upon mankind; you must never hear that story – for the sake of your sanity. For all that you believe in is about to be challenged. All your scientific understanding of 'how your world works', or worked.

MIKE PHILBIN

28
YOU THE PEOPLE
OUR WORLD IS SACROSANCT

Eventually, you run out of food. Well, not you. The local Co-op warehouse.

You hadn't actually left the North Hincksey Industrial Estate since Bless You had been taken – what was her real name? You'd noticed it, that first time you were down there. Noticed the cars filling up with whatever they could carry away from the Co-op warehouse. You went in. You found food. You stayed there, for as long as you could. There were plenty of tins still in situ, free to eat. So you stayed. You ate. But the food ran out. You were threatened by thugs who wanted food. Finding none, they took out their anger on you.

You'd resolved that, after all this time, you didn't even care if you were swallowed up in some Solo's gaping maw, how much worse could it be than this? You resolve to return to Oxford, catch yourself chit-chatting with several people as you go. Everyone you meet is upbeat, hopeful. No wall bars your entrance. You arrive at the Town Crier position that was always the centre of Oxford's informational highway. A crowd has gathered.

Oxford has yet to crumble like so many towns and cities on Earth but it's getting there. An obvious degradation of this ancient town is already taking place. The outskirts of the town are indeed returning to the wild; broken flagstones accompany pitted roads left derelict, new trees are growing up on the spaces cleared by structural devastation. Sewer pipes and water pipes had busted but now there's not even power to cause further spillages. Edwardian and Elizabethan buildings have continued to sag and crumble, as they always have. Rot setting in; even here, in the town centre, the more modern aspects of commercialism have already fallen (or been pulled) into the street; corporate signage, remodernisations, CCTV cameras.

The assembled audience have just been listening to a speaker at this prime location in the centre of town. Men, women and children talk amongst themselves. You make your way forward to the Speaker's Position and await the attention of the mumbling crowd. You hold up both your hands, finally. You're not sure where you should start or if this is the right time.

But the words come, and once they do, you're relentless. Somehow, you stumble and flounder until you arrive at what you really wanted to say all along, what you've been driving toward for all these days and nights in utter confusion up on the hill. This is the important bit:

"...and we have to salvage an ethical future for mankind, from this insane genetic slaughter of his species," sermon over.

Really, that's all you wanted to say, your little bit. But the faces are so expectant, you can't resist adding a few extra thoughts on the subject.

"Re-Wilding the planet is fine, great sentiment guys, nice counter-move well executed. But we have to want it, still. We The People, working together to make Free Planet a better place, have to really want this new future for our children's children. We have to really make it work and make it be sustainable and make it so that our children understand why we did it. I can see many of you brought your children to this meeting," you take a sip of water from a leather pouch. "Of course, it'll be natural to them. By the time they come to read history books about what we did to our Prison Planet. Our children's children will remember real history and see how empire always fails, how ambition is only an illusion, how despotism only leads to bloodshed. They will see that the only real way to live is day-to-day, like this, in the moment; bravely, yes, bravely. In the face of all the trials put before us, in the face of such glorious natural beauty, a world replenished, a world re-opened to exploration for all."

The crowd gets edgy, comments shoot forward.

"But we have this already," proclaims one voice.

"Where are you?" you look about for the owner of the voice, "There, you, what did you say?"

"We have this already, we already have sanctuary in Oxford. A place that will never collapse or crumble for the next couple hundred years. The Bodleian Library."

"That's great, who else? Any ideas?"

"We lost everything when we lost our military dominance," some old sergeant-type in the crowd grunts before getting buffeted and near killed by the assembled pacifists. Your response, direct and to the point, prevents them from lynching this man. You're a survivalist now, and common sense must over-rule fantasy and action must trump idealism.

"Stop, please. Stop, you, leave that man alone. You put down that rock. He's right. He's right; we may have to reboot the C4ISR global space network so that we can 'gain the upper hand' on the warring Re-Wilded that's still eating everything in its path and fighting to be top dog of their world. Of course, that's how it will always go when you turn ruthless capitalists into rule-stripped animals, give them teeth and claws and wings. I'm sure it seemed like a great 'poetic' idea at the time. A must-do kinda thing..."

As if on cue, one of the winged Re-Wilded drops out of the sky at freefall speed. It slams into the outer edge of the crowd, sending men, women and children stumbling and tumbling and spilling all over the street. Feathers fly, beaks peck, claws grip clothing, tearing through material into flesh and bone. This is obviously a juvenile, some dumb kid who remained plugged into his/her Evertainment during all four days of the Natural Lottery Show, watching the talking birdy. Some gangly, gawkish kid with wings tries to steal someone's daughter to have for his lunch. But the crowd beat him back. There's a scream. A girl's hand has popped loose. Utter silence falls upon the crowd. The gangly bird flaps its wings madly, the hand in its beak, trying to get airborne again while one brave mother hangs onto one of its legs.

A much more ferocious animal hits the crowd like a bowling ball, one of the Properly Re-Wilded; a natural hunter, adult proportions. It's solid muzzle like some Egyptian river god, its back like gleaming tiles of patent leather, its forelegs much larger than its back legs; teeth like flint, fingers sporting lethal claws. It spots you and its tiled back becomes like liquid gun metal, smoother than silk. You literally shit yourself, your bowel dropping into your trousers. You back away, a sensation of utter panic in your guts, pulsating in your spine. This beast skull-hammers a couple of these people out of the way. It seems intent on getting to you, and you alone.

This four-legged beast moves in, stalking you for its supper, as people between you and it scatter for cover. You've nowhere to go. Sooner than you think, you've stumbled, and it's upon you, pinning you to the floor. Its skin like sheets of lead. Its mouth, rows of chipped grey teeth, that Elvis-like sneer.

"You know nothing of this Earth," the words chew its awesome features.

"Who are you?" you ask, as someone attacks the thing's flank with a fence pole. The beast shrugs off the attack as mere annoyance.

"Timi forgives you for what you did to her. Remember that," he looks into your eyes and you briefly see a man behind the raging beast, a fleeting compassion.

From off shot, someone launches a projectile, a rock. The beast snarls. An arrow. Then a spear bounces off his carapace. A gunshot is heard. It's like the concept 'projectile' itself is evolving over time. A group of men clad in archaic suits of shining armour approach from up High Street, shooing away the beast like it's some sort of 'bad doggy', hammering it on the side with annoying pitons and falchions. And they have a communal war cry, these amateur knights of old reborn for your protection. It's just all so surreal. It's like your mind's regressed historically to a time before jet fighters, to a time before tanks, to a time before muskets; you've literally slipped out of the natural stream, the moment by moment of linear timeline.

After much screaming and battling, the armour-suited mob goad back the beast off you. These shiny armoured heroes push too far, and the beast angrily swipes at the nearest assailant, carrying off one of the screaming members of the defending pack, almost out of spite. To de-can later. Enjoy, fingerlick by fingerlick.

"You know nothing of this Earth," it snarls back at you, over its shoulder, as it retreats with its struggling prize.

The juvenile Re-Wilded who'd clumsily battered into the group from an awkward descent finally gets airborne with its trophy, a torn-off child's hand, while the mother continues to chase after him screaming, begging for its return. The daughter once-owner of the hand moans and falters on the edge of consciousness, nearby. A black shape flaps feather-shedding wings into a milky Oxford sky.

You scramble to your feet and turn on the crowd, the armoured mob who'd rescued you, "See! This was bound to happen. They got fat bellies to fill. Egos to nourish. You realise they're still human inside those hideous disguises? I mean, you have been told about this? They're not sterile mules. They're humans. And they're going to multiply. They're literally going to empty the planet if we're not careful.

"We gotta get back in control of Free Planet, if only for everyone's sake, so that there'll be someone somewhere next year, not just one big fat genetic centipede sitting on a hill burping with a hundred stomachs from a hundred mouths, just sitting there getting fatter and fatter. You The People being like nothing more than food for this new machine. Worse than all the Corporate Wars put together. Worse than all the insurgency and counter-intelligence games.

You are 'Custodian' now. You always have been. But You forgot. Or someone neglected to tell you. You overlooked the obvious in exchange for a cushy life on the corporate chain gang," your eyes are wild now with a fanaticism that Asalah Al Faghori would be proud of. You wipe away a tear.

"It's not the job of some crack squad of specialists to protect this world; such a police force is always corruptible. It's **our job** to continue the good work started by those lost friends. Their methods, their genetic solution, was not a mistake, but it has brought its own problems with it. We're all gathered here because of it.

We need to reactivate Oxford Wall.

We need to redefend our ancient past, our home.

We need to stamp our own identity onto Free Planet so that it doesn't remain in the hands of those who have always been ruthless enough to kill and rape and plunder in the name of win win win.

It's our job to re-ignite industry, to create a technological future that has an ethical basis in terms of poisons and pollutants used in our gadgets, our tools. We must learn that harmony with our homeworld is of utmost importance. Let the Custodian Liberation's ultimate sacrifice at least to have not been in vain. We must create our own automated network of flying taxis so that we are safe at least in flight. We must create our own solutions to mass communication so that all members of our Diversity, here," you point to the spot you're all standing on, "there," you point to the skies, "or in any secluded place mankind survives, can communicate. We've got to reunite under the Custodian banner and prove to all who look up to us, our children's children, our future dependants, that we can make this work and mankind can come out the other side; brighter, bolder and more brilliant than ever.

"We need ambassadors to communicate with the Floating Homes and the members of the Diversities. We have been kept apart for too long, and this is our world. We are its guardians. We can't just be put in floating jails and told we've been a very naughty boy. We don't deserve this incarceration in someone else's jail, again. Can't you see this has to be our story, our world?"

And now that you've started, you find that it's where you should have always been, stood at the cross-roads of history channelling the spirit of Human Ingenuity to achieve greater things than simple productivity and profit. To push beyond the need to benefit from human industry. To fatten one's own portfolio.

"Sure, you'll want justice. You'll want to at least see justice done. Maybe you'll even try to reignite the flames of the ancient martyrs murdered long ago in this very town. I understand that you will want your pound of roasted flesh. But there will be no witch hunts in the name of Free Planet," you say.

You would never have thought that The Public Platform would have suited you, but as they say, if the glove fits.

"Bringing down the shimmering towers of the Conglomerate stronghold will be its own punishment, denying those who're playing the wrong game of their toys. You might think it appropriate to go hunting for the Israelis for 9-11 or the Bankers for the collapse of the economy or the military for all their murder and D.U. legacy across the world. But it won't help.

Remember Henry Ford," you've started but where to go from here? "Henry Ford, founder of the Ford Motor Company and assembly line innovator, the man who gave us a deadly machine to kill millions of innocent people every year? A profit-based decision to put control in the hands of sleepy, impatient, stressed commuters and delivery boys. What a stupid idea. It's a crime, only if we look back on it as such. We have the power to do that. It's our big brained scourge.

But is it something worth digging up the body of Henry Ford for and exacting some form of abstracted 'justice' on maybe the

Ford Foundation or other beneficiaries of the corporate game? These 'structures', these corporate games, are just accidents of intelligence, misplaced intent toward the wrong value set, namely profit.

This year, if Free Planet achieves anything it will be this – to make people realise that they have always known the difference between right and wrong. They have always known that too many children means too much deforestation which means too few places for wildlife to flourish. They have always known that crime is the result of the need to pay and pay the jailers and the slave-masters as they have been allowed to become."

And surprisingly, for you, because you've never felt compelled to give a public speech and have never received such, the crowd erupts into spontaneous applause.

A stinging tear comes to your eye, and you find it hard to swallow. Is this what hero worship is like? But that's not what you want. It's not what the gathered sovereign individuals here should want. You want, your planet needs, strong Custodians who can share the responsibility, not more doters, voters, floaters, rabble rousers, backroom stabbers, conspiratorialists, yes-men, slaves. That's not where Free Planet can be allowed to go. It must not devolve (again) to that sad consequence.

You try to buoy up the fighting spirit among your audience, "If I had a global microphone, I'd say that we the silent majority have made the world the wretched thing it is today, our complacency in the face of obvious tyranny, because it benefited our lives, has allowed this reign of terror to ruin our one true home.

Us.

We.

You The People of planet Earth need to take responsibility for Misplaced Intelligence. You're all clever, all of you. Your big brains have given you that terrible burden. Don't act like slavering pack dogs. Don't act like lemmings. Don't act like warrior ants. As necessary and intriguing as these roles are, they're already filled by the re-wilded animals we share this planet with. Let them be led by the nose ring.

We're far more intelligent than that. Rather than merely reacting to basic sexual or hunger drives, one of the human race's greatest strengths is that we actually think.

We must forgive, but we must never forget how close we came to totally destroying our home-world, eradicating its wildlife and enslaving its populace. We can do this, all seven billion individuals huddling together under the same umbrella of realisation, if we want to.

It is our Free Planet, after all."

People start to mob you like you're their Messiah. And it's not what you want. Not at all. This isn't the way you wanted this to go. Free Planet, as you understand it, was meant to be about togetherness and sharing and unity and all those things that have been missing from your life, from society on this planet for the last few decades, centuries, millennia. You wanted everyone to take hold of the shoulders of the person next to them and let them know that they are the most important thing in the universe.

Not this hapless redirection of intent, this pathetic worship in broad daylight.

You start to berate them, in your head you have thousands of words that could maybe help rally them to love their neighbour as themselves and all of that tosh, but you're exhausted, speechless. The words just don't come. Only the hands of strangers, bearing you aloft like a hero.

29
THE CUSTODIANS
NO MORE COVERT WORLD

Let's examine those fat-controllers who (think they) run the GCG or *Grand Chess Game* from off-shore havens like it's a Covert World of Games to be Played, Wars to be Won. Let's look at those piece movers, those strategy makers; those Tavistock, those Hitler, those GIABO or *Global Insurrection Against Banker Occupation*, those Think Tank ideologists, those revolution makers.

Google, Facebook, Twitter, Arab Spring, 9/11 and all the other FFT or *False Flag Terror* events. That was all their doing.

MOD or *Merchants of Dissent*.

CIA or *Citizens In Anguish*.

JFK or *Just Fucking Killed*.

And that's what the patent-swapping Custodians were, nothing more than a clockwork toy, a clever ploy, a seeming sacrifice on the GCB and nobody bothered to check if there were any covert pieces secreted away in sock garters.

You'll notice how it was an Oxford-originated plan to make it look like mutiny? You'll notice how they were all fee-paying foreign students to make it look like terrorism? You'll notice how it was a Jerusalem-like Georgia Guidestones-inspired final solution Eugenics-bowing idealism to make it look familiar, like something we'd all seen, all feared before? What was the opening line of that poem, that song?

And did those feet in ancient time
Walk upon England's mountains green?

These people's minds are filled with such senseless slaughter; these self-protectionists.

Do you think these real rulers of the world be seen dead plugging their god-given brains into the Evertainment system along with the gawping masses, agog at the projected illusion of reality? You think you'd see an RMI or *Royal Master of Industry*, were you to recognise them in public (unlikely for Joe or Jane Public) wifi-engaged with the GEN or Global Evertainment Network, nodding along like a mascot? Come on.

They know exactly what that shit, that radiation, is doing to the collective consciousness of the lambs-to-slaughter. They know it is like some sort of CSM or *Cynical Social Metronome,* sowing seeds of doubt and diversion into the billions of minds, orchestrating the ultimate OFC or O*rdo Ab Chao* or *Order From Chaos* problem-reaction-solution to keep everyone slaving to the tick-tock, tick-tock of insatiable Supply & Demand.

You'd never see a Global Elite Chess Player ascending the corporate ladder. They're exempt from that blackmailed shame, that ever-pending humiliation. They don't need to earn bonuses or reap rewards or show results. There are no honours in their world, no heroic badges pinned to chests for everyone to aspire to. There's nothing you can give them, the Global Elite exist in a constant state of ambivalent exile from what you and I call reality; no ™ needed.

It's just theirs, an island in the sea fueled by slave ships and serviced by an army.

They're effectively out of the game, not a part of Covert World inc.

Their SBI or *Space Based Intranet* (as it was first called in the sixties) is separate from the GEN used by the wifi-hungry brains of Normal Folk™. They needed this 'break from the public sewer' this private club of Chess Players. A dusty old meeting room in a private estate out in the middle of nowhere.

Out in the middle of space.

They don't even care if Free Planet exists, that's not what gets them out of bed in the morning. They're exempt from such consequence, they don't even care how their world is run. Sure, what The Custodians did will seriously influence their game for the next few years but it'd be naïve in the extreme to think they'd been beaten. You don't live this off-shore a life for millennia, exiled for your own protection and complete rule of those beneath you, and not have contingencies or back-up plans, emergency exits from the blazing building should it all go up in flames as sometimes happens in the BBW or *Big Bad World.*

The once-patent-owners, the once-global-financiers, the once-respected-now-forgotten superstars of the BFDBG or *Big Fat Dollar Bill Game* who sat there in their stolen palaces in the hills, their temples in the mountains, raining pronouncements down upon their flock in the name of Global Agenda, thinking of better ways to torture you, to enslave you, to murder you. Buy more shit, cut that bottom line, maximise goodies for me me me. That will literally always be their driving force.

The Global Elite (let's leave them at least with their military decoration of their title intact) aren't going to I.N.T.E.G.R.A.T.E. They're never going to 'come down from their mountain' and adopt temporary positions of influence within the masses. Are you joking?

The global elite sometimes wish they didn't have to live in these isolated castles in the ground, these Deep Underground Military Bases of the conspiracy world. These buried palaces that don't really exist, in the classical sense, in the accounting sense. These off-books black-housing projects. Shielded off from any physical insurgency. Able only to associate with their kind, their tight-knit global family, their private army, their robots.

Assassinating any 'accidents' of birth that might occur due to a lack of discretion party-time. Watching that trendy game of Us & Them from a safe haven, out in space maybe. In another dimension entirely, maybe. They will not be invaded or eaten alive or used in some deal to suppress and protect. They will be the viewer, not the participant. That's their burden, for ever. Their strength, their weakness.

Theirs can be the longest waiting game, the longest siege of the keep mankind has ever had the privilege to take part in. They can be starved out of existence in the most cruel and abnormal fashion. Their lands can be used as a toilet for all the shit and piss of the Re-Wilded. Tonne after tonne of hybrid effluent raining down on Them (for a change) so that they're made to scrape their own roads and scrape their own buildings with their bare hands, their nails shattering back to reveal blood and bone as they scrape and scrape and scrape to keep up appearances, darling, as they strive to make it seem like 'nothing has changed for us, dontchyaknow?'

We are the Global Elite, know us by our name, we will never change.

But that name, that one royal luxury that is so hard to give up, much harder than Bollinger, than Caviar, much harder than fist-fucked stolen children. Such a hard thing to give up, one's Name. One cannot afford to lose one's Name. And that could even become a Bargaining Chip for them, if only mankind knew the rules of engagement.

Mankind was busy, like proper busy for the first time in recent millennia, busy looking around him and assessing the damage centuries of Empire had wreaked upon his delicate homeworld. All around the globe, grown men stood with their children by their side and wept. Simply sobbed their mortal hearts out at the vast global destruction the CWFP or *Corporate War For Profit* had wrought upon their once-beautiful homeworld.

Mankind was busy holding a delicate flower in his hands and sniveling like a child, the tears of absolute joy running down his face and the snot from his puerile sobbing pouring over his gaping mouth. Child-like wonder restored unto a world where Rules & Regulations had basically imprisoned mankind behind a false facade of adult-ness.

Mankind was busy hugging and kissing and congratulating his fellow man, woman and child for their brilliance, their sun-like shine of uniqueness. He was keen to forgive all the bad things he'd said and done and thought and imagined about his fellow man, from any country, from any part of the world, any (fake [assigned]) role in corporate life.

Mankind was hoping to forget the Dark Years, as history will now remember them, now that TAJ or *Truth Armed Journalists* were setting the record straight, now that the lies and deceit of Corporate War for Profit were being unveiled, sifted through, and mostly ignored. By the masses. Ignored. No one ever really reads history, unless they're keen to change it. And mankind doesn't like change. We all know that.

Mankind likes things like Family and Togetherness and Solitude and Boredom. Mankind is a contradictory animal, but that's what life's about. As long as the goal posts stay where they are, mankind can be happy, contented, unstressed, creative, passionate; mankind is far too busy rediscovering the global kinship the Divide To Conquer game had robbed him of for all those years, those decades, those centuries of slavery to their legacy.

Can't you see, Dear Gods of Olympus, in your slave-built temples and native-built castles, can't you see that your reign has come to an end and your significance is now – *POOF* – gone.

Evaporated, or rather sublimated, in a flash, in one night of total donation to the Custodian Cause, of their souls, or at least of their flesh. But we'll examine the souls issue at length, later – when you're gone and forgotten. When you've all been 'dealt with', shall we say.

Oh, yes, dear Elite Game Player, Free Planet is coming for you, eventually. Mankind has a long memory for unkindnesses done to his fellow man, his global family. Mankind's ire can stretch back aeons. He is more of an animal than those re-wilded beast of the forest, the plain, the skies and the sea. He is an intelligence with vengeance as a prime controller. Well done for breeding that into him. The Art of Never Forgetting, never forgiving.

But that's not where this story is taking us, just yet. That would be too easy a cop-out, to invade their realms and take them by storm. That'd justify their greatness in many ways, lend far too much credence to their influence in the Grand Scheme of Things. Where they actually have no lasting effect at all on a totally revamped and reunited planet, bent on only Do Right By.

Before then You The People have to lose all sense of normalcy and subscribe to the fact that your life will never be the same again once Creativity, Passion and Kinship are your ambition, once Do Right By is your guiding mantra, once Free Planet starts to flourish and regrow and replenish.

You The People have a lot of living to catch up on.

Failure must (once again) be hailed as the highest form of human achievement. We must allow all of the sovereign individuals of Free Planet to share their own and others' failures. Why? Well, for decades, centuries, millennia, our failures, our human weakness, our blackmailable fetishes were held over our heads like the corporate sword of Damocles. Everyone is ashamed, by deed of Original Sin, of their own wants and needs, their own physical urges and desires. And that's such a leverage and guiding principle for the Global Elites. They've used it time and again, they've made compliant drones of once-living beings.

Even the elites, the glowing Gods of Olympus in TOL or *Their Own Lunchtime*, are victims to this shaming of their inner souls, their innate failings (as prescribed by an invented 'society,' small 's.') Even these so-called Global Game Players are subject to the arbitrary rules of the game. They're unwitting pawns within their own dissolution. And they don't know it. But they will.

Soon, the whole world will witness the cowering children who never grew up – the shadow in the corner, the beast in the mind.

No More Covert World will be the cry.

And you'd imagine that'd be the end of their reign over humanity, but that's where The Global Elite excel, in the subversion of the innocent. They had already taken it upon themselves to 'recruit' from the zombie hordes, the disaffected re-wilded, the corrupted bastardised genetically entangled Uber Beasts or *Menshenjagger* of the wilds. Their networks of influence, though injured by the death of Evertainment and The Industry, still existed and there was always a price that one assassin could be paid to eradicate an enemy.

Revenge was sweet when tales were tallest, and boy could The Global Elite tell a tall tale to get their minions to do their worst. Let's call them Cleaners, these amalgamated monsters, these scraps of desire and lust and wretched psychological sickness, these 'things that could never be eradicated' in the first wave of Free Planet's existence, these hyper-sexualised throwbacks to an MK Ultra'd world of corporate espionage, their lingering Manchurian Candidates; these slavering mongrels of total control.

Mission objectives were set and payment drops in living child flesh were orchestrated, all from the contented comfort of some off-shore off-world(?) satellite or enclave. It has to be put like this because Nobody Really Knows where these elites reside. So better not to speculate. They're un-visible, anti-discoverable. Not even their own family members are allowed access. Parties are always arranged at 'some other property'. Initiations are always arranged at 'some other property'. Awards, murders, punishments, bonuses – all take part at 'some other property'.

Even now, they're convinced their Free Planet is as its always been. Playable, manipulable, ownable. Let's let them rot in their pit for a while. Let's let the sleeping dogs lie. Once they're integrated back into the reality of ninety billion souls. Made to bear witness. Made to repent. Made to make amends. Then we'll see.

30
YOU THE PEOPLE
IF YOU'RE HEARING THIS BROADCAST

As beautifully as the tourist literature paints the carved wooden ceiling of the Divinity School, above ground isn't really the safest place to be right now. You know, what with potentially hundreds of Re-Wilded ground crawlers and sky swoopers and tree climbers and dirt diggers lurking around the feeding zone that is Oxford, their aching bellies groaning for sustenance. You just don't wanna be caught out in the open, if you can help it. You certainly need to regroup with your kind. You understand that, right? Such self-preservationary thinking brings us to the underground pyramid of corridors, catacombs or storage rooms that comprise the Bodleian Library on Catte Street.

Okay, while we're momentarily celebrating outside the 17th century School Quadrangle of the Old Bodleian Library, hoisted in the air on the shoulders of your disciples, your back to the Divinity School, let's notice the twin towers of the Orders of Architecture: Tuscan, Doric, Ionic, Corinthian and Composite. If you make your way to a position directly under the archway between the pillars, on the left, you come across a locked door.

Once it's opened for you, make your way through (don't dally, and remember to lock it after you) into the stairway. Notice the musty scent despite all the ducting attempting to clean the air of moisture and disease.

Directly, you will gain access to a descending wrought iron staircase that leads down to the Bodleian Library's real treasure trove, a vast underground space dedicated to scholarly learning and ancient history. Nothing like the gormless sheoplefood you get on the (defunct) Evertainment system.

This place is like a Dream Factory, where ideas you'd never come across, concepts you'd never considered, histories you've never read about are presented to the willing in physical book form. Just sat there on a shelf for anyone who can get down here to read, learn from, study.

There is a pre-Industry tannoy system that cuts through the place like veins through anatomy, delivering useful information to the inhabitants of this underground world. It would have been installed for summoning some weathered librarian or some crumbly archivist to some internal meeting, presentation or debriefing, or it would announce the arrival of some requested tome that'd finally made its conveyor belted way to some pickup place or depot, plucking you from your studies in one of the amazingly old chapels of research.

Today, on this Free Planet-yet-to-be the Bodleian Library's tannoy system carries *muzak.* As you enter for this first time, ushered along by the ever-enthusiastic ever-questioning crowd of admirers, is the Vera Lynn classic, *We'll Meet Again.*

You know how it goes, this War Time song that brings tears to the eyes and a lump to the throat of any old person who lived through the horrors, foreign and domestic, of the Second World War. Here's the few lines you hear...

We'll meet again
Don't know where
Don't know when
But I know we'll meet again
Some sunny day.

Keep smiling through, indeed. *Just like you always do*, eh? And it's okay, you *can* smile. There is light at the end of this tunnel you're in, this heinous narrative journey of the senses and the sensibilities. You have survived your first Re-Wilded attack. Congratulations. They're ferocious fuckers, aren't they? Not at all human in their movements, their intentions, even though you know they're still human on the inside. They're like something from another planet but, remember, a nugget of humanity drives these ravaged souls; or maybe it's just misplaced ambition at the wheel, the worst of all man's sins.

Citizens Band Radio and Pirate Long Wave Radio had experienced something of a resurgence and self-appointed Disc Jockeys, as they used to call people who were paid to put records on turntables and announce the title and artist, were once again broadcasting local-to-local across the re-commissioned analogue system, so recently neutered by the digital change-over.

The analogue signal would fade in and out like the good old days, at the behest of weather or atmospheric conditions. And it wasn't even needed. Okay, it was good for keeping in touch with family in neighbouring towns, distant neighbours you no longer met face-to-face, allies you'd like to gather around your Free Planet cause. It was good to know where and when the next band of Re-Wilded would strike. It was good to know which warehouses or supermarkets still had stock. Which petrol stations hadn't run dry, yet.

But this was only interesting if you were abandoned to the old ways, the time before the Custodian Liberation. And that was a very small percentage of the population of the northern hemisphere, truth be told. The Atlantic cables were still all connected, it was just a case of reverting to an earlier form of Evertainment – they used to call it *The Internet*.

The Bodleian Library was actually designated a Diversity by the EPA or *Emergency Powers Act* out of what remained of Parliament re-founded by the scavengers (well, survivors) who would come to rule, once again, the northern hemisphere. We're talking about those sovereign individuals who'd not been connected to the Evertainment System by choice or luck and who may have set aside and accrued the supplies they'd thought they'd need if (one day) the shit hit fan and all hell broke loose in their villages and towns. Basically, people had been preparing themselves for a day when a Custodian Liberation-like happening captured control of planet earth and tried to pull Humanity kicking-and-screaming from its corporate prison cell in search (once again) of *Real Life*™. People who would have great difficulty giving up their country for some concept of freedom.

Yes, even in the corporate days, people actually lived like that, an overnight bag forever packed; rations stashed.

'Bodleian Library' was the first official earth bound or terrestrial Diversity i.e. one that had its foundations on the ground, in the ground; as opposed to having its foundations in the sky or in the ocean somewhere. It had roots, and those roots tunnelled deep into both the mantle of the earth and the memories of the humans who had come before; the rulers or at least re-writers of history.

So, this is where the rejoicing mob, in their dolt-like ignorance had carried you, their reluctant Messiah. They didn't realise you were just a Pavlov-dog-like spokesperson for LGI or

Larger Game Inc, those mocking elites who really still controlled you, controlled the game, through sycophantic (or unknowing) assets like yourself, and made sure 'God' was on their side, even as their Eugenics agenda scraped another few hundred thousand slaves off the bottom of the barrel to make sausages for tonight's tea. A literal Cannibal Holocaust.

The Bodleian was an underground maze of two floors of shelving stretched back towards the Sheldonian Building and onward to the New Bodleian Library building across the bottom end of Broad Street. Automated ten years ago, and eventually digitised, this knowledge base had never made it onto the Evertainment Grid. *Defendu! Histoire inconnu!*

Think of that old Hollywood apocalypse cliché, "If you're hearing this broadcast, you are the resistance."

Well, that exemplifies what it means to be under siege like this in an upside down castle in the ground; a rat in a sewer.

You've not been long down here when you come across two amazing pieces of ancient history, framed under glass and evocative of a time when the Anglo-French connection was much more blatant in the English canon. One is a Franciscan Missal from the mid 14th century, titled *The Crucifixion of Jesus*. The other is *The Mirouer Historial Abregie de France*, a mid 15th century depiction of the battle of Hastings. As splendid as that pair are, the thing that sits between them, also under glass is the most intriguing.

It's a small thing, old and scruffy looking, also under glass. A declaration that had to be read out loud, by the researchers in ancient times, when confronted by the library's staff. And this really used to happen. You had to be prepared for the confrontation, ready to leap to your feet, tap out the embers of your pipe, and recite these words on the card you were issued along with their permit to read, such that, "I, the undersigned, deign it a sin in the eyes of God to tear pages from any volume in this worshipful dwelling and use the crackling sheaves for toilet paper."

Seriously, a lovely memento of much more civilised times.

Bodley's Bell dictates every communal meal time. The loyal subjects of the Bodleian Library Diversity gather in an underground dining room to discuss the ideas of the day and to air the many grievances of subterranean living.

It's like the entire population of greater Oxfordshire, from Banbury to Newbury, from Cirencester to Aylesbury, those who had remained human, had rallied together and decamped to Bodleian Library; proud that their Oxford was the site of the first permanent (i.e. geographically fixed) Diversity. Not some flimsy helium balloon floating on the wind or some seaweed floating on the sea but an actual castle, albeit an underground one.

Nightly News or *News at Ten* (depending on your global territory) returned to prominence in the lives of those people struggling to survive in a world that had just shat out demons onto the dinner plates of those who were so used to the lap of luxury.

Sure, bills had ended. So had taxes. But also, so had wages, so had water distribution and sewage removal and other such domestic needs. The promise of de-patented local solutions to these simple human comings and goings had started but production of such was nowhere near the volumes it needed to be to be fully functioning, useful for all who had avoided or escaped (thus far) incarceration in the floating homes of the Diversity Movement.

Sometimes, it all got too much, and you had to escape outside, for the sake of your sanity.

On one of these illicit occasions, you spy through a ground floor window Dafyd Atkins, Head of ESI or *Eye Sys Industries* (now defunct) and his ex-industry cronies undertaking the Oxford Wall Reignition Ceremony to which you weren't invited. Lots of Freemasonic symbolism, the chalice, the aprons, the checkerboard rug, the twin candlesticks. And you wonder what this Diversity really is, what sort of secret sin is it?

In the sky, you see the now-enhanced Oxford Wall rising and curving right over Oxford like a spectral dome. Just one small hole at the top where the electromagnetic mathematics fall off to infinity or divide by zero. It was good enough though for most protective situations.

On another illicit occasion out in the open, you spy, by the Radcliffe Camera exit of the quadrangle, The Monster aka your old boss in The Industry meeting with Dafyd Atkins and three more delegates of New Oxford. Two of the three extra delegates, if you'd have been part of the original Custodian Liberation's 'Group of 38' rebels, might have looked an awful lot like Patent hackers Frank McCardle, USAF and Damon Hoskins, BsC. Maybe it was their combined skills that had helped reactivated Oxford Wall? Maybe their double-crossing activities to Creativity, Passion and Kinship is why the Free Planet idea never recognised its full potential.

Hands are shaken, in fact cheeks are kissed; followed by congratulatory hugs. It's evident that this impromptu meeting marks a coming together of political allies in a world that's just (supposedly) been stripped of all that tosh. That such an occurrence can only bode ill is reinforced by the image of The Monster handing Dafyd Atkins a package; an oil-stained brown-paper sack. Hands slap shoulders, manly laughter.

The last time you see the Bodleian Library, you'd made your way up St Mary's Church tower, overlooking the Radcliffe Camera. "Opened in 1749," you muse, realising that you've suddenly become an elitist snob with your knowledgeable nonsense about unimportant things and if this were another time, you'd find the cheeky peck of Madame Guillotine's razor-sharp lips on the nape of your scrawny neck for such global treason.

Out beyond the extremity of Oxford Wall you can see the hunters and the hunted. Lone or in packs. Congregated in herds. Respectively. It surely is a wondrous site, seeing nature from this safe distance. The sheer beauty of families of these genetic freaks, communing, grooming, loving. You can imagine huge herds of these creatures making their way across the shortest part of the English Channel, roaming from continent to continent, not sure of what animal armies they'll meet on the way, whose territory they're about to invade. It's all starting to sound like this might just work, but there are other considerations to contend with before we're all linking arms and wassailing the night to bed.

You're looking down over the ledge when one of those considerations assaults you.

Remember Abi Chopsticks, the floating Peanut Taxi-like entity, stealer of humans, impregnator of Floating Homes? Well, she's got you, gulped you into her interface-laden interior.

You cry and beat her inner walls with your fists, scratching with your fingernails until you draw blood. Abi Chopsticks seems to just pass through the Oxford Wall, unscathed – maybe it can let people out? Maybe she has a special affinity with the wall? Maybe she's one of them, the elite who are still calling the shots in Oxford despite what the radio and TV might tell the world. Does this render false hope upon those imprisoning themselves behind this wall?

"I will not be exiled to a Floating Home, I am a Free Human!" you yell at her, all around you. You have no idea why you've been kidnapped. You have no idea that this Solo is none other than one of the original Custodians, of which few remain.

Keen to minimise damage of her inner self, she sucks the oxygen out of her lungs, this is where you're seated (within her chest cavity), until you pass out and she ferries you off to an insane life of imprisonment in one of the many Floating Homes or Diversities.

MIKE PHILBIN

31
THE CUSTODIANS
THE FIVE NOBLE ORDERS OF CHROME

And it's like this suffocated moment in an airless organic hijack species was always destined to happen. Bang on time. Big on tone. A single phrase, held magically aloft as if it had resonated throughout the length of human history, precluding the dinosaurs, precluding the birth of the sun, precluding the cooling of your sector of the Milky Way galaxy. The lung-rattling rasp of your death transforms into sex with the sun and communication with the entire living consciousness of the Universe.

Or that's the way it seems, interstellar relations; star orgies.

Keep that erotic tone, that crazy dreamy sleazy standing wave, in your mind for as long as you can. Concrete the erectile tissue into the neurones and synapses of your brain. Reinforce all that you think you've learned on this planet with the innate knowledge that you're more than the sum of your tiny molecular parts. Imagine this tone, this song that structures the super-structure of galaxies, thrumming and burbling along like an old jalopy. Imagine this echo from the first gasp of intelligent life in our universe caressing all the anarchic axes of creation with its unifying song.

If such a feat seems beyond you right now, fear not. You're not alone. You will receive help. A single dot. You can imagine that, right? Now, turn that dot into a reflective sphere, like a drip of chrome hanging in the sky. You can see it, can't you? A single, 100% reflective unity that embodies all the physical properties and psychological magnitude of deep, starless space.

Don't worry about the vertigo at this point, everyone goes through a brief spell of vertigo when faced with the incalculable. The incalculable is easy to grasp though. It's a point of reflection, sitting, pulsating with universal reverberation. There are no sounds here, no sights, even, certainly no matter. Other than this 'memory of chrome' and the you-ness it contains. This what-you-are-ness. Your substance. Your meaning. The hidden sensation of potential. You won't collapse under your own ego-phrenia. You've come too far to fail now.

You can imagine this seemingly impossible scene. This is your real strength. The ultimate demonstration of your power as a Glimpser. Your ability to enhance and experience something called The Big Picture.

You remember that you're split across four representations of yourself, the thinner you, the fatter you, the female you. Imagine your thinner you starting to turn, slowly rotating head over heals with its arms and legs out like da Vinci's *Vitruvian Man*. He turns and turns on his axis like a spinning disc.

Your thinner-you lives inside you, obviously, but as he spins, he starts to form a plane; in your chrome: within the reflective substance of you.

Imagine a fluid centre of chrome spreading out as it spins, faster and faster.

This chrome disc is like a mirror expanding out along one plane filling the whole of space, and slicing it in half so that you have two regions of space: an 'in front' and a 'behind'. In the front face, stands your thin you, as you remember. In the back face is the feminine aspect of your thin you; this is something that you've never seen but always suspected was there. And though it may seem obvious now, you didn't spot it at the time. You didn't spot that each of the four aspects of you would have counter-sexual alter-egos.

Remember when you were in the dusty old room with the eight wrinklies sat in a semi-circle warming their archaic socks before the embers of a fire? Didn't you see that there were four either side of the fire place. Four wrinklies on the left side of the fire; three male, one female. Four wrinklies on the right hand side of the fire; one male, three female.

Doesn't it make sense yet? Can't you see that this is how it has always worked. This four-facing-four across the glow of the fire grate, the four points of one face of a cube opposed by the other four points?

Keep in your mind the image of the four corners of a cube being opposed by the four opposing corners; mirroring the entire universe within their shared space. Can you see that? Can you visualise with that much attention to detail? Can you create with that much fidelity?

Your female thin and your male thin version of you stand facing each other, reflected in the unit-thickness plane of chrome, each on their separate and distinct half of the universe.

Another chrome plane starts to spin, driving like a mighty engine within you. This plane starts to spin and expand, you see that it is perpendicular to the first one, slicing right down through the faces of the thin-fem thin-masc you've just invoked. It slices through your thin-fem and thin-masc such that the left eye of the thin-fem lives in a completely separate part of the universe from the right eye. And each left eye of the thin-masc lives in another completely different part of the universe from both the eyes of your thin-fem and its own right eye.

Though the resonant frequency is the same, your body starts to shudder as this is taking twice as much energy to maintain, twice the mathematical effort pulsing through the same algorithm. One mirror, takes a certain amount of concentration. A second mirror, more than double the concentration because of the inner reflections of each surface in each other reflected surface.

A third mirror slices through your centre like a horizon, pouring out into space forever spinning and reflecting your fat male self and your fat female self, as above so below.

A chrome sphere pulled in so many dimensions like this can't maintain its form for so long and eventually manifests 'you', the physical floating you in the centre of this these six versions of you bisected by these spinning planes of chrome. The planes of the mirror shatter, leaving behind only the six versions of you represented by six spheres of chrome.

Transmutation of the First Order has just taken place and you sense that one billion human beings, wherever they might currently be hiding, are attached to each of these chrome nodes. Imagine that, and them not knowing it, one billion humans are (potentially) linked to all your physical aspects at this point. Though they'll never find out how this came to be. They'd always be unaware of the origin of their connectedness, until you activate the Second Order of Transmutation from chrome into soul.

Each Order of Transformation assigns a square root to the share of chrome, such that after all five level of chrome have appeared as tiny chrome pricks of light in the starless void. A lattice of ninety billion stars? Fifteen billion chrome souls of the Glimpser per cubic plane. Each human star-being an integral part of their own star, the Sun, that they orbit on a daily basis, thinking it nothing more than a heat and light generator.

If any human could see this, he would understand that at the centre of every galaxy of ninety billion stars, there was a similar function that split the mutli-dimensional realm of chrome out into the universe. Always in this specific mathematical relationship; exact and never altering.

Each of the six billion humans now had intimate connection with fifteen living chromes each, shared across five communal (and compound [and inter-dependent]) orders. Sharing of the Chrome AND of the Orders being the key to understanding man's ability to travel through the stars without moving, being at all spaces and at all times, at once.

That's why the six billion human population figure was so important, method in the madness.

To physically by-pass the eight.

Jumping straight into the centre of the cube.

The only place from where all eight points of the cube are visible.

That's what mankind brought to the table.

His/her contribution to Free Planet.

Raw, basic, clumsy Humanity might be a four-point four-gamete planar-version of universal reality, but it can occupy any of the six faces of the cube, at any time. Even with its limited control of the great multi-dimensional machine. Humanity can still cause irreparable damage, like it did in the nineteen thirties with the first atomic tests.

On that occasion, the cube of Humanity actually suffered a one-face loss leading to a momentary pyramiding of the whole of the universe (as we see it.) As a double dilemma, this allowed entities that should have been quartered within their own limited version of reality to 'slip across' into the human realm.

This is the reason for all sorts of ghost-related, UFO-related or ET-related business throughout the history of man.

This pyramiding of the human cube was the disruptive mechanism that masked the first signal of six billion from planet Earth; literally put Earth's most important point in its history into UCM or *Universal Cloaked Mode*. This second chance, then, this vicious routing of mankind by the Custodian Liberation, was Earth's opportunity to get it right this time. A second alarm bell for mankind's true awakening before CCC or *Critical Colony Collapse*; our destiny without galactic intervention from the Nomadix, the Glimpsers.

Six billion is the way its always been; it's the number that works for bi-lobes like You The People. It's a number that planet after planet of your kind has exploited to Ascend to the Next Level of Being.

And by six billion, no man or woman, no boy or girl, no one is excluded; no one left behind.

The Re-Wilded fighting through a Natural Lottery of new experience and adventure, the Solos scooping up free humans not affected by the show's genetic influence. The Floating Homes where the humans are retained, for their own good. The hybrid creatures, the lust-fuelled centipede zombies roaming the fields and meadows fucking everything they find. The elites, who thought, hoped, prayed, that their idea of a Private Castle was enough to spare them inclusion in the whole empathic soup that constituted the Human Race.

All six billion of them are represented here, on five different levels of existence; Five Noble Orders. Each of the six billion offered this ultimate gift of fifteen (inter-connected and co-dependent) Chrome souls. The masses are exalted by this occasion and become the Glimpsers, the Nomadix, and a world of No Secrets is instigated, press-ganged into reality, extruded through every human failing and twitching guilt we all possess.

Officially, this is the moment of The Eradication of Original Sin. A reflective dust will settle upon the every separate entity in the human grid like a whisper in trees.

* * *

IED or *Intermittent Evertainment Dislocation* corporate ident doesn't fade or flicker this time. It hangs there flirtatiously, like the opened night gown of a glowing whore star. Impossible to look at for more than a few seconds without going blind. But you don't need to physically 'see' it. You know it's there. Solid, indelible, softly mutating from font to font. IED, *IED*, <u>IED</u> forever secreted in your back brain, anchoring you to the truth of your existence here on Earth. You can smell it, touch taste hear know it. A controlling stake now exists in the company of your mind more powerful than any reprimand from parent to child.

"This is mankind's future, whether you like it or not," let's say.

32
YOU THE PEOPLE
BATTLE FOR THE SOUTHERN HEMISPHERE

As you know, most of the northern hemisphere was plugged into the Evertainment Grid during the four rambling episodes of the Natural Lottery Show. Do you understand what this means? Most of the workers of the world 'break the law' and tune into Evertainment during work hours, after school, during lunch hours, some even leave that shit plugged in while they sleep.

Most everyone in the northern hemisphere, where The Industry is the only respectable way of life for the planet's corporate drones, was plugged in. A bizarre life, no? Live to work. Evertainment's your paid-for perk.

Which means?

You got it, most of the corporate drones in the northern hemisphere got Re-Wilded.

Except those who earned themselves a disengagement clause to their Corporate Non Disclosure Agreement by insanely pledging their genetic legacy during the four days of the Natural Lottery Show. And no-one knew this would be the outcome, that normality and a return to the good life would be their prize.

* * *

Large swathes of India, China, Africa, South America still didn't have access to the perk of 100% Evertainment saturation. The Third World as it remained known for centuries, was still what you call a Growing Market for such insidious dogma, such omniscient propaganda, such perpetual mind fuckery via psycho-violent re-ordering of the creative mind, like putting bars on a kid's imagination.

Over and over until the magical *ib, sheut, ren, ba* and *ka* of the long-forgotten concept of the soul is bolted down under layers of steel, tonnes and tonnes of suffocating programming.

The Custodian Liberation can come across like a bunch of tyrants themselves. They set everyone up to be subsumed into the Natural Lottery escape plan, the great global gene-splice in the name of Free Planet. Were they any better than the Corporate War Oxford-educated banksters and military leaders who preceded them? Well, they'd put into place definitive Checks and Balances in the form of the Re-Wilded and Floating Homes. The aim was to have a Liberated majority, adopting all sorts of diverse lifeform configurations to repopulate the land, the sea and the air, and to have a Protected minority held captive (for their own good) within these floating Diversities. A Diversity was a floating structure that could both liberate human Creativity, Passion and Kinship and also allow for the planet to heal from the onslaught of rampant Commercialism that has marketed Earth as nothing more than some slave to be raped and abused.

Diversities allowed the planet to heal. That was how the northern hemisphere looked now, where most of what the planet knows as The Industry had had its base. Re-Wilded, Diversitied.

The southern hemisphere, despite decades of trying to catch up and be invited into the global rape-fest known as Capitalism, Democracy, Communism, Religious Fundamentalism – call it what you will, were left behind in many ways.

Sure, in the northern hemisphere you had been effectively taxed into submission, a slave to the game, but the people of this UnterVelt, this southern hemisphere of social depravity and financial austerity, were some of the poorest humans on the planet, struggling the hardest to 'make ends meet' in an unjust knee-jerk reaction to not being in the Need To Know game plan, not even in the role of a pawn.

Whole southern continents refused access to Evertainment, refused access to The Industry; whole countries with nothing to do but beg and scrounge for benefits and charity from the United Nations, the World Bank, the Players.

It didn't take the several billion Re-Wilded of Cordwainer Smith's *Menshenjaggers* long to exhaust the food chain of what remained of the northern hemisphere. They were hungry and they were ruthless. As per their programming, their upbringing.

Imagine a huge mass of centipedes and other amalgamated giants composed of twenty, thirty, forty lust-zombies crawling across the face of the Earth, refusing to become Floating Homes, insistent that their solution to the re-wilded planet was the best place to be.

An Exodus south ensued, on the wing, on the hoof, on the waves, to lay claim to the remainder of the human resource; to corral and farm and perpetuate for themselves the supply of human meat. To fill their own bellies. Spawn their own children. Rule their world.

The nuclear deterrent was incapable of use. Everyone knew that nuclear weapons were only as good as the nuclear weapons your enemy had. You never actually intended to use these insane things, the costs were too great.

The costs to both sides.

They had conventional weapons, these southern states, but there was no way they were going to *en-ma*

sse slaughter the Custodians. There was corruption in the making, the doing of deals to prevent the invading marauding starving Re-Wilded from eating the citizens of their countries. And the human sacrifices that happened in Maya culture were re-commenced, re-industrialised. Virgins offered to Kong. Thousands and thousands of southern hemisphere citizens per day sacrificed to the status quo once the Floaters discovered they didn't have to Dirty Dozen into Floating Homes, once the Floaters learned that their zombie-like lust of terror could be waged on the human survivors of the Evertainment scam known as The Natural Lottery.

That's always the way mankind has done business: deals with his devil.

The northern hemisphere got the chance to re-wild, the buildings of the cities allowed to crumble, the roads leading into and out of the Empire-centres allowed to fracture and crack and dissolve over time, forests encouraged to grow once again, covering all the government grain deserts that had ruined the landscape for six months of every year. The new Gods of Custodian transformation were living among the terrified, the worshippers. The southern hemisphere became a Living Hell for the innocent individuals who had been able to survive thus far on minimum subsistence rations.

There were never enough Floating Homes. It's like when the RMS Titanic went down, there just weren't enough life boats for the screaming passengers to escape via.

Gigantic colossuses soon roam the landscape of the southern hemisphere, literally living tribes of bestial hunger, roaming around, fighting fellow Re-Wilded, making deals with subordinate humans, pro-creating with their own.

And this is what everybody overlooked. Everybody. The things that Asalah Al Faghori's clever DNA tech generated wasn't like the barren mule of commercial breeding. The things that emerged from their rainbow-filament egg-casings were still human. No matter what their physical appearance, the personal traits of their Re-Wilded war paint. It's not like a goat trying to mate with a kitten. It's not something that's unlikely to bond at the gametal level. It's not like chalk trying to taste like cheese. The Re-Wilded were 100% human, and they could inter-breed and re-populate within their own personal herd instinct, their chosen clique.

From altitude, from the protection of your 'floating homes' Diversities, you can gaze in awe as huge swarms and herd and shoals of these amazing creatures tear through a human territory with such utter hunger, such enormous savagery, such ruthless delight. You can see, from this lofty perspective that what's happening below is right and is the way human life should have always been.

A Free Planet is the worst, and the best, thing that could ever have happened to the Human Race.

And besides, not that many Re-Wilded were devout carnivores.

Sure, you get a massive hit from the blood rush, the meat rush, the lust rush of carnivorism but some of the Re-Wilded just couldn't take it, many decided (on their own) that it wasn't right, others were just natural herbivores. It was a cosmopolitan spread of culinary tastes, wants and needs.

The amoeba-like flying Solos and the collective Floating Homes – let's not forget there were swimming and digging versions of these variations too – mostly used a form of photosynthesis to convert solar energy directly into transmutative potential, they'd devolved some of their functions or functionality to enjoy liberation from the chore of physically taking food into a mouth and digesting it and in many cases benefited from extended lifetime.

Swings and roundabouts.

In fact, the war for the southern hemisphere soon fell into a tactical status quo, with the odd sacrificial rite held in honour of the Re-Wilded, to acquiesce the Reborn Gods as shamanism, tribalism, aboriginalism saw them. They understood what had happened even if they didn't understand the patent-derived mechanism that had allowed it to flourish so rapidly across the northern hemisphere.

Many shamans and holy people of tribes that still existed promoted the Re-Wilding as the only way Earth could have gone and implored their 'new gods' to show them the way, allow them to share in this new landscape of opportunity and adventure. Though this never happened. There would always be an us and them. It's just the way humans are, it's the law of competition. But that's not to say the world remained the same.

Even despite the wars, mostly among themselves.

And they were real wars, with real goals – assets and territory. Those of a carnivorous nature and those of a herbivorous nature soon found themselves at opposing ends of the food chain. And the whole Natural Lottery, that had been mostly eradicated from this planet in the name of deforestation and trophy and zoo, was running once again. There were weekly winners, and as with all gambling games there were mostly losers. But using the cliché of Darwinism, those that weren't killed trying to propagate their species, evolved.

Children were born to the Re-Wilded people of planet Earth. Real children who would be brought up now, as then, in carnivorous or herbivorous roaming Diversities, playing the hide-and-seek danger game, living life to the full. As has never happened before on Earth, not since man crawled out of the trees and started building walled cities to protect his weak ass.

In the skies it was no different.

Living in the Floating Homes was a perilous nightmare for some humans, finding themselves assaulted by hordes of winged monsters ripped from the myths and legends of mankind's creativity. These marauding bands would try to down a Floating Home by sheer weight of numbers. And safety was in numbers for both sides. Basically, the bigger and more interconnected the Diversity, the more chance it had of surviving an attack from north or south, from east or west, from above or below. Sure, the molecular formations would buckle and stretch and twist and bend. Sure, there would be repairs to make, there would be scars to heal and ruined FH's to abandon to the Re-Wilded.

And this happened more than anyone wanted, whole Diversities had to shift camp, decamp, flee in their Peanut Taxi escape pods, their DNA-fixated Solos, one at a time, from the steaming pile of bone and blood that their Floating Homes had become, fed upon by those land-eaters, those air-eaters and those who had crawled from under the soil to devour the living meat, the coralised flesh of a Diversity.

It was simple war of survival without the corporate agenda.

And though it was still war, W.A.R., it was better than the slavery and stagnation of The Industry that had, like a festering gangrene, spread itself across and within the very living fabric of Planet Earth, its human conveyancing couriers, the carriers of the virus-cum-reason to live. Such a sallow infection had been healed and 'normality' of a sort had been returned to the Human Equation. The Natural Lottery devoured what it needed to and rested when it was sated. There was harmony once again, but still, it wasn't easy.

This was the southern hemisphere and weapons were still aplenty. Many had been imported from the tactical plethora of American military bases in the now totally Re-Wilded northern hemisphere. How long would it be before some southern hemisphere despot got hold of an Intercontinental Ballistic Missile and launched it into what had been called a Living Hellhole i.e. the northern-most landmass of this once-Prison Planet.

In many way, it was the people of the southern hemisphere, or those who hadn't yet been liberated from their old territorial ways, those who still hung on to their language of conquest, those who still thought barter and bargain were worthy pursuits for their one and only lives. It's obvious to anyone with eyes to see and ears to hear that the rumblings of resistance to the Custodian Liberation were imminent. Why did humans have to war so greedily? Why did humans have to destroy instead of cultivate? Why did humans have to invent lies, fears, paranoias instead of just living a life of Creativity, Passion and Kinship?

33
THE CUSTODIANS
FINITE NUMBER OF SOULS

He had taken a Heckler & Koch HK-4 pistol from an oily brown bag and shot her; once in the face then twice in the stomach, right where her bulge showed how fat the hybrid babies in her womb had grown. Asalah Al Faghori had fallen to the floor, on her side, cradling her unhatched charge with her left wing.

She had asked the obvious question, gasping for breath as her life blood poured out of her in a growing red pool.

Her once-pretty beak hangs open where the bullet had torn away that side of her face, severing facial nerves. She coughs up a choking froth of bright red blood, marbled with a strange white fluid. She coughs and shrieks and wheezes and tries to puke out the hurt, retching ineffectually. Not even a sour pellet of part-digested prey pops out.

You know, birds (even hybrid-human birds) can't really support themselves on their arms, on their wings. Their once-hands are structurally inadequate to support their weight, their elbows no longer up to the task. Too lightweight, to airy. Asalah knows her right wing will be mostly invalid and useless once this is over. Having said that, she is not convinced she will survive this inquisition. So what? She's had a good life. She's lived to the fullest of her potential. Her parents would be proud, her people of the Nile would be proud of her. She can see it now, the river shimmering at the outskirts of Qena which she can still picture with the clarity of youth; some things can't be rubbed out, can't be erased.

In a rising hyper-incredulous Welsh accent, "Why did I do this, Miss Facorry?" Dafyd Atkins, the acting head of ESI at their Oxford patent factory shoots a fourth bullet, right at her face. She flinches automatically, prepared to meet her maker. But the rage and insanity of his aim sends the bullet wide, grazing her on the upper left side of her forehead.

A brief jet of blood dribbles out of her feathery head, spotting the floor.

"Why did I betray all that we've agreed, together, you and I, these last few months of our *unbeatable global game plan*?" his face grows in to a fuming mask of freckled pain, and it looks like he's going to have a heart attack.

"Why did I jeopardise all that we'd put together, all that we'd agreed would happen? All our pre-calculated futures?" he crouches down beside her. Puts his fuming face up close to hers. Adjusts the gun so that the barrel is right under her beak.

"I've seen the CCTV of you and your dog-friend."

Asalah Al Faghori doesn't understand, of course.

"That was my fucking son, you animals!" he spits in her face.

There's a brief moment of realisation on Asalah's face, then.

"Yeah, the truth really hurts, don uht?" he rattles on in his rabid Welsh way, "Imagine that hurt stalking you for years and years as you visually rot in front of your family, as your life is just shattered and no longer worth sustaining. Have you see how much fucking weight I've lost?" he pulls up his jumper showing his soft, round, white, flaccid office belly.

Asalah is busy remembering her first live meal, the shameless meat she shared with Rotimi, her lover, father of her children. How glorious was that virgin moment. A moment of adrenalin-sexual thrill ruffles her feathers, despite her fatal injuries.

He stands back up, punching the air with the gun still in his fist, "I will Shit all over the Custodian Liberation until every last genetic freak among you is Wiped Off The face of this planet, you fucking Animals."

"You say that but nobody cares. You're too late. You think a few guns and a few missiles can combat a Free Planet?" Asalah dribbles blood out of her broken beak.

Atkins stands over her, shaking the gun at her, "You filthy… birdy! Your kind make me Physically Sick. You fucking Traitors! We are Human! Didn't you understand that when you made your decision to Murder and Cannibalise my Son? You're *still* a human, no matter how stupid you look in your feathers and your Stupid Broken Beak," waving his pistol about.

He shifts his feet apart to get the most stable pose. He has plenty more bullets in the HK4's magazine. He takes aim at her. Cradles his other hand round to steady the shot. Asalah's beautiful dark eyes close; ready and willing to accept the inevitable: prepared to 'be at peace'.

Finally.

Dafyd Atkins explodes, right there, on the spot. Like someone had kicked him between the legs with a semtex army boot. A wet splatter momentarily rained down upon Asalah Al Faghori and a pink dust settled within the volume of the room.

"Hennessey?" Asalah coughs up blood, readying herself to produce the longest death soliloquy in Hollywood history.

"Don't speak; we'll get help for you."

"I have to say this. I have to share this with you. In case the world forgets," pain races through her again, as it did when she first tried to explain her thesis, back when she first suicided her old self in the name of the Custodian Liberation.

Hennessey (a fellow hybrid) cradles his dolphin-like strangeness beneath her, moving the boards foundations and the floor and the carpet around her like a crescent nest, "Don't speak, Asalah Al Faghori," he takes her (negligible) weight.

"I have to," she fixes the mid-distance with a manic glare, "Ninety billion souls. That's all we are, Hennessey. A finite number of units shared between all living things. The more human souls there are, the less animal souls there are to go around. The less plant souls there are. This means a starved over-populace, and this is what happened to mankind. This is why we're here."

"I don't need to hear this, Asalah," Hennessey tries to calm her by resting his body against her.

"Hennesey, when a soldier torches a village of children, as part of his orders, does he lose his soul? Well, obviously not, so that leaves two options. There is no punishment for evil for an entity with a single soul; no morals, no guilt, no sin. Or... there are more than one soul in each of us? A soul for each conflicting occasion of our complex lives?" pain flutters through her, but she continues in a delirious state.

"How many souls do each of us have? Three? Fourteen? Fifty? And if we have souls, do animals also have souls? And how many? And how do we categorise our multi-soulness? Is it based on sociability, say? Isn't it obvious that, as a communal race, we feed off each other, so maybe we share a finite number of souls between us all to cover for these 'seemingly immoral moments' we're forced to partake in, or allowed to partake in because of our 'role in life' at that time. And so do the 'other wild animals' we share this planet with," her wing snaps just then, like a thin dry twig, she doesn't even seem to notice that she'll be dead soon, her life ebbing away as she continues on in her sing-song catharsis.

"So we're better off, because as we all share a finite number of 'character souls') there's soully salvation around the corner for what could have been a decaying planetary fauna. But we're not better off, we're not better off at all. Humans having souls – and perhaps sharing them with animals – is not the real problem. The soul itself is the real problem."

"How so?" Hennessey is intrigued.

"We have to look at what a soul is. As stone is dead. A table is dead. Water is dead. It has no soul. But what is the exact definition? Well, it's about the transfer of energy. The soul, in our newly defined form, becomes a system that has the ability to convert zero point energy from one form to another. A living system, if you will.

"Like a plant photosynthesising the sun's energy. Like a wolf digesting an elk. Like an earth processing the radiational energy of the sun through the mantle and atmosphere. This gives us a whole new perspective on what the soul might be. No longer is the soul the 'sole preserve' of humans, but we can now extend that out to other living systems, other pain-feeling systems, other energy converting systems. Even the earth has a soul, as a part of the solar soul entity."

She pauses momentarily, takes in as deep a breath as she can manage.

"And now here's the real earth killer...this...*this* is why we're truly fucked as a planet. Human Technology; you know what I'm talking about, the periodic souls of the water kettle, the petrol car, the digital computer, the nuclear energy plant. All these artificial energy conversion systems, when they're working, act in the same way as organic souls.

"And if there are a finite number of souls, the proliferation of these artificial energy conversion machines are eating up the number of souls accessible to the organic world. What's basically happening is akin to the Borg infiltration of the organic universe. For a star the size of our sun, for a planet the size of our earth, only a certain number of energy conversion systems can be accommodated at any one time. It's like an accounting table. Energy can not be created or destroyed, and as souls are a mechanism of energy conversion, the more likely we are to eradicate not only all other life forms from our once-glorious world but also ourselves."

Hennessey is riveted.

"Think about what Evertainment was. An extension of the human soul, at least it is an extension of or dislocation / bilocation / relocation of human memory. What's the first thing you do when you can't remember the name of that film about a washed-up boxer who makes a comeback and wins the trophy for Adrian? You extend your organic soul into the artificial (or illusory) soulscape that we call Evertainment. That touch of the organic and the artificial could spell the end for all of mankind," she wavers, then. On the edge of life. Literally only a single act of valour away from dissolution. Her eyes clouding over, the eyelids heavy.

"At the intellectual level, the Custodian Dream was perfect," Asalah Al Faghori rallies, a crazy light igniting in her eye as she fights to defend the method and the madness of where her treasonous infiltration of ESI or Eye Sys Industries has led mankind and the members of her cell.

"'No campaign plan survives first contact with the enemy.' Ninteenth century field marshal Helmuth von Moltke the Elder," Hennessey impersonates a history professor.

"It was the right thing to do," a fever shivers through her feathered ruin, her body a shattered remnant of its once-resplendent beauty.

"You sound like the mad Adolfus Hitler," you call from the shattered window.

You've been carried here by the (shadowing) Solo who bonded with your DNA when she first abducted you from the streets of Oxford. She'd opened her 'doors' to revive you just before your late arrival at this death scene.

You're sat upon the distended chair-tongue of this thing, hovering outside the window where Asalah Al Faghori's last moments of fleeing sanity had been witnessed. Asalah on her side in a pool of her own blood, seemingly reconciling her spirit guides, demanding Contrition from her Lord.

You step down, onto the narrow balcony, open the patio doors and enter the pink-dust filled room, coughing dryly as you inhale a lungful of the abrasive air.

A soft rippling movement in the worn boards of the floor, the paint-chipped skirting boards and the under-coated plaster of a nearby wall catches your eye for a split second, but the enigma is quickly forgotten. Evaporates. Disperses.

On the floor lies a mortally-wounded and savagely infected hunter of the skies. Beside her, the gun that spelled her ruin. You're thinking...*Suicide?*

"Why?" you ask.

"Oh, I couldn't take it any more," she coughs dramatically, a wing to her brow. "The world was so close to ushering in a Free Planet. My life's work, I just couldn't stand the pressure. I opted for 'the easy way out'. I had my fingerless wings all the way out there on the other side of the room and shot myself three..."

You realise that the gallows humour is a mask for mortality. You both understand that within sniffing distance, the Re-Wilded will soon find this death-nest and chew to bits whatever they find here. That's the way of Free Planet from now on, the Custodians will always ensure that nothing goes to waste and everything will be returned to fertilise the world so that their children's children can live in peace and be ready for any environmental emergency.

The Free Planeters will be the toughest humans who've ever lived; solemn yet dedicated to the continued cause of liberation from all slavery.

Ruthless killers when they need to be.

Kindest mothers Earth has ever had.

Re-Wilders, re-sourcers, re-finers.

Asalah offers you her bird-dog-cat children, cocooned in their protective egg. She does this in a most spectacular way that spurs your gag reflex into autonomous activity. She can't use her broken beak, so she uses the claws on her feet to open the bullet holes in her belly. First one, then the other.

Asalah gives birth right there, tearing her guts open in the ultimate offering a mother can give to her young; blood spatters her feathery face and her unravelling guts settle where her children would normally find them, feast on them; survive on them. Her head goes back one final time, the eyes cross. The egg that contains her brood, in good condition despite having been shot at from close range with a pistol, bobbles out of the gory disembowelment.

Cradling the fracturing egg of her hybrid children back into the Floating Home of your Adopted Diversity, the first of the Human-Re-Wilded reunion that is makind's only salvation.

MIKE PHILBIN

34
YOU THE PEOPLE
7.8 HZ OR THE SCHUMANN RESONANCE

It's the sound that assaulted you on your first ejection from the mouth of the Abi Chopsticks solo into this shared domestic space, this Floating Home; attached to its Diversity.

It's this constant low-frequency throbbing. This guttural thrumming. This relentlessly hammering sound. It's like your head is about to cave in, or explode – you have yet to decide the graphic special effect that will dispatch with your head. You feel nauseous. You feel ugly. You just feel assaulted.

It's a noise that's being generated deep in the coral structure of these cloud-like floating living spaces, a noise that's made within the hidden (and obscenely mutated) vocal chords of the beast. It comes at you from all angles, day or night. You can't get a fix on it, but it's there, assaulting you, literally hammering you across the skull, every living breathing moment. It's a sound that's produced in such a way that it doesn't appear that air is passing over a vocal chord; you can't put your hands over your ears to shield yourself from the noise.

It's all around you, like the walls and floors and ceiling themselves are bludgeoning you with this resonance, this chorus of out-of-synch frequencies resulting in the earth-centric Schumann Resonance.

In a time before the Natural Lottery, when people had instant access to Prison Planet Evertainment, you could just ThinkTiVate™ search terms like "binaural beats" or "Schumann resonance" and you'd be given the answer. You couldn't trust the answer. You couldln't trust any answer Evertainment provided because you had no idea of the agenda any item of information might be masking, adding to, convoluting. You weren't in the Need To Know loop, you were sequestered, compartmentalised off into your level of knowledge cell. And that's not a lot. But yeah, you could get an answer to 'any question', you might even be given a sample of what the answer to the question might sound like. On headphones, you could experience the crack of lightning rattling around inside earth's atmosphere that produces the 7.8 hz noise, this Schumann Resonance.

But you don't have such luxury as Evertainment here.

It appears to be a truly devolved world.

And everything you once knew just stinks like old joss sticks or worse, faeces.

This place literally stinks. It's ripe. Over-powering. Distorted and disorienting in a truly alien fashion. It's like the entire structure is festering, from within. You feel physically sick all the time. You don't yet have your Sky Legs. Every time the Floating Home you're being held in encounters an air pocket, turbulence or changes its attitude in that disorientingly off-centred way, your stomach rises bitterly into your mouth. You're Floating Home is part of a Diversity with many such units attached to each other in various carbonic permutations of Organic Chemistry and such linking configurations.

You're there a couple of days before you forget the constant noise, it becomes like…remember normal passenger airlines, how they used to hum when they flew? How the passenger cabin used to buzz like a bee? It was insane and deafening when you first encountered it, right? But you got used to it. The brain 'filtered it out' over time. Well, same thing happens here. Except what the brain doesn't do is 'filter anything out'. It just feels that way. What's actually happening is any noise or interference in the electromagnetic spectrum is attuned to, thus nullifying it. You start to resonate at that frequency and you don't notice it any more. It's a part of you, sort of.

And it's that following day, when you wake up in some salvaged bed from the late twentieth century, some wooden affair that creaks and groans all night when you toss and turn in bed, you lie there and something flickers at the corner of your eye.

Something catches your eye; you don't know if it's intentional or not, but your attention is grabbed.

You get out of bed and go to the kitchen area where raw food is being prepared for the morning meal. Raw food is the new microwaved, by the way. All naturally sourced, properly organic. Trust me, you don't wanna know, yet. But you will, as they all know, eventually. They all find out where their food really comes from, these prisoners; these salvaged humans.

No, let's forget that the inhabitants of these Floating Homes are prisoners for a moment, that's a negative interpretation of something that's actually very positive, in fact it's so positive as to have been the only way it could have gone. No one in their right mind would have willingly volunteered for a life-saving race-saving mission such as this in a pilotless coral factory in the sky. Maybe one or two idiots, but not in enough numbers to make it viable, to ensure the longevity of man kind and Free Planet. So, a few hundred thousand humans were stolen for their own safety, to protect them from the horrors that were taking place below on the Re-Wilded planet. Mankind was always at a disadvantage in the Natural Lottery, where ruthlessness and brutality were the way all cookies crumbled.

You pick up a scraped carrot and bite down on it. It gives a satisfying crunch. Tastes authentic, like a carrot should taste. But you're too enthralled by the external wall to even have noticed if the carrot had been propped up in a dog turd prior to your eating of it.

Not the view of the rolling cloud formations and your Free Planet neighbours attached alongside you as far as the eye can see. Glorious as that is, that's not what's making half-chewed raw carrot fall from your gaping mouth. There's a flickering in the external wall, like it keeps shifting from fully transparent to vaguely opaque. But not in a misty or uniform fashion, we're not talking about condensation here. We're talking about images, pictures. And in your head, voices. You hear children laughing. You see through time and space to other connected Diversities.

"It takes a few days for your brain to ignore it, doesn't it?" Bless You offers you a bowl of porridge. Oats cooked in water, salt added.

You'd like to be shocked to see her, but actually you're not. You take the bowl from her and tuck in, as the wall continues to play its broadcast. The porridge tastes gorgeous, like a nutty flavour you've never noticed before.

"What's the spice?" you ask her, unsure why you've accepted her 'survival' so easily.

She laughs, looks around at her co-guests, "All in good time," she says.

All in good time? What does that mean?

"No, it's very nice," you take another spoonful, "Tasty porridge."

"It's not 'porridge'. But anyway, the view, isn't it spectacular?"

"Can't you see the pictures, hear the voices?" you ask her.

"That's what I mean, dummkopf. It's The Schumann Connection. Luckily for you, I've done quite a bit of research into these connected entities, these floating homes made from the copulating juices of a dozen, and only a dozen, complimentary genetic units."

The Diversity sways on its non-centred axis and you stagger to your left. The milky wetness of your gruel spills out of its bowl onto the floor. You don't feel well. Bless You guides you back to a place where you can sit down. This woman who brought you food to eat. This beauty you'd not seen in the two days you'd been here. Acclimatising. Getting used to.

"NMS it's called,"

"What?" you frown.

"*No. More. Secrets.* It's all part of the whole Free Planet story: no secrets, no subterfuge, no espionage mindset. These homes that we're fortunate to live in now..." she raises her hands up towards the ceiling like she a religious nut in praise of a levitating god, "...they have a pact among themselves and their inhabitants of *No More Secrets* to deal with the fact that there are No More Countries and No More Rules and No More Regulations laid down by a single umbrella operation once known as the New World Order. Its been deemed the best way to vet any new additions to The Family; any New Inmates. *No More Secrets*, get it?"

"That's a lot of Proper Nouns there," you joke, or try to.

"We like truth, in Diversity. The pictures you're seeing and the voices you're hearing – they're insights into the occupants, they're like the living memories or whoever is aboard this one Diversitiy at any one time. You can go up to them and rewind, replay, re-edit, to your heart's content. There's nothing that's secret from anyone here. We all know already what you are and what you've been up to in your life. We know this and, so far, we all accept it."

The living spaces aren't separate, there are shared walls that pull back to open up the space, there are certain space that are able to be lifted up to create spaces so vast. You'll agree with me that they're like Cathedrals in the Sky. You don't like the religious terms being used. You wonder if this is a Mormon or Muslim Diversity.

"Neither," she has her hand on the external wall, "Come on over here," she instructs you.

You put the bowl down on the floor, and unsteadily make your way over to her.

"Put your hand right on here," she shows you where to place your hand, palm facing forward. You do so and aren't prepared for what happens.

You are no longer standing in one space, with your hand on a wall, you occupy someone else's physical and cerebral space. All your limbs feel wrong. All your thoughts feel wrong. In fact, they are wrong, in that they're the attributes of somebody else, someone who's not you. NMS is about to show you why the Floating Homes go black every now and then, seem to shut down; sleep.

"Don't!" Bless You shouts.

But it's too late, you've panicked and pulled your hand free. The snap-back into your own body/mind is too great. You can't compute. Your brain is too conflicted. You spasm unnaturally, your legs buckle and puke pours out of your mouth the colour of the gruel you've just eaten as you're falling face down into the wall, the skin of your face smearing as you slide down it. On the floor, your body convulses softly like you're having an epileptic fit. This spell doesn't last for long.

You awaken in the arms of this woman.

"April. You want to know my name," you see that she has her hand on the wall, she's prying into your mind, "You have so many questions. When you get used to our Diversity, you won't need to ask any more, as the answers are already there."

"Like Evertainment," you summarise.

"Don't you dare blaspheme in this place," she lets your head drop to the floor and bounces up onto her feet.

You reach out to her as she is darting away to leave you, you heathen, to your sin. You have an idea and drag yourself to the nearest wall. You put your hand out, palm forward, "I'm sorry," you try to picture the woman, April.

You now understand that everyone in your Diversity, all the occupants of all the connected Floating Homes, (Cumulo did she call it?) can hear and see and touch and taste this panicked connection. You see them all pretending not to hear, backburnering it until some red flag emotional spike comes to kill the curious.

"I know you're sorry," comes back the instant response, like you were already inside her head. While you're connected, she adds, "Come and find me, when you're feeling stronger, and I'll show you how this place works and why we're totally self-sufficient. Free to be wherever we want to in the world. Free to enjoy any diversion that takes our fancy. Free to exist, finally. For the first time in mankind's modern history. Free of the empire. Free of slavery. Free of debt and taxes and sanctions and maintenance. This truly is a wonderful place, even though I'm sure it doesn't yet feel so. You being a prisoner here like all the rest of us. But it's not only for our own good, it's for the good of the planet and the lives below that still have to regain control of a delicate homeworld, there's still a future to seed. There's still a Free Planet to awaken, and it'll take time."

You think you've heard that sort of spiel before, you're reminded of Asalah Al Faghori, another idealist you once met, ever so briefly, on the two occasions which ultimately led to her death.

"When you're ready, come to me, bring your hybrid children with you." the connection is (abruptly) broken by the second party. You've yet to learn that.

* * *

If you were looking down upon Earth from space, you would see that it hasn't really changed that much. It's maybe a little greener where grey cities have rotted to their foundations and clear-cutting has stopped, allowing stunning regrowth of the flora of the planet.

It wouldn't look that much different than it did before The Custodian Liberation tried, in vain, to break the rules of the game of the global elite.

It was fundamentally changed though, and everyone knew that.

35
THE CUSTODIANS
UP YOUR FUCKING BORSTAL

"I hate you! I hate what we do, in the name of profit!" she snarls into the camera. In corporate infiltrations such as these, there's always a single eye, a living lens turned, a paid cameraman to capture the Money Shot that'll seal the deal and activate the Dead Peasant Insurance software.

For every covert action, there's an equal and opposite contractual obligation.

The Mommy had always realised her girl would be the weak-point of her defence strategy should she want to extricate herself from The Industry one day. But nobody expects the Inquisition to cast its eye upon one. She'd known all about the mechanism of threat and retribution, she'd been a key player in The Industry for long enough. These were the tools of her dreadful trade, and she'd used them to her distinct advantage. She blithely thought, desperately hoped, that such would never be visited upon her, or if it did that they would spare her child.

She knew all along, in her heart of hearts, that this is how the rungs of her particular career ladder would shatter under her, just when she thought she'd made it to the Penthouse or the Treehouse. She had no idea what they'd done with her child, what they might be doing to her right now, on camera – those fucking bastards.

"Come on, Mommy," screams one voice, spitting filth all over her face, bringing her back out of semi-consciousness, back to the real world.

"Come on, Teacher," another voice, "I'm sure we all understand the legal term Double Indemnity Insurance," they all had a good laugh at that, because they were a funny lot, these fuckers, these torturing bastards.

Five pairs of human hands had taken it in turns to perform CPR or Cardio Pulmonary Resuscitation on the chest of Erotica, on the chest of The Mommy, on the chest of Teacher, on the chest of God Knows How Many Other Aliases, how many other Cover I.D.s, how many other lied-about lives.

Boisterous laughter and boyish jostlings for position in the rut take place somewhere nearby. Eager dribbles of spit and semen sputter down upon her exposed breasts like exhaust from a dying engine. A dirty football crowd, a baying pack, a lads night out; movement in the the dank and rancid shadows.

Don't look there, you won't like what you see.

The image will be too upsetting, too confusing for you.

Even a flashing glimpse of the Flocker's roiling silhouette will be sufficient to assail your delicate sensibilities, chill your spine and curdle your blood. This is something you shouldn't remember. You may look, if you're brave or foolish, but you must forget this ever happened. That'll be your only salvation, that the Flockers don't come looking for you.

Fragile pathetic human scum.

This had been the umpteenth time Erotica aka The Mommy aka Blahblahblah had passed out from her trial by the baying pack of Flockers. She didn't even feel the cold cobblestones grinding into her back any more. She had gone through too much already, and her interrogation hadn't even really begun yet.

This mob called themselves *The Borstal Boys* in honour of that film their leader saw when he was a kid. They'd been snooker-ball socking each other and *I'm-the-daddying* each other for what might have been hours, these dumb fucks, these thugs. They had this derivative *i.e. stolen* script they all seemed to have learned by rote. It was like a test of initiation – you had to play the game properly, or you weren't allowed into the foreground. You could stay back there where the guts rotted like cabbage farts and the brain dribbled like bloody snot from a bitten off nose.

"But, sir, I barely touched the cunt," they'd complain camply as several of the Mommy's bones jutted out of her flesh like living fresh-grown razor blades, unsheathed white swords catching the light pouring from a nearby street lamp. They always worked, like this, in piss-stinking alleyways; always by the jaundiced illumination of a street lamp. It just adds to their mythos, their *scandale*.

"Fuck off with the *sir*, you sucknuts; what's that then, eh?" one of them rises to prominence in the glaring pit of the foreground like an engorged phallus rising up into your face. He's pointing this strange arm at the shin bones of Erotica aka The Mommy sticking out of her skin like at nasty accident, blood pouring out of the brand new hole, the gorgeous gaping cuntbone to be. "What the fuck's that, lad?"

Another voice, unsheathing like AIDS, "Who the fuck! Own up!" and it's like Mommy's going to faint again, you can see it in her sluggishly rolling eyeballs.

"She slipped, sir," some other cunt offers from the growling back ranks.

Uproarious laughter, then a crazy-mad frenzy of Top Dogishness ass-fistery and head-butting, someone's ear gets bitten off and a yelping sound makes ya think of dog fights in pits dug in the damp ground. *Get him, lad, bite his fucking throat out. Go on, lad. Go on, my son.* You couldn't even hear yourself scream, such was the din.

They were always doing this. They always lied. To each other. To themselves. Especially to themselves. Denial was better than truth. Better than the real things they do to get by, to stay alive, to get near enough to lick the arse of Top Dog and be one of his Rutters Supreme. You don't wanna get on the wrong side of any one of them, no-fucking-sir. But then you don't wanna come across as a suck-dick, on your knees, yes-man; that was a recipe for disaster in any clique.

They bickered constantly.

That's how they bonded, bloodied knuckle and swollen eye socket.

There was a funny smell to Flockers, a collective rutting nausea. But (much worse than that) there was a distinctive and unique stink as each hard-nut reprobate of the Flocker Crew put himself forward as periodic pack leader. A stink of tobacco. A reek of beer. A stench of piss. Bowels. Old Spice. High Karate after shave. The wintergreen tang of the rugby changing room. The exhalation of a coffee drinker right in your fucking face, because you're nothing more than a piece of crap under a shoe. The ruminant pungency of cum in soiled crusties that have never been washed.

They communicated by a series of head-buts, knee'd groins, snooker-balled sock attacks, in your face spitting contests, nasty sly backstabbing auto-erotic group action on the less tooled up members of their Flock. They were a proper nasty bunch of back-shafting shirt-lifting bastards, all of them male; I mean, who wants a woman around giving orders and thinking she's

Margaret Fucking Thatcher all over your fun and games, your Free Planet japes.

How did any of them retain any sense of personal identity?

A brief history lesson will aid your confusion. When the Natural Lottery poured its message of human benediction into the Evertainment grid, when the patents were flouted for microsecond transactional rape, when the systems that had ruled the Royal European Empires for centuries suddenly ground to a rubber-burning, metal-shrieking halt, distinct clans erupted through the human genome. Eggs grew in rotting dorms and these were the fucked up results.

All the determined, competitive, arrogant bullies became the Re-Wilded.

All the thinkers became the Solos.

All the needy gathered together to protect mankind within the 'floating bosom' of their mobile Floating Homes.

All the docile, non aggressive, humble, bullied, shat upon, downgraded, ass-suckers like you, me and all our broken brothers and sisters, became the Flockers; the lawless posse of lusting under-achievers whose sole aim is now to ruthlessly protect the one rule *Do Right By Free Planet*.

The Flockers were really the 'forgot to grow up' foetal stem-cell fixated members of the great global Custodian manifestation. Why decide to be a Solo or a Floating Home or a Re-Wilded when you could exist in this constant flux of possibilities, fighting like a cancer for the most exotic solutions to the common problems of the day? Why not revel in your once-in-a-species moment of bio-genetic glory? Why not really rip some ass, and get some well-earned payback for wrongs done to your race or in your name. Flocker mentality meant no boundaries to human creativity, neither moral nor legal; anything goes.

The Mommy was in a bit of a state. They'd roughed her up something rotten, sir, yes they had. She'd slipped and slipped and slipped and slipped in the virtual shower their sick and vicious communal minds occupied, bars of soap forever at the ready.

She couldn't talk, not because she had all her teeth snooker-ball socked to shrapnel but because of something much more insidious, something much more worthy. They'd taken it in turns on her, all relentlessly contributed to her current state facial disfigurement, every kiss they placed on her angry snarling mouth made one more tooth root grow out through her maxilla and her mandible, her gums and her lips, like bleeding tusks on a stuck boar.

The touch of a Flocker is closer than anyone's ever touched you. Deeper than fisting. Harder than a clitoral climax. More long lasting than multiple womb shuddering contractions. They had touched her all over, and she had not liked it. Not one little bit.

Boners: that was where they touched her – in her fucking *boners*. It was the way their sick, illiterate MK Ultra'd minds worked, broken words, broken deeds.

They touched her in the boners – in the physical architecture underpinning her humanity, her translation of sexual longevity into the visual realm.

You know, it causes unbelievable pain to redirect a tooth root to some other spacio-dimensional location. You can actually watch a scythe of pain pour out of the victim's face like a molten rainbow, each microscopic move of the rebelling toothroot like a million diamond-encrusted needles slowly searing through flesh that (because the kiss from a Flocker is so fucking weird, genetically) keeps growing back with each fresh wound just like Prometheus's liver.

"You knew. Don't embarrass us with a denial."

A sheath of writhing communal foreskin writhes back to reveal, not a head or penile glans, but one more of their zombie-like lust tribe, another full human torso in the Biogenetic Centipede that is so much more than a single line of connected insect segments. A centaur, right, get that in your head. It's a human torso placed on a horse's body. Right, that's in your head. Now, imagine the human torso on top of the horse torso slitting down the back and another human torso flowing out, each time gouts of blood dribble down onto the thighs and hooves of the centaur.

But this is not a centaur, it's more like a writhing slither of snake after snake wriggling and sliding over each other in a rutting lust, each part of the nest trying to reach up higher onto its vanquished, dominating the sleaze pack. But there's something missing, it's all too 'smooth' the image needs a rough edge – imagine a tree that's fallen over in a storm. Its branches are all dirty and shattered and wretched but it can still move them, they still heal. It roots can crawl about wetly, scuttle all over the moss-covered surface of the bark, legs can carry this fallen tree everywhere it wants.

Now, imagine all those competing images combined. And understand that each side of the living organism has its own personality, and soon, these conglomerated colossuses will learn to incorporate support structures into their army of lust and then giants will roam the earth once more, enormous living structures underpinned by core columns from teetering skyscrapers or held together by wires from crumbling suspension bridges rotted from lack of maintenance.

We're talking giants, but that's not happened yet, the Earth doesn't have to deal with that – yet.

"Erotica can't speak, can you love? Stop fucking taunting her, will you? And get your mouth off my fucking cock," it was The Monster; you remember him, don't you? They'd brought him forward, through the de-sheathing process of puss and veins and ball sack, expelled him from the roiling mass of bone and flesh speckled with the occasional rip of vein or burst of eyeball.

As far as the Flocker mass was concerned, the Monster had been assimilated into the engine a couple days ago as fuel for the anger of these insanely wronged employees who used to infest his cubicle with their petty demands for decent working conditions, agreed schedules and no team pizza i.e. paid overtime. They didn't even suspect that he might have been a plant, a covert agent, or even that he might have volunteered for such a 'obvious suicide mission'. Once they'd tortured the sleazy confession of his Corporate Life Story from him, this was the first place they'd arrived at; the secret location no one knew about.

'Monster loves Teacher,' 'Monsty luvz teachy," and other such crap rose from the aroused mob, and at that point, Monster, as dumb a corporate fuck as he had been, finally realised that this would be his end. This was going to fucking hurt. He knew this as sure as eggs is eggs.

After all, these were the monsters The Monster himself had created via Corporate Buggery in Dusseldorf and Oxford, and it looks like they were about to make their once-fist-master the

Master Bater of his middle manager, aka Erotica aka The Mommy aka Miss Twisted Inside Out and tortured with the rippling bones and nerves of her own pustular, eviscerated body to be.

What ensues is a long protracted torture scene involving shoving The Monster's face into the living shattered bottle of Erotica's shuddering vagina, a sing-song massacre of manhood for all their chuckling entertainment. Retribution, grim and dismal as it always tends to be, when the gloves are off, when those who are allowed to pass judgement are given free rein. Bar Teacher, bar the Monster, a whole lot of creative fun was had – ghosts were exorcised, demons laid to rest.

And that's what Free Planet offers them, these tortured souls, the right to protect and serve that thing they need the most, the Mother Earth upon which we all live. They will be the police, and sad as it is to say, there was no one else worthy of the roll than the under-privileged, the down-trodden, the abused and used of Corporate Duty. The underdogs bite back.

The way they see it, any attack on Asalah Al Fargohri or the members of The Custodian Liberation is an attack on Free Planet. Especially at this stage, where she's carrying the first hybrid babies to be born to the new world.

"When we thought we were barren, we may have opted for near-immortality as Diversities. But this, this gift, we must protect," that's what these centipede zombie conglomerations of once-humanity are mostly thinking, that's their driving mantra, their *raison d'etre*. Protect Free Planet from all assault, actual or implied. Never, in the history of humanity, had there been such a ruthless punisher, such rough justice.

At that moment, the girl rushes in screaming, "Mommy, Mommy!" and throws herself into her mum's embrace. Cuts herself instantly on a razor sharp tusk. She screams as a quick spurt of blood dots her soiled white summer dress. She pulls herself free of her Mommy's barbed wire situation, all the bones and nails and teeth and nerves of her spilling out all over her body. It's amazing the girl wasn't more damaged by her impromptu hug with Mommy.

"Mommy?" the girl succeeds in pulling her Mommy from whichever Hell her broken mind is residing in.

"Hi, sweet peaches," Mommy says through a disaster of a mouth, the words like wriggling worms on fish hooks.

And only then does the girl see the living horror that is a centipede in full arousal. She screams like no one's ever screamed before. Her mommy pulls her close, despite the cutting pain and razor sharpness of such a protective act.

Five or six pairs of hands pry the screaming girl loose of mommy's embrace. One of them touches the mommy's pubic bone and a slithering, curling, narwal-like tusk grows from the bone and cartilage like a curving sword refined by super-fine living vines as sharp as any laser. The hands of the living mound of torture grip the thin arms of the girl and present her to the horror that has become her mommy.

And you know they're gonna fucking film it. You know they're going to show the world the evidence of who tried to kill their Free Planet.

36
YOU THE PEOPLE
NO PLACE TO HIDE

Having said earlier that you're not likley to recognise one of the Global Elite were you to meet them in the street, you can bet your life you already know one.

They'll have run their own mortuary services company, they'll have been a charity worker, a donator of excess profit to a string of charities. They'll have come by money somehow, made their way. They may even be your friend, they may have married into your family. You'll know them, they'll have appeared on Evertainment every now and then to bathe in the limelight of their charitable or informational deeds for humanity, as they saw them. They love the adulation and they especially love the winning of the game.

Sure, many of them won't have been so cavalier, they'll have quietly got on with their lives pouring vast amounts of acquired family wealth into hair-brained super-longevity programmes, sat in their off-shore castles somewhere they can't be found, somewhere that may not even be mapped.

You all know that Area 51 in the Nevada Nuclear Test Range, where many B-52 and Stealth Bomber prototyping was done, wasn't actually on any Ordnance Survey maps until very recently? Of course you don't, you slaves of Evertainment, that's not the sort of thing they'd tell you; not the sort of thing a global consumer needs to worry their pretty little head with.

But it's the truth.

Your common or garden elite – you know game player – real world ruler. The sort of guy who suggests what continents to raid, what economies to trash, what presidents to off, he's probably someone you know already.

He'll have been some star of Evertainment, like a disc jockey, like a disinformation legend, we're not talking about the government shills here who will have shat out the party tripe on command, the Brzezinskis and the Kissingers of the global kissy-kissy game for favourable backscratchings and borrowings of global power for a few relevant microseconds of need.

Nah, your real Elite will have been a documenter of the Chaaange from corporate Global Gulag to Free Planet. Yeah, as insane as this may sound, you'll have probably been goaded into setting up a Free Planet with such a person's help.

And he'll have put loads of money into the effort too, and just to make it even more believable, he'll have had You The People continuously donate to his cause so that he could continue to deliver the psychological manipulation that would have encouraged those with a Georgia Guidestones bent to have pledged their DNA to the Custodian Liberation across those four nights of the Natural Lottery.

Why?

Because, even though they don't really share who they are with any old wage-slaves, they do like to rub it in your faces, the power of influence on a global scale that they can wield.

They're self-centred, sure, but their motives are purely of a 'breeding' nature – they want the right people with them on their planet – the rest, it's just human zoo.

Even with all the so-called freedom and liberation of this new world, even with all the Creativity, the Passion and the Kinship of what has already happened to mankind; the Re-Wilded, the freeing of the patents into family hands, the floating homes isolation of the human race while the planet replenishes herself; can't you all see that it was a perfect set up from day one?

Some of them will have even been shepherds in the Custodian Liberation, they'll have been the public figures of dissent on a punisher world of corporate finance that seem to have been able to reveal any secret files to the world and not been hauled into jail for an instant fisting up top or down under. They'll seem to have skirted with the law, been threatened by the Police State, maybe they'll even have been arrested every now and then to give the appearance they were One Of The Resistance.

What better way to stay hidden than to be right out there, in the public eye, seemingly fighting for the good guy, embodying the values of Creativity, Passion and Kinship to an ambivalent audience keen only to save themselves the bother of thinking in a Consumerist Psyche-scape.

But the important thing here is audience.

They'll have gathered a certain survivalist audience around their revelations of a G3H or *Global Government Gone Haywire.*

You'll remember the shows. They'll have been informing you of how to get into gold. How to close your bank accounts. How to stock up on survival foods. How to get yourselves prep-d, locked and loaded for the Civil War to come. How to hunt, how to fish, how to enjoy nature. They'll have been the Best Friend of certain partially-eye-opened Corporate Drones who laughed among themselves at the tin-foil-hat agents spilling their crap all over the Evertainment grid, not knowing that all the 'crap projected as facts' for their stuntified minds were the real fiction.

It don't matter what you hear, just how you hear it, might have been one of their catch-phrases. You'll know them. If they did what they should have done, to have framed their own kind to their own standard of survival, then you'll have been one of them. Yes, you, in your ordinary mind, there, reading this thinking, *I'm not some global elite scum!* it's probably true that, if you survived somehow the routing of mankind to Re-Wilded state, if you're in some sort of floating home right now, if you're on your own island right now, enjoying the extra space and the enriched bounty of a revitalised world, you're probably there as a result of one of the global elite's media army having schooled you in the way to escape your waged prison cell.

Your common or garden Global Elite, as they still are, would not be brought down by some sort of amateurish Free Planet effort. Such an unprofessional scam wouldn't get to first base without the concerted input from the Masters Of Strategy. And it really is dog eat dog, for control of the human race, for ownership of Free Planet.

They'll live near money. Near gold. Near oil. Their families will have had involvement with The Military, why do you think all the Royals are forced through military training even though they're rarely put in danger on the front lines. Rarely, unless they're being taught a lesson, as was Prince Andrew during the Falklands invasion. Punishment and reward works at all levels of the social pyramid. Never forget that.

And that's how it is with this particular Global Elite who thinks he's been uber-wise, thinks his decades of dried meals and canned goods and water purification machines run by solar power and filtered using all the latest easy-to-generate minerals from the sand whereby he lives, thinks he can just expand his clan into the grounds of his protected property. It'll probably be some ranch, somewhere, out in the American wilderness, away from the cities, separate from society. That's how it is with these elite types, these global survivalists.

Or it might be right on the outskirts of your dustbowl town.

Remember *Dallas*, the TV show about the Texas Oil Men – that's what it'll be like; several generations of elite family members will live in the same residence, wherever that may be. The grannies, the grandads, the family and the kids. And this guy, the guy who maintains his slice, thus far, of the global pie, will have seemed so virtuous, not religious, but pious and personable. He'll have raged with evangelical anger when he needed to. He'll have shared his sorrow with his public when the 9/11 or Utoya missions tugged at your heart strings. He'll have been a news reader, maybe. A disc jockey. Or some sort of Evertainment Public Speaker, a chat show interviewer, a Topic Of The Day sorta guy. He'll have had his Elite Friends on the show, for shits and giggles, dispersing the disinformation among the true details of the Globalist Chess Game.

It will have been right before your eyes, right under your nose, and you'll have never suspected.

"Him?" you'll have sneered, "Nah, he would never be *One of Them*. He's a good guy. I love his whistelblower show," that's what you'll have said about him. That will have been your reaction.

Well, watch his reaction now as he shoots up his home with his collection of guns 'n' ammo.

"Fill me up another gun, Jay-junior," he'll be informing his younger son, while his elder son has his back, shooting up anything that moves as the Octopus moves in.

The Octopus hunts down members of Octopus; how ironic. But we'll see real soon the details of this claim. We'll understand real soon why those we though were our friends in the fight for Liberty, Truth and Full Spectrum Information were really our jailers, our daddy.

"Keep shooting, Ronald," he'll say as they both back off to the bank vault-like Safe Room they'd installed in this walled residence way back when the threat of nuclear conflagration was uppermost in the minds of the mass media, back to a time when the press was convincing You The People that a school desk, as long as you were under it, could protect you from All Out Nuclear Conflict.

In those more primitive, more innocent times, when you were just as gullible as you all are today when Evertainment propaganda is enhanced with viral marketing pharmaceuticals pumped down your personal datahole gullet. You can do nothing but believe, but that's been Humanities Achilles Heel since long before the Aztecs were tearing out thousands upon thousands of human hearts to help the crops grow this year in the elaborate cities of Teotihuacan. You know, before the Spaniards came with their viruses and microbes and their armour and muskets.

Even among the so-called global elite game players there'll be an implicit 'need to know' mechanism that masks off certain tactical areas from prying game minds. Put it this way, just because you 'think' you know all the moves that have ever happened on the global chess board, just because you're an advocate of 'those who don't follow history are doomed to repeat it,' just because you'll have studied all the rulebooks of engagement with the enemy, doesn't mean you'll have knowledge of the exact form of move that will be employed. You can only exist within your own particular flavour of existence; and there are many flavours of existence: many ways for life to just seem 'too darned strange'.

Take this family, this isolated remnant of the global elite who thought they might be safe from all insurgency, safe from all the stress and strain of a Re-Wilded world, free to do as they please as they had done since first footfall on American shores, shooting up their own property as something they can't comprehend seems to want to take what's rightly theirs and murder what's not meant to be murdered. They've been betrayed by their own, and they will fight to the death.

A door explodes, and this global elite parent shouts to his daddy, "Did you get granpappy and grammy into the Safe Room?"

There'll be a kitchen between them, for cinematic purposes. And the camera will be running at at a phenomenal frame rate, to show the explosion effects of a poltergeisting whirlwind smashing up the place, causing black and white tiles to explode from the floor, causing fridges, freezers, cookers, microwave ovens, plasma TVs, fitted cupboards, marble work surfaces to shatter into tonnes of shrapnel with no visible source for the destruction.

"Get your ass into the Safe Room, son," his daddy will order him, and he'll obey, "Go through the pool room."

And through the pool room, this once-rotund now-cut athlete of global survival will battle through the pool room as gallons of water assault him from all sides, as stolen floor tiles from Cretan ruins explode under his feet, his children shouting and screaming beside him, "Hurry up, daddy! We're nearly there!" and no one will see the shadowy black shape with a bulbous human head shimmering through the roiling surface of the pool, tonnes of backwash rolling ashore like an Asian tsunami.

No one notices that they're being herded.

They didn't see it when they paid their taxes.

They didn't see it when they took their vaccines.

They didn't see it when they thought they were right in supporting a *Corporate Global Gulag* with their blood, sweat and tears.

There comes a time when even the most intelligent among us can fall foul to a clever bit of herding, in the name of global compliance.

And this family of global elites, these major game players on the stage of Human Consumerism are being herded. Their conviction in the shelter their Safe Room will offer them, able to withstand Nuclear Holocaust, will protect them in this dire situation, this assault on their precinct, their castle.

All eight members of the family, are protected now, ensconced within the steel-reinforced concrete and lead-impregnated walls of their underground base. They gather in the chapel, for even here God is their guide and their succor. The father, his wife, their two sons and daughter, the father's dad and mum and the granny on the mum's side; the classic combination of three-and-one one-and-three. All kneel in a semi-circle facing the elaborate altar they'd had installed, down here, in Sanctuary.

"Dear God," their family prayer begins. The father, the son and the holy ghost are all present, except the real Holy Ghost in this tableau is a hybrid-human like Hennessey. Remember Hennessey, the strange dolphin-like peregrin-falcon decorated beast of electromagnetic impossibility? Well, since then, other such Hennesseys have grown, been born, come into existence. This one, as we've mentioned earlier, would look like a human headed octopus, could it be (somehow) liberated from its incarceration in the solid matter of the architectural world.

Now, as the family bow their heads in solemn prayer, tears down cheeks, the octopus takes command of the floorboards and the marble and the rock beneath their knees, and slowly, before anyone can really notice what's happened, he's curled his tentacles around them all.

On global link up via the capturing Re-Wilded, people will try to hurt them. People who weren't party to the ins and outs of the global game will try to extort some sort of retribution from these abstracted human filth that used to enslave the world. But they have to be shown that these elites, these living horrors of a New World Order that was abated, are excellent fathers and mothers, they have to be seen as loving husbands and wives, as essential parts of a shared future for Free Planet.

Who they've always been, for millennia – pity them their closeted existence, their lack of unity with the global collective. Pity their ambition, their loyalties, their lack of shame.

These monsters (these genius tacticians) must be left to fester in their own worlds of self-inflicted isolation, their castles and caverns, their own names Diversities of rock and cave and island. But they must be held periodically accountable to the other ninety billion souls within their universal sphere. They must be part of the transformation from slave to sovereign.

Resistance is futile, would be the classical Hollywood cliché of what's happened here. The Free Planet equivalent, no less corny or contrived would be, n*o place to hide, everyone is a part of the whole.*

But there'll always be exceptions to every rule.

MIKE PHILBIN

37
THE CUSTODIANS
WE BORROW IT FROM OUR CHILDREN

All around the northern hemisphere, in fact as far south as the Tropic of Capricorn in some continents, Diversities of all sorts of colour coordination are landing on rock, embedding themselves into protective formations, the circling of wagons that used to happen in Wild West times now protects their human charge from the slavering onslaught of the Re-Wilded world.

Each of the Diversities conjoined with as many of their fellow Diversities as they could summon at such short notice, great swathes of human homing arranged on the the floor, like complex living hydrocarbons. Within, their hands placed on retinal walls, their eyes and minds shared with the world, the captives of these living refuges; these lifeboats in the disaster.

Simultaneously, across the globe, the tribal resonance of each Diversity connects with the living rock of the planet and a single tone begins to form. If you were outside, you could hear it, but you'd have no interface to the rest of the sensory experience. You'd just suppose a very mild, very sustained earthquake was happening in all places.

All around the world, families are at one with their floating homes, conjoined within the hearts and minds of the global broadcast.

All around the world, those elite families who thought they'd got the Monkey of Humanity off their collective/isolated backs, are forced by their entrapment in the concrete and wood and steel and marble and porcelain and glass of the architectural world to listen.

All around the world, the Re-Wilded look up from their Natural Lottery of who dares wins, sniff the air, send up hackles and cackles.

"Ladies and Gentlemen, survivors of Free Planet," some voice emanates from all points of the compass, a living sound that might be the combined Creativity, Passion and Kinship of thousands of Diversities speaking as one, "Welcome to our once-Global Overlords. Glad you could join us. Sorry that there was no escape from reality for you and your lineage," the announcement continues, "We're gathered here today to celebrate the birth of the first Free Planet Institute Of Creativity, Passion And Kinship, to help those who have questions or want to send their kids to school, learn new survival skills and educate their families protected in Floating Homes."

And the voice, it is a vaguely female voice though it has that quality of *eunuchness* that some sound labs are able to produce by time-blending several people reading from the same script, edited together, compressed, stretched or otherwise folded into a single tone real, live, and at that moment. Imagine what sort of power the minds who could make you think like that had, the power of the Glimpsers, the power of the Custodians, the power of You The People.

And everyone sees the next bit, everyone shares the moment, experiences the pain and the suffering and the heartfelt joy of the birth of the first Free Planet Institute Of Creativity, Passion And Kinship.

Generated from six mating pairs of floating homes, these Cathedrals in the Sky will extrapolate the No More Secrets ethos of localised Diversities, where contact allows for sharing on a personal and emotional level. People are starting to discover that these 'Floating Homes' are a totally living transformable architecture. They're not dead. They are the still-formulating result of rampant sexual climax that had ossified for the moment into rainbow-like shelters of human occupancy; lust and frenzy forever frozen in mid ejaculation.

Every dozen Floating Homes, intimately linked in their Diversity formations, are able to perform this amazing feat, this magical trick, of Diversity to Diversity communication.

How strange that these first Cathedrals in the Sky, these noble castles in the air, these floating crustaceans, these nematodes, these balloons of living flesh crenellated by the crippling miasma of the abrupt death of of the creative urge, the murder urge, the resurrectionist urge. Cathedrals in the sky, based on this second-stage offspring…real, living Creativity, Passion and Kinship – skies of coral cathedrals shimmering like the southern seas, clear and vivid, alive and spectacular – launching themselves into the air to light up the sky like a glowing firefly or levitating squid, pulsing on and off as it progressed through the heavens.

Floating Homes reproduction is hermaphroditic, meaning each individual produces eggs and sperm. When twelve Floating Homes mate, they exchange sperm as a trade. They usually do not fertilize their own eggs; they reproduce asexually by toroidal fusion. The Mating Diversity constricts at the midpoint, and the circumference is gathered in, twist by architectural twist. After a few hours of toroidal fusion, the Diversity rips apart at the constriction, leaving a newborn in the crackling air space.

Now ascended, and fresh from the birth toroid, everyone witnesses the first Free Planet Institute For Creativity, Passion And Kinship rise into the sky. Satellite FHs hanging off the side of it like pilot fish on a shark.

"In this first sermon…did I say 'sermon'?" the female voice stammers.

A classic Yellow Brick Road moment. A shudder of Emerald City dread. A flutter of nervous laughter. The first indication that the global audience was really listening, really panicking still. All those faces, all those minds, all those souls. Questioning (internally) where this Free Planet ride is taking them, will take them. What have we gotten ourselves into? Is this just another One World Cult about to raise another ugly head from the gaping cervix of the corporate hydra? A stunned silence.

What had the Custodian Manifesto promised?

Crime - most crime on this planet was a result of people having to 'find cash to live in a consumerist debt-based society.' As Free Planet belongs to all people there is nothing to steal, no 'wealth' to accumulate, so there's no need for crime. The prisons can be shut down and people (even the psychopaths, even the elite Risk-players) can be reintegrated into relevant cultures to contribute fully. There will be no centralised (nor global) governance, nor surveillance state.

Culture – cultural Diversity is the key to returning control of Free Planet to You The People. Moral issues should be dealt with at the local Diversity level. If you live in a Diversity you must embed yourself in it, live like them, you must not promote your culture in an aggressive fashion to other Diversities. Everything is permitted on Free Planet - science should be our friend.

Defence - on a Free Planet, it makes no sense to plan for, budget for or equip 'our enemies' with the weapons they'll need for us to blow them to smithereens. There are no enemies, we're all trying to make this place the best in the entire galaxy. Come on, people, grow up.

Economy - there is no longer a Corporate War Game running on a Free Planet, that's not what we're here for. We have realised we are not slaves to feudal planetary-conquest ambition and we will no longer tolerate their penny-stolen castles in the sky. We all benefit from a cleansed planet. We all work together as a race of specialised Diversities so that all of the planet benefits from our blood, sweat and tears.

Education - don't pussy foot around difficult issues as political age-relevant education has done for millennia – tell the children the truth. Don't distract them with their corporate role, their make-believe android status. Let them dream freely; dogma is of no use to Free Planet.

Energy and the Environment – it's already happening, science liberated from the military leash is starting to equip the world with the most ethical (i.e. least polluting) sources of Free Energy. There was a lot of research in this area in private government hands. Freeing the patents into the custody of You The People makes it possible to see proper local revolutions in the name of Free Energy.

Food and Re-Wilding - encourage ethical food (and water) and a return to a more vegan lifestyle for a few decades while Free Planet 'Re-Wilds' and the planet's diversity restocks. We must allow this to take place. Science is mandated to feed the world, ethically.

Foreign Affairs and International Trade - it's a round world, last time I looked – Free Planet means just that; no more boundaries to creativity, creed or race. The fun will return to this world.

Health - as energy is free (and locally generated), ethical food and water is free, so is health care - but it will focus more on prevention rather than drugging and chopping and blasting with nuclear radiation and chemical poisons. Big Pharma has gone too far and we need to return to understanding how we can stay healthy.

Housing and Planning - despite the global ownership models that are currently in place, this is a very unstable world upon which we live. Floods, earthquakes, fire storms, asteroids, solar storms are all part of the activity of our region of space. We must be able to react to these changes and this means investigating in 'mobile housing' that will support such. We should aim to Re-Wild Free Planet with a big push away from cities.

How We are Governed - You The People know, in your hearts, what's right and what's wrong. We will all soon understand what's right and wrong for Free Planet. At that point, the whole of humanity will rejoice at its liberation from the arbitrary ruleset of feudal slavery. We will be in control of our own destiny again.

Immigration - we are all guests on this alien world, we should all be allowed to move freely across any border and live where we want to help Free Planet return to her original beauty. We are not the property of our corporate states.

Referendums - we all know what's best for Free Planet.

Tax - Free Planet doesn't need any 'funding', will not tolerate organised crime.

Transport - automated travel modules will get us from point A to B and Free Planet-funded research into other exotic forms of long-haul transportation will open up the Solar System. A beautiful future lies ahead for the members of Free Planet.

Diversity Rule, *Local Solutions* and *Do Right By* are our guidelines.

An authoritarian, fatherly male voice breaks the silence like a rumble of thunder, "I'd personally like to hear suggestions from others, suggestions less based on unifying propaganda and more on day-to-day hands-dirtied reality."

And yet another voice, the crackling voice of a truly aged person asks, "Is this how we are to self-govern, like this, arguing across the airwaves like spectres or puppets?"

"Why can't I believe in a God or a Satan?" asks another.

"What is this demon worship hardware we're all trapped in?" asks another voice tinged with northern European chill.

"When can we go back to our own countries, our own land?"

Sure enough, the humans (from all across the world) are trying to fuck up that which is, potentially, a way for them all to save themselves, save their race, save their planet so that their children's children might have a chance to explore life as it's meant to be explored.

"We have no currency. We have no job. We have no arbitrary government. But what do we do?" whines an imploring Chinese tone.

"Welcome to the real world, you can now start to make a real difference to Free Planet," stabs another voice, ready for a fist fight with the whiners. All this flak erupting all round the world without a care for translators, just people connected via the rock of the earth, able to understand. People move toward each other, in this strange disconnect of connect, alliances are already being made. They are working out for themselves how it can be done; this leaderless, moneyless, prisonless world they had all given birth to.

And then, from within the global voices of disdain and their quiver-trembling sulky-puss faces of anger and fear to match, their ever-disjointed minds, comes a single child's voice, like a bell. She speaks in her hesitant tones, and such is the commotion, she has to say it again, for her words to be heard, then stronger, "Leave it better than you found it."

That's what she says.

That is the catalyst that brings some order to the airwaves.

"Only when the last tree has died and the last river been poisoned and the last fish been caught will we realise we cannot eat money," suggested another South American voice as the ruckus dies down, a Cree Indian Proverb.

"There are no passengers on spaceship earth. We're all crew," suggests a man from what used to be Kazakhstan, quoting Marshall McLuhan.

"When we show our respect for other living things, they respond with respect for us," and this actually sounds like a member of the Arapaho tribe sharing a wisdom with the world.

"After one look at this planet any visitor from outer space would say 'I want to see the manager'," suggests an Arab voice badly-imitating the drawl of William S. Burroughs. This received an appreciative round applause from those global elites who'd found themselves drawn into this Free Planet mess. Humour is gonna be a structural component of the world to come. A world worth fighting for.

Finally, the sermon giver, the female voice who'd started off this birth of the Free Planet Institute, summarised for us all so we all had something positive to take away from this first meeting of the Diversities of Free Planet, "Treat the earth well: it was not given to you by your parents, it was loaned to you by your children. We do not inherit the Earth from our Ancestors, we borrow it from our Children - Native American proverb."

We borrow it from our children – no wiser words have ever been said.

In fact, they want more than that, our children, they want a better world for *their* children, that's the least they should expect. They want their children to live on a healthy, sustainable world where diversity of life is paramount, where all the people are responsible for all the world and corporations don't lazily benefit from labour; our blood, our sweat and our tears are meant for *us* to appreciate.

MIKE PHILBIN

38
YOU THE PEOPLE
THE CHILDREN OF ASALAH AL FAGHORI

There's a sudden commotion of whooping and hooting and snarls and hissing. Two new lifeforms scuttle about in the steamy dank underworld of one of the Floating Homes of the Cumulo Diversity. Down here, under the living quarters, is where the Floating Homes orchestrate all their own essential business; that which sustains the Human Families they have chosen to protect.

This basement area, in the (literal) bowels of such Dirty Dozen union, is the living food, heat and water centre of cloud life. Human waste makes its way down here and is converted by enzymes and bacteria into dried fertiliser for the channels of food creation that are auto-watered from specialised bladders that pump their damp mist into the air. Carbon dioxide makes its way down here from the humans up above and plant yield is phenomenal.

It has its own *exotic aroma*, this place; one that takes some getting used to.

Kids don't give a shit; they'll play in anything as long as it's familiar to them and they're allowed to have fun. Look at the pair of them. Twins, sure, but nowhere near identical. The girl has the flattened plates of her father. The boy has the down or feathering of her mother. Both have very human faces, maybe a slight underbite/overbite issue. Characteristics have been passed across the genetic division, if you like. Each child is its own 'person' but that personage is formed from the unique pairing that furnished their gametal genesis. Watch them, scooping up big musty handfuls of processed bedding material and flinging this nutrient gloop around like it's snow. Dodging and tittering as they dash about, full of the life donated to them.

April (you remember, Bless You's real name?) looks up from tending one of the organs, applying some 'herb' to an infected area, making sure it all works properly, efficiently, "You brought your hybrid children with you then?"

You step out from around an enormous spleen swollen to a new function you can only guess at.

247

"It's a lot stronger down here." you open with that. Man, you're some sort of conversationalist genius, aren't you?

"The Schumann Resonance, yes. Imagine, twelve human brains per FH. Twelve human hearts. Combined into some self-amplifying organic organ. I'm surprised you're still on your feet, you must be getting used to it.

You approach her, but getting too close to the heart is…not painful – just strange.

"We're in the Heart and Soul of Free Planet," she enthuses, "Where food and water and shelter come at a price, and the price is sacrifice of the 'dozen souls' for the good of Creativity, Passion and Kinship. By the selfless who've allowed us into their Floating Homes. You wanna know what that means, touch this, here. Right here. Come on, come over here. It'll not bite."

The kids continue to play, noisily, screechingly.

You touch a large red round organ with many chambers arranged in a doughnut shape, pulsating and throbbing grotesquely.

"That's someone's actual heart, well, hearts. You can count them by the number of chambers, two four six eight ten, you see?" she asks, "And up there, thats where someone's actual skin shelters the inhabitants from the sun's rays but also allows itself to be suntanned, turns that tanning process into some sort of energy transfer. I've no idea of the technicalities but I've been asking around, learning about maintenance really. You know, in case.

"All over the place, this is the intestines, lower and upper, it's all in here, cleansers and fertilisers, we've never seen vegetables, fungus, bulbs, beans and greens grow like this on Earth. There's no need for chemists or Big Pharma on free planet either … you've seen these FHs go DARK every now and then? Melatonin production. Big Pharma has known that blue-light sensitive 'cryptochrome' receptors behind the eye have regulated the mopping up of free radicals for decades, but they kept it secret. The FHs cut themselves off from the electromagnetic spectrum so that they can 'simulate sleep'. They use this trick to fix the numerous cancers that grow every day as their hybrid cells deteriorate. It's like we're finally immune from cancer here, in Diversity.

"We could self-sustain for decades without ever landing. It's a very complicated, very specialised bioscape, eh?"

But you're not taking much notice of April's marketing spiel, you're looking into her eyes, smiling; hoping. You're thinking about how she would taste, you're seeing yourself and her growing closer. Faces moving nearer each other, lips parting.

"Daddy-daddy," the hybrid girl screams at you as her brother shoves mud in her face; at least you hope it's mud.

"Timmy, Sally," you call the kids over to you.

"Really?" April asks, rubbing under her nose with the back of her wrist because of her soiled hands. She's is looking at you like you've done something wrong.

"Temporary names, temporary names," your hands are up defensively, "You know, in honour of their parents and all that. They get to choose their Custodian Names when they're able, of course," and then you're thinking out loud, "Maybe they'll keep their names. Maybe names really are that important to people. Something…resonates…around a person's name? Right? His spoken self? Maybe we do create the world of our inheritance," you bumble through your reasons for pet-ifying the hybrid children of Asalah Al Faghori and Rotimi Ogunjobi.

April raps you on the forehead with her small, sharp knuckles, like she did when you took that trip out to the Industrial Estate to see how The Industry really works, how it treats its slaves.

You catch yourself, a sudden palpitation of dread gushes through you, but nothing extra-dimensional happens. No excruciatingly insane parallel universe of Nomadix/Glimpser cubic hell assails you. You're not transported off to some alien void and accosted with cracker theories and lunatic rationales that you can never really understand, the realm of dreams like a stalker; a predator: a sworn enemy.

"You okay?" she frowns, lowering her head inquisitively to look into your face.

A sudden jolt blasts through your Diversity. April grabs hold of your left shoulder to steady herself. Her face lights up.

"Scared the shit out of me," she grins moving to the exit from this lower section, rubbing her dirty hands on her jeans.

"What's happening?" you stand there like a scared boy.

"Oh, you'll like this. We're moving out, honey."

"Moving out?" you look haunted.

"Man, you need to be less harsh on yourself," Bless You chuckles, "We've just de-coupled from our CUMULO Diversity. We've been cut loose. Come on. This should be wonderful."

You look down and realise she's left a dirty hand mark on your shirt, white shirts are made to attract dirt.

* * *

You and April are above deck now, looking out from the wall-width window of your shared, separated Floating Home. You can see the exact location from where you decoupled from the Diversity. The hole is quickly filled by another Floating Home that was docked alongside in an excess port, waiting to become an integrated, structural member of Cumulo. You see that there are other Cumulo wannabes hanging off the sides of the main structure. Patiently awaiting their turn in the mix. Waiting to become invaluable. Other FHs joining where yours just detached.

Your Floating Home drops suddenly and banks hard right, shocking you with its ease of movement.

"Yeah, they move a lot faster when they're detached from their Diversities, don't they?" April pours an arm around your waist. Fairly soon, your Floating Home breaks the low-hanging cloud, revealing a beautiful world, sprouting up through the ancient city of London, the Thames snaking through the greenery like a viper. Packs of Re-Wilded (showing all sorts of mouth-to-stomach weaponry) stalk herds of other Re-Wilded. Solos (showing all sorts of flight enhancements) slip by, moving even faster than your Floating Home. As you approach the Folkestone/Dover coast, you see the GIANTS, those Flockers who have adapted artificial structure into their ant-like river-crossing colonies, show them lumbering and rolling across the rejuvenated landscape like a Boschian horror tableaux that might rival *The Garden Of Earthly Delights* in its vibrant ferocity. These enormous entities move toward the English Channel, some of them step into the water, heading east toward the French coast.

"Put your hand on the walls, like I showed you." April points to the wall where you'd had your 'connected' experience when you were part of Cumulo.

You do as she tells you (will it always be that way?) and try to sense the other members of your Diversity, "We are only four."

"There you go, you see what Diversity means now?" she kisses you on the mouth, full and warm. Looks into your eyes. Smiles, "It's me and you now, and the kids."

"Daddy-daddy!" the whirlwind approaches.

She seems to have timed this perfectly, as the kids arrive, running around you and April, still screeching, shouting 'daddy-daddy', still full of beans, still alive and breathing; how insane is this world is, eh?

"I think those people who pledged their DNA to the Custodian Liberation on that Natural Lottery show will be 'left untouched', taken to the Floating Homes, saved. Everyone else who was logged into the Evertainment Grid will be re-wilded, left to compete for resources. Alongside the people in third world countries, and the global elite who had their own digital playground, there'll be like a 60/40 split between hybrids and humans."

"Then that means you...."

She smiles, "Yes, I was always the clever one. How do you think I've survived in The Industry for so long. That fucking place chews virgins to bits and spits them out. As I did for you, my mercy release."

"I'll never be able to repay you."

"You flirt," her cheeks redden; is she actually blushing?

The hybrid owl-dog twins look up at the pair of you with all-too-human eyes, chuckling and touching, whispering and stroking, a contented trill of joy burbles in their chests. All eyes turn to the fully transparent wall as your Floating Home approaches the French coast, dipping down to treetop level with a sudden drop in altitude. As France speeds below you, you see that it's even more re-wilded than England was. It's like a whole new place has just been grown over the top of what used to be mile after mile of industrial food deserts, devoid of hedgerows, ruined beyond usefulness. Now rejuvenated, reborn.

Your Floating Home banks southward, sniffing for the Seine to guide the way in country.

"Now then, isn't that a better place to bring up the children," she smiles and you look at her for the longest time, desperate to see a mocking smile. But no sneer arrives, no sarcastic look scampers across her face. She is deadly serious.

Below them, the Seine comes into focus, and the Floating Home tears along following its course.

"I have no idea. This feels like it's just the beginning of a longer story," you say.

"Well, of course it is. Where shall we go now?"

"I was thinking Rio!"

"Rio, that dump? Anyway, we're not heading for Rio. I was thinking somewhere by the beach, Paris for instance."

You were about to say, 'Paris isn't by the sea,' but instead you say, "*Paris plage*," with a fake French accent, "Very good. You know that's just down stream from Notre Dame Cathedral."

"Oh, who's been catching up on their homework?" she seems genuinely proud of your efforts to learn what Evertainment tried so hard to obfuscate and mask. She ruffles your hair.

"And it still exists," you add confidently, taking her in your arms before realising what you're doing, "We could go in, appreciate the view."

You pull her in close, feel her crushing her pubis against you. The kids disappear, instinctively understanding that to be elsewhere might be better, right now. You look into her eyes. You've got to kiss her now. Seal the bond. She watches your mouth, knowing that she has you. Hook, line and sinker.

What on Earth comes next, nobody knows.

THE END.

EXCLUSIVE EXCERPT FROM
LIBERATOR – FREE PLANET BOOK TWO
by Mike Philbin

2102 hours.

"Sir, the Free Planet Simulation has just gone live, sir." With military efficiency a topside security operative is on the space-blower to his section chief.

Major General Johnson P Wildefire of NATO COMMAND in the South Pacific, answers his vidphone in shirtsleeves. He's still zipping up his trousers. You can still hear the toilet cistern filling after the flush. He takes his seat, adjusts himself in his chair. A half-smoked cigarette depends from his lips. He clears his throat with a phlegmy cough, "Speak your piece Butterscotch or so help me God–"

Lieutenant Butterscotch (that's actually his name) hesitates a fraction of a second, gulping back his fear of what he's about to reveal.

The Major General crushes his cigarette into the all-seeing-eye glass ashtray on his expansive oak desk. Exhales a grey lungful to one side of his mouth.

"What I mean, young fella mi lad, before you shit your knickers is, 'Would you like to repeat your initial comment. Please. Repeat exactly what you just said as I came out of the lav'.'"

"The Free Planet Simulation, sir--"

"That's... that's what I feared you'd said." the Major General speaks in a controlled fashion, as if to a child/imbecile, "Now, the FPS or Free Planet Simulation, as a soldier with your clearance should know, is an Eyes Only Black Project that has no GO CODE for another," he checks a wall chart over his right shoulder, eyebrows raised, mouth pulled down in contemplation, adding and taking away in his head, "Sixteen months and … one, two, three days, by my reckoning. I have the Go Date right in front of me. Now, unless somebody knocked me out while I was 'in the little boys room' and I've just been brought out of a lengthy coma, I'd suggest you have a really good reason for suggesting otherwise."

"I'm monitoring ahem... Evertainment, sir. Hoo-hoo, that's Hands Off Only, sir. Double blind surveillance. Absolutely no psyche-contact. Sir." he does this weird two-fingered scissors-opening salute from the back right of his head.

Wildfire's eyes burn, at this revelation, "If I find even one of my satellite crew are into that fucked up shit, I'll come up there in Space Command and personally murder that S.O.B. with my bare hands. I mean literally wringing chicken necks and watching them dance. Do you hear me?"

"It flag'd. Sir." cuts in the soldier.

"Flag'd did it?" the Major General reaches for the stubbed out cigarette in the ashtray. Picks it up. Examines the crushed and twisted stub before placing it carefully back in the ash tray. There's an ancient pack of Marlboros on his desk. He picks it up and scratches the side of his face with it. Then flips open the hinged top and pops one into his mouth. He picks up his lighter and prepares to flick it on.

"They're using the designated call sign, Natural Lottery, sir. It's what you call an Evertainment Infestation, sir. Patent hackers. It's on all the channels, right now, and I mean Total Saturation, sir. And there's another thing..."

"I don't wanna hear it," the Major General winces, the blood literally pulls back from his face, making the skin look like old parchment, the lips go blue; the cigarette depends from his lower lip, quivering.

"Major General, sir?" asks the lad, "What shall we do? We haven't war-gamed this..."

The Major General takes the unlit cigarette from his mouth, ripping a fine strip of skin from his lower lip and hissing, "That's a fucking suicide mission, boy. God help us all if they're running that scenario already. Keep your eyes peeled. On Us, and Them. Any deviation from 'expected outcomes'. I want an instant report. Day or night. You got that, soldier?"

"Sir, yes sir," the contact is broken.

Forty stories below the Pacific seabed, just off the southeastern edge of the Hawaiian archipelago, sealed inside a cube of living plasma hotter than the surface of the sun, Major General Johnson P Wildfire puts on his stripes and intercoms his p.a. or Personal Attaché, "Get me McCardle and Hoskins on the sat-link, immediately. I don't care where they are or what they're doing."

"May I ask what this is about, sir?" the male p.a. asks in faultless English brogue, as if he's taking notes for a whistleblowing book he's writing.

There's a pause, "Are you testing me, soldier."

"I'll have them on Vid One, pronto, sir." the contact is broken.

Wildfire talks to the mirror in his tiny office 'en suite', "You know, I kinda like it when T.S.H.T.F.," he actually says out loud the acronym for The Shit Hits The Fan...

**For more from Mike Philbin, please
visit him online at the following sites...**

TWITTER.COM - @CUST0D1AN

CHIMERICANA BOOKS at SMASHWORDS
Smashwords.com/profile/view/ChimericanaBooks

FREE PLANET NOVEL SERIES BLOG
FreePlanetNovel.Blogspot.com

MIKE PHILBIN BLOG
MikePhilbin.Blogspot.com

MIKE PHILBIN

23335788R00142

Made in the USA
Charleston, SC
17 October 2013